THE

RESURRECTION

BY

RICHARD CRANE

PREFACE

The burly man had to find that book he had seen so many terms ago. The collection of books that he had been extensively looking through was old, and barely legible. Many of them were so tattered that he was afraid to even try to handle them in fear that they would fall apart in his hands. The covers were so heavily coated in dust that he had to wipe several binders with an old rag just to see the titles. The illumination pod, which he brought with him, was sitting on a nearby table and cut through the darkness of the room so good that he could see the far wall. Every dust particle he had disturbed danced lightly throughout the chamber in the pod's radiance. The disruption had made him sneeze three times and he had to wipe his watery eyes upon his sleeve, twice. After regaining his eyesight, he looked at the collection again.

He knew that the complex had an extensive library, in fact three separate rooms, and that there were some books that would bring in a lot of rolets. He had been in the collection many times before, but it had been a while since he had the chance to come back to it. Many cycles ago, he had happened upon it while he was wondering around the complex.

The main, and most important books, were in the far west side of the complex. Those books he would never be able to get his hands on for they were very well guarded and used a lot. They would be noticed if they went missing. The second one was a bunch of odd and end items that Medico used every once in a while. But this third library, tucked away under several dusty tarps and boxes, was never touched. He had made a list of them before, and had lost that list, but still knew some of the titles. He even found another entrance to the area that gave him access without entering from the main doors. The complex was so vast that nobody would notice anything missing, particularly in this part. As far as he knew, Medico never came to this side of the complex.

One book, in particular, was going to get him about ten thousand rolets, and he had seen it the last time he was here. He knew a shop that purchased books, and when he told them about this book, they reacted like it was a lost treasure. He had used the store many times, knew the owners for many cycles, but had never seen a response like that from them before. Of course, the offer could be higher in numbers if the book was in a good condition. Mint could even double the expectations.

He started to drift away thinking about the reason for the payout; an object that he had been wanting for a long time. An object that was so rare, people killed others for it, and he knew where one was available. He dreamed of having it in his hands, feeling its power, and using it. He could be calm and relaxed knowing that anything, or anyone, would never intimidate him again. This object was in high demand and was going to need a lot of rolets to acquire.

For a while, rolets were never a problem for him because Medico paid him well. Jobs came few, and at times many, and for the last few weeks he had been nonstop finding items for him. He had a small stash saved up, but he needed more, a lot more.

Thoughts of the past struggles clouded his now dreaming mind. He was only twenty-six cycles old when had had first been hired by Medico. He was unusually large for his size, and strong; which was the muscle that Medico needed at the time. His mind, on the other hand, was not so strong. People had picked on him for many cycles because he just couldn't think as fast as them, or have the common sense that every rotation people took for granted. They threw things at him, they wouldn't acknowledge him, and they even called him names. He was a real Dooferdoo.

But Medico really changed his life. He didn't have to live from dive to dive anymore, or fight for a decent meal. He was given a place to stay, food, and rolets whenever Medico needed something done. He was given a purpose and a future, and a sense of completeness. It didn't take long for him to become a loyal worker for Medico. In fact, Medico not only became his employer, he became the only family he had ever known. Born on the streets; he fought, scratched, climbed, begged, and stole to survive. Now, after that first job, he accepted the offer to work for Medico all the time. That was almost twenty-five cycles ago.

Years of service had made him a strong ally for the complex. Jobs were odd at first, but he soon got used to the things that Medico needed and continued his service to him. He knew to never question the jobs; just do them in a timely manner and get paid. Other people would find them offensive, wrong or even cruel, but growing up on the streets like he did, his conscious never bothered him, so the jobs didn't bother him either. All thanks to Medico.

Medico was the only name that he knew him by, for he never knew his real name; that is if he ever had one. In fact, he only spoke to him with either "Sir", or "Boss. It would be too personal and improper to say anything else. He guessed Medico's age to be somewhere around seventies, but he had heard stories that it was a lot older than that, in fact, older than most people could live. He also heard other stories as well, but gossip never attracted him, and he always saw it as a distraction from the truth. He could care less anyway; talkative people annoyed him.

The man sneezed again, bringing his mind back to the present and the pile of books in front of him. He started shifting through the pile once again and after several taps, he saw the book that he was after.

He slowly picked it up, and a smile grew on his face, and it sparked an inner joy. When the dust once again cleared, he looked deeply at its condition and saw that it was very neat, colorful, and bold. There was not a scratch upon it. The title, although, was hard to read. Not because the letters were damaged, but because he didn't understand the words. When he told the store about it, he handed them a piece of paper in which he had written several titles on, and this was the one that caused the reaction. Writing the title was easy, but pronouncing it was impossible. All he knew was that it had something to do with science.

He still could not understand the concept of science, even though he had been around Medico's experiments for so long. The strange things that he had seen still could not be explained, nor believed. Many things went beyond natural evolution and could only be labeled as "Creatures." He never would question nor interfere with the experiments, for Medico was one that you did not cross. Many had, and were never seen again.

He cleared his thoughts and looked deeply at the book in his hands, the book that will bring him salvation. He could easily afford the device he wanted if they paid the price according to their reaction. See if anyone ever calls him a Dooferdoo again.

With a grin on his face, he tucked the book into his carry bag and headed for the exit.

CHAPTER 1

Walking along the street was almost like a dream. The sun was just rising and everything had an odd look to it, making images not clear but rather fuzzy in appearance. A light mist filled the air and you could smell the odor of fresh water. It looked like a typical day in the port, but the noise level was low, almost nonexistent, and eerie. You could even hear the echoes of your own feet hitting the pavement and resounding off the solid walls around you. Slight sounds of dripping water, a brown beetle shrill, a wind gust, and even a person coughing down the street broke the silence but just gave a little notice to the stillness around. Another gust of wind just tried to make everything seem the same, just like nothing had ever changed.

Then, stepping around the corner, the regular turned unfamiliar. The smell of burnt wood filled the air, clutter still was thrown about the street, and that regular walk turned into a frightening nightmare. The surrounding area was different; the brisk morning had turned into a chill down the spine, objects were not fuzzy but completely unrecognizable, and it seemed that the noises that were noticed before no longer existed. Nobody even coughed.

Stopping at the entrance, emotions and images started taking control redirecting thoughts. The door didn't look that bad, in fact hardly touched, and even the lock still worked, but the windows had been blown out and were now covered with boards and police tape. The sign, that usually stayed lit above, was now dark and lifeless. The place used to hold lots of life, fun, and feelings of comfort, but now, it displayed the death that had surrounded everyone in the last twenty-four courses. Hurt, worn out, and barely holding its own, the building looked sad. It needed someone to breathe new life back into it and make it feel young again.

A sparkle of a key broke the dimness of the area as it was pulled out of a pocket and inserted into the lock. A hard twist to the right, and the lock clacked open, splitting the silence with a sound that shouldn't have been as loud as it was. It took a strong shove to open the door and it argued the motion with cracks and creaks as it was forced. By the time it was fully open, the echoes of its strain could be heard throughout the empty building.

Suddenly, a flashlight bulb split the darkness in the room and things became a lot clearer. The damage was substantial, but salvageable. But who would want to start it all over again and bring it back to life? Who was willing to find the time and money to bring back its glory? Could it ever be the same?

The light proceeded to wander toward the left where several stools still stood next to the bar. Reaching the counter, the person walking the flashlight turned it upward and set it upon the bar's surface. The reflection off the mirror and the ceiling illuminated more of the room giving another spooky feeling of death. No music played, no lights flashed, and shadows danced around the once active stage. A little sound of trickling water was the only apparent noise happily bouncing off of something metal.

Steve pulled out one of the chairs and sat down on it. It creaked but held firm. He let out a long sigh of relief and anguish, taking note that this all happened so quickly. He had spent the night at Katrina's apartment where Base Security talked to all three of them for about two courses and cleared up everything about the destruction, the deaths, and the outcome. After the Police left, they all got something to eat, and then Steve took a shower. When he returned to the room, Jason and Katrina were having a drink, and he joined them. They each had a couple, and then decided to call it a night. Not much was said, for they all were still traumatized from the events, but they soon ran out of energy and went to bed. Jason and Katrina slept in her room, and Steve slept on the couch. He had tossed and turned all night, and then realized that it was futile to sleep. He got up, got dressed, and walked to "Little Chicago" to clear his mind. That proved to be a mistake for the visions started running through his head again about the consequences leading up to this point.

At first there was the explosion here, then, the second explosion at the Tower. That was all followed by Veronica's death, Jason's death, Sheila's death, Jason's return, then last, Hawk's coma. Seven deaths total, on the ground, and many in the air. He had no idea how many people were on board Rodger's ship when Sheila blew it up, but they all deserved it, especially Rodger. Good riddance. The thought of even attempting to enforce Davi rule made him sick to his stomach.

He still couldn't figure out why Rodger got involved with the Davi in the first place, especially when he was from Tennessee. During his whole life, Rodger was a United Nations citizen and had a good upbringing. He was from a rich family, went to the best schools, and was given all the comforts of home. Everything that he stood for was the complete opposite that the Davi enforced. The United Nations stood for peaceful, non-controlling countries who had adopted a declaration to grant freedom and equality to all forms of life and needs. Poverty was a thing of the past and together they combined their knowledge to find cures for many diseases and provide food for the population. Cancer, hunger, diabetes, brain disorders, and even psychological disorders were long gone to the past. Hell, even the animal life on the planet had protection. Life became precious and the respect for others was just a natural fact. Racial discrimination was gone, animal cruelty was gone, and even money was gone. People were granted allowances per day for use and nobody profited off of the other. We all lived together as an equal and were happy.

Then, the Davi came. The Davi wanted to rule everything on Earth. They believed that their government was the answer to organized spiritual enlightenment. Anyone who did not join them, were marked as inferior and exterminated. They quickly gained control of land that was major energy sources for the planet and used its control for demands. Several countries were lost across the continent of Europe and were formed into either Davi supporters or massive grave yards. They had gained control of almost half of the

European continents and were establishing themselves as the only true race. Then, of course, the war dragged on for years. Steve enlisted to help fight and was a marine fighter on the ground. He had been through many battles and had the scars to prove it. After four years, he transferred to the air force to become a fighter pilot flyer. He went through the most heavily guarded runs and missions to where he had shot down many enemy targets. His size, skill, and victories gained him the nickname 'Badass of the sky'. When he was transferred to the station at Ford Base, he was assigned to drop the bomb. The bomb, in all hopes, would end the Davi occupation and take out the leaders. Taking out the world was not the plan. Nobody would have guessed the outcome.

It only took Zeus about twenty minutes to find Steve's OAJ, and another forty to get him onboard. After meeting Jason and Rodger, the three of them became determined to find a future. The star charts that Zeus contained gave the three of them possible destinations to pursue. They were only in space for six months and even then, they had plenty of supplies to last another three years if needed. The ship that Zeus was contained in had four sleeping compartments; each with its own bathroom, a kitchen, a pantry, and a large gathering room with plenty of electronic entertainment devices. Essentially, it was an apartment with no yard to upkeep. They kept themselves busy and with the information that Zeus contained, they would never run out of topics to learn. They had heard of individuals who had become 'Space Happy' on long deep space explorations, but at least they returned home. The three of them had no home to return to.

Steve sighed and turned his head toward the floor on the other side of the bar and something caught his eye. "Well, I'll be damned," he said out to nobody as he got up off the stool. He then grabbed the flash light and walked toward the end of the bar. He really didn't have as far to go as usual, because the end of the bar didn't exist anymore, for it was now in fragments all over the room. He stepped and crunched his way over broken glass and wood until he found himself at the object he had seen. He knelt down toward it and shined the flash light upon it.

The large safe under the counter didn't have a single scratch on it and it was still closed. He hooked the light under his left arm and with his right hand, started turning the combination lock to its numbers. After four turns, the door clicked, and Steve swung open the door. He crouched closer to the ground to get a better look and pointed the flash light into the large safes' contents. He was quite surprised what he saw.

None of the money was burnt, a lot of the building's assets were still intact, and glistening in the light were three bottles of Kentucky Whiskey. Not one of them was broken. He reached in and gently pulled one out.

"Hello, sweetie, nice to see you," he said as he twisted the cap and heard the seal crack upon opening. "This is going to feel good," he said as he lifted the top to his lips and took a slow sip. The liquid, even though it was cold, gave a warming sensation as it went down his throat. He then took a deep breath and slowly exhaled.

A scuffling sound came from the front entrance door, and Steve hurried to his feet to see what caused the noise. He took the flash light and aimed it into the direction of the disturbance and blindsided Jason right in the eyes. Jason quickly put his hands up to block the lights and cocked his head to the side. "Steve, is that you?"

Steve aimed the flash light down toward the floor and sat the bottle upon the countertop. "Yes, it's me. I couldn't sleep."

Jason smiled and walked toward the bar, "I thought that you would probably be here." His voice still sounded tired and weak. The past few courses had really taken its toll on him and it showed deeply in the lines in his face. The thought of him being dead earlier still felt like a dream and he couldn't shake the image. Of all the different stories that he had heard about death, feeling a calming serenity, seeing family that has passed before you, or even seeing a light, he remembered nothing. Maybe he wasn't dead long enough to experience it. Maybe the afterlife wasn't what it was believed to be. Maybe there was no afterlife. His thoughts drifted back to the present as he looked at Steve and noticed the silence of the room. "Are you ok?"

Steve pointed the light toward the bottle on the counter, "I will be after a couple of swigs of this."

The light bounced off and through the bottle at the same time and glimmer lines bounced off the walls. Particles danced through the room around the beams and lightly floated to destinations unknown.

Jason's eyes squinted and he got a better look at the object in the light, then he started to develop a slow grin across his face as the bottle became clearer. Memories started to fly through his mind as the past was brought back to him. Many times, were recalled; the relaxing nights, the quick sips, the party nights, the 'how the hell did I wind up on the garage floor' nights.

"Well, I'll be damned," he said as if repeating the echo of Steve's previous words. "Did any of the glasses survive?"

Steve turned the flash light back up the counter, "have a seat and I'll find out. If not, we can drink it straight out of the bottle." He turned and started looking through the debris around the holding area.

****

A bright sunny day shone through the glass and the morning animals started their elegant chirping. A gentle breeze slowly crept through the crack of the open window and blew across her body on the bed. She started to stir, for her body was still half asleep and her alarm did not yet go off. Her thoughts drifted in and out of consciousness as they toyed with her reality. Soon she would be back at work enjoying the company of her friends. She would be going through the transcript reports of incoming and outgoing shipments and trying to decipher who had priority one. After a busy morning, her coworkers and she would enjoy lunch together at some nearby eatery and laugh until someone would squirt arura juice out of their nose. Then they would return back to the office and continue; getting the next day's schedule report ready and in order. Her thoughts turned to her friend's eyes and she watched their expression turn to horror as objects around the office room started to slowly melt. Intense heat started to build up around her as her friends' faces turned from shock to pain as their bodies caught on fire in front of her. She started to reach out for them, but it was too late. The walls around started to explode out, slowly, and fragments splattered everywhere. A blaze appeared on everything and grew larger with each breath she took, up to the point of being entirely engulfed in the dancing fire. She looked up once again toward her friends, who were now nothing but two flaming figures reaching out with arms seeking for help. The words came out painfully as they said in unison, "HELP ME!"

Katrina bolted up in her bed and screamed. She was so disorientated that she didn't understand what just happened. Her arms were quivering so bad that she started rubbing them to calm them. She was taking short, gasping breaths, and tried to shake the dream from her head. It felt so real that she even checked herself for burn marks. When she realized where she was at, she thought that she had spilled water in the bed because her body was so drenched in sweat. She lifted her hands and wiped the sweat from her forehead toward the back of her hair and down. She let out a large breath and quivered upon its release.

She was in her room and things looked the same, but different. Jason was not in the room and she quickly got panicked upon his disappearance. Was he still dead? No, Sheila changed all of that. Did he leave? No, that would never be the case. Maybe Steve and Jason were in the front room and her nerves were playing overtime.

She swung her feet out over the side of the bed and that's when she noticed that she had slept in her clothes, and they were soaked. She attempted to stand up, but the action seemed a little more effort than any other time. Her muscles ached and she had little energy. Her body was still quivering from the dream, but she managed to stand fully up and shuffle herself toward the closet. The back muscles on her calves screamed in agony as she reached the doors and pulled them open. She first took off her pants, then her shirt, her brassiere, and finally her underwear. Turning toward the right closet door, she looked upon her naked body in the mirror. Several bruises scattered over her body and the dried blood upon her cuts still stung. She felt like she had fell down a flight of stairs.

Still locked into the dream that awoke her, she shook her head and had to tell herself that 'it was only a dream'. She reached for the house coat hanging on a hook inside and put it around her body.

Once again, she attempted to walk with her pain in another direction and went to the door that opened into the front room. When she reached it, she grabbed the knob to turn it, and noticed that it was cold. Shaking her head again, she tried to disperse the thought of everything being hot. She turned the knob and entered the front room.

Nobody was there.

She started to panic again, until she saw the note on the table in front of the couch.

"Darling, I woke up early and saw that Steve was gone, so I decided to look for him and pick us up some breakfast on the way back. I won't be gone long." It was signed, "Jason, your sexual play toy."

She raised her left eyebrow in a response to the last comment. Odd, why would he... her thoughts were interrupted by a low toned bell, in two ring intervals, informing her that a call was coming in on her Vid. She reached over on the couch's arm, grabbed the remote, and hit the receive button. The screen turned on, audio only, and the ringer stopped.

"Hello," she said with a raspy voice.

"Miss Williams, this is Port Officer Stone. We have you as a contact for Miss Veronica Stem's body. Sorry for the loss, but we have a few questions."

Katrina swallowed hard and slowly sat herself upon the arm of the couch, "Go ahead, officer."

****

Coldness, darkness, low sounds around me. Body tinkling, eyes cannot see, nose cannot smell. Hands start to move, body is pulled upwards, and needles are inserted. Electricity is humming, water current is moving fast, and flashes of light can be seen through my eyelids. I pass out. I awake to see another room with cold hard floors, three solid walls and bars holding me in. A large plate of food sat on the floor in front of me. My body senses are all functioning and I can see really clear. My ears are so attuned that I can hear screams and groans from the other chambers around me. I feel strong but yet alone. Someone comes, I panic. As they open the bars, two people enter my room with more needles and I start to burn inside. My actions seem too fast to see and I swing after my jailers. Burning, BURNING SENSATION THAT WILL NOT STOP AS I SPIN, THROW, BREAK, RUN, AND FLEE. I FIGHT, CLAW, CLIMB, FIGHT AGAIN AND ESCAPE! I SlowlY StARt TO CalM DowN and mOve on. At peace, I now try to find refuge. I slept in alleys during the night, and continuously walk by day. Further and further, I take myself away from the beginning, away from the pain. I find transportation and find myself planets away from the pain. I'm hungry, cold and I find a place to rest. Terms pass as I become aware of myself and my abilities. I find ways to get an income, ways to become normal. I find rest in a bar. I break up a fight and discover that I am no longer alone. Relaxed, I establish myself with my new friends and try to make a normal life of it. I even feel more comfortable travelling. This is easy; I could win all the time. Oh no you don't, you're not GOING TO STEAL FROM ME!!! I FIGHT, CLAW, SCRATCH, SMASH AND KILL. I WILL NOT BE, Be, bE, be cheated. My friends calm me down. Life goes on again, another game, another challenge, another cycle. I start learning how to better control my change in emotions and what they bring forth. Several terms pass and I'm feeling more relaxed and confident in myself. Wait, you think that you're Not GOING To PAY ME!!! FIGHT, SMASH, HIT, KILL!!! Run. This time, I calmed myself. I'm getting better at controlling these emotions and my actions. When I return home, I find a beautiful lady. Start to develop a new friend and relationship. Feel totally different and really relaxed. Explosion! Chase, hit, catch, kill. I return back to the room. Roni? RONI??? NO!!!! I START TO CRASH, SMASH, THROW, WRESTLE, AND DESTROY. MY FriEnDs oNce aGAin calm me down. Revenge, is what we all need. We plan, travel, transfer, and kill, KiLL, KILL!!! We become victors but at what cost? JASON? JASON? NO!!!! SHEILA? SHEILA? NO!!!! I CAN'T TAKE THIS BURNING!!! I WILL NOT BE ABLE TO STOP THIS BURNING!!! I WILL NOT BE ABLE TO REGAIN CONTROL!!!   I CAN'T..

****

"Welcome to the midday news on Largo's number one station, AJBA Vid station 20. The news starts now."

The screen cut away from a picture of the downtown hall and focused in on two reporters sitting behind a blue desk with a glass top. The female, on the right, was blond, and had a dark green blouse on. She was smiling at the camera, but the look of worry was upon her face. The male, to the left of her, wore a light grey suit and expressed the same empty look.   The desk in front of them had nothing upon it, but the report screens under the glass could be seen illuminating. Behind both reporters, the wall was a large visual screen, which at the time, flashed blue, red, green, and yellow streaks from left to right and dissipating into the station's logo.

"Good day," the woman said, "I'm Sherry Owen."

"And I'm Jack Lorns," the male added. "Welcome to the mid-day report."

"Following up on the tragedy around the port last night," the woman said as the screen behind them became flooded with pictures of fires, injured people, and emergency vehicles.

"Authorities have informed AJBA that the people behind the devastation have been killed. Reports from several flight crews and companies say that a massive vessel in Largo's orbit was hindering shipments and was the one that broadcasted the message we heard yesterday. The following message is that broadcast."

The camera switched imaged to only show the blue wall screen and the audio with words of the broadcast.

"..........Attention people of Largo. We, the Davi, are in charge. All incoming ships and outgoing vessels will now be controlled by us. Preedom is no longer available. All operational and financial control will run from our main vessel, the Duress. In keeping with our request, we order that the vessel known as "ZEUS" be turned over to us immediately. If you do not comply within the first rotation, more destruction will occur......"

"The destruction that did occur," the male continued as the camera refocused on him, "was the destruction of the communication towers in all of Largo's port bases. Kelly, Cosal, and Stuart base towers were all completely destroyed, and many lives were lost. Seven of Preedom's main branch offices, as well, were destroyed and had massive loss of life. Here in Serin base, not only was there the explosion and destruction of the tower, but a separate explosion occurred at a location called "little Chicago"."

The screen behind them changed to a burning building with several people trying to contain the fire.

"The local club was a favorite among the port citizens as well as visitors to relax and unwind." Sherry continued, "The connection between the port explosions and the club has not yet been discovered. Ongoing investigations are being done by Largo Base Authorities and Police factions. AJBA tried to contact the owner of 'Little Chicago', but no one has been able to find him since the events."

"In another story," Jack said, "a woman's body was found brutally murdered in the Grand Gate Hotel. Authorities say......."

The large Vid was turned off by a remote.

Aiden, sitting on her couch with the remote still in her hand, immediately punched numbers into the remote to dial 'Little

Chicago'. She had been relaxing all morning only in her pajamas and had just finished her third cup of Kedy brew. After a couple of ticks, she noticed that the call didn't ring. The vid screen displayed that there was a disruption at the source. She disconnected the call and then started punching in numbers again. The two consecutive clicks, told her that the vid was ringing at her dialed location. After three sets of clicks, the video flashed on, showing a short woman in a house coat that was rapidly drying her hair with a towel.

"What's up, Aiden?" the girl asked.

"Remy, have you been up to date with the news?" Aiden's voice sounded nervous.

"No, I went to bed when I got home and just been listening to music all morning," she stated as she rapidly rubbed her hair with the towel. "Why, what's...."

"'Little Chicago' was blown up last night." Aiden expressed.

The girl on the other end stopped rubbing her head with the towel and leaned closer to the screen. "What? Is anyone hurt?"

Aiden swallowed hard, thinking about all the people she knew and loved at the place. She had the night off last night and took advantage of it with a long hot bath and a bottle of Sindi wine. "They didn't say," she said as she tossed the remote on a side table in frustration. "I can't get a connection to the club either."

"Let me finished getting dressed and I'll meet you at your place. Give me about thirty taps."

"I'll see you in thirty, and then we can both go to the club and see what we can find out."

The vid clicked off.

CHAPTER 2

It's an odd feeling what the mind does when it is so inebriated. Things tend to move slower than what they really do. Things look hazy and much unfocussed. Noises sound like you're underwater, and your head doesn't want to sit still. It just keeps pulling toward the right. You feel like you're going to spin out of the chair and even when you try to scratch your nose, it feels weird. Your skin has the sensation of rubber and your eyes can't move as fast. In fact, everything seems like a dream. At times, your lips will not cooperate with the words that you want to speak and you come out sounding like an idiot. The coordination in your hands is lost and the room looks like you're in a foggy mist, or perhaps a steam room. And when you belch, oh boy, when you belch you can taste the drink all the way back up into your throat. It burns, but you swallow it back down anyway. The cool sensation of the liquid still holds in your mind and you can't get enough. Even when you lift the glass just for a sip, you end up downing the whole drink.

When you first start, the alcohol makes you light-headed, woozy, muddleheaded, squiffy, tipsy, a little lit and dizzy. Your continuation of the ongoing celebration gets you to the next level of being half crocked, soused, toasted, pie eyed, stewed, and slap happy. Most people stop at this point because they can neither function or they get so tired they need a nap. But then there are the exceptions who continue on. They pour down liquid like there is no tomorrow. That next level brings them into that category five emergency situation where everything is lost. They become loaded, plastered, sloshed, hammered, and bombed. Coordination is lost to the ability to making a total ass of one's self. The ultimate level is beyond anyone's control. You are now blind drunk, snockered, zonked, drunk as a skunk, drunk as a fiddler's bitch, three sheets to the wind, and fizzucked. You are royally shitfaced.

And in all the confusion, you start asking yourself goofy questions that could only be replied by goofy answers. 'Am I really touching my nose?' 'Is my chin filling up with rocks?' 'Are my shoes still on?'

You find yourself pulling even more things up from you mind and concentrate harder on your emotions. They feel stronger and more intense than you have ever felt them. You start to cry, thinking of the times of pain. 'Why did my frog have to hop away?' 'My doggy got run over by an ice cream truck!' 'Why did she have to die?' 'Why do bad things happen?'

You ask these questions in hope that someone will help you, but nobody does. You try to wash them down further with another drink and it takes you several tries to grab the bottle. As you lift the bottle and try to fill your glass, part of the liquid pours on the table but you manage to fill the glass once again. The situation looks funny and you start to giggle. You start to giggle a lot. In fact, you can't stop giggling and then your mind starts to develop more questions. 'Why do I have to have knees?' 'Why can't I have wings on my back?' 'Did my nose fall off when I scratched it so hard?'

You reach up to your face to find that you nose is still there, but it still itches, so you scratch it once again. You can hear the sound of it echoing inside your head and notice it sounds weird. You notice that everything sounds weird. Then you start to say things just to hear your voice, 'Macaroni, kumquats, garbanzo beans, and loopy!' Your giggles dance between the words and you laugh even harder. You lean over the table and grab the person's hand on the other side. 'Did you think that we have a chance to win the game?'

You fall back and grab the bottle again, this time forgoing the glass and connecting it with your mouth. Three, (was it three?) gulps later, you set the bottle back down, carefully and slow so not to tip it over. You lift your arms in triumph because it successfully sat up straight. You feel the liquid going down your throat and it warms up your chest cavity. The warmth gives you feelings of calmness, stress free time and fatigue. Then, your thoughts get serious. Your mood changes once again as you look as deep as you can to the person across the table. 'Is the room shrinking?' 'Am I an ok guy?' 'Do you love me as much as I love you?'

19

The last question made Steve reach over and pull the whiskey bottle out of Jason's reach. "I think you have had too much of this," he said as he pulled it toward his side of the table.

"There is never too much, sailor," Jason yelled. Then he started to giggle again and Steve started to laugh with him. "We almost finished two," Jason added. "Let's down this and start the next!"

Steve knew that this was the way that Jason always vented off his anger and pain, so he slowly slid the bottle back toward him. "Ok, you can have the rest of this, but I'm saving the last one for later."

Jason grabbed the bottle and cuddled it with his arms. "Why? Is there a big shindig coming up?" Jason started to giggle again as the word was added to his list. "Shindig, shindig, shindig," he repeated as he laughed more.

Steve started to laugh with him as he stood up from his chair to go get another candle. The one they had lit on the table was almost gone, and even though it was day outside, the fire had darkened the windows with soot and ash. No light could come through. Steve staggered a little bit and realized that he also had too much to drink, but clearly Jason was beyond that. He doubted if even Jason would be able to get out of the chair.

It has been a long time since he had seen Jason this drunk, in fact, never this bad. The last twenty-four courses had been very devastating and he truly needed this release time. Steve still was trying to comprehend it himself. Did all of this really happen or was it just another nightmare. Maybe he was drunk as well.

Shaking his head and refocusing, Steve grabbed another candle from a box they found in the back and brought it to the table. He saw Jason, as he approached, teetering on the stool to the brink of falling off of it. He would wobble to the right, his body would jerk to set him back straight, them he would teeter to the left. When Steve sat down, Jason lifted his head up and a surprised look came across his face.

"Where did you go" he asked as Steve sat back down.

"To get another one of these," Steve answered as he upended the candle and lit its wick with the burning runt on the table. He then tilted it sideways, dripped wax onto the surface, and then stuck the candle into it. All this time, Jason was very intensely watching the action. When Steve readjusted his chair, he looked across the table to see Jason who had a really serious look on his face.

"Well, do I?" Jason asked with a serious concern in his eyes.

"Do you what," Steve asked.

"Do I have knees? Because I don't think I can bend my legs."

****

The large home could not be seen from the road that led to it, for an iron fence, ten feet tall, surrounded the entire yard and was topped off with several coils of barbed wire. The fence was black and was barely visible in the night's fog that engulfed it. The fence alone explained the importance of what laid within it. It was a home not only built for strength and security, but also represented a major power in the area. It belonged to one of the strongest organizations on the planet, and Tego had a lot of them. They all had their own territories, fought often to gain more ground, and each had their own small army. The gambling casinos and the skill games on Tego not only held power and strength, but were very dangerous to become a part of. Here, money came first, and then your life came in second.

The planet had no organized police, for each group had their own task force, and even the landing ports were controlled by an owner and his empire. Most areas had posted laws, and if followed, you would never be noticed. Step out of line, or become a problem, you might end up with a couple of bruises as they 'escorted' you out, but most places were run to attract people, not to frighten them away. A lot of the businesses presented themselves with pride, enjoyment, and customer satisfaction. Without that, there would be no money flow. Money could be made here by means of ownership, or by being a big winner. Each held its own reward and the bigger the better. Success was a wonderful thing.

But punishment was saved for the real problems, like here, now, in front of this fortress.

The peaks of Marre trees could be seen rustling in the light breeze as they danced above the fog. Favino bugs filled the air with their loud shrilling chirps and added eeriness to the area. Seen from the front gate, the flood lights in the yard split the night with a haze that provided no relief to the view. The gate itself had an electrical control panel imbedded into the left wall and contained a surveillance camera. An armed guard stood next to it.

The guard had a medium built body, but was tall, and cradled in his arm was a long-barreled GEO gun. A very precise weapon that was so accurate, it could pinpoint a Stacnat off the ass of a JC rat, without hurting the rat. He had a large collection of guns, but the Geo was his favorite. He was deadly accurate with it and combined with his strength, it was clear why he was placed at the front of the gates. If anyone needed to get in, they had to go through him first. He enjoyed his job and had been with this power for almost seven years. Because of the pay, he lived comfortably, enjoyed his off time with lots of pleasure, and owned everything he had ever wanted. His life felt complete and he was ready for anything.

Except this.

The front gate electronic device beeped several times and the green light upon it went dark. The guard turned to look at the device and saw that the camera port had no power, and he started to reach for the Comm button. Then, the small sting he felt in the back of his neck felt like an average Stacnat sting, but the dizziness that followed wasn't expected. He didn't remember hitting the ground.

Seconds later, past the cut open barb wire to the right of the gate, one of the flood lights on the ground went dark. The fog blended into the night as darkness over took it. The guard in the right tower box, saw the blowout, and noted into his log that it would need replaced. It was a very common thing for the fog to build up enough condensation to blow the ground lights, in fact, it happened often. The other lights had more protection.

That's when the tower light went out.

The quizzical look on his face as he leaned back to look at the bulb above him, was comical. That's when he felt the sting.

The right back flood light went dark.

The left tower light went dark and another sting occurred.

The three remaining perimeter guards walked to the center of the yard where the one remaining flood light stayed lit, and a low conversation was engaged. The faces of each one was lit up in the illuminating beam and combined with the fog gave them all a ghostly appearance. Without cause, the light above them went out.

The entire yard was cast into total darkness. The three guards quickly turned on their hand-held lights and split up in different directions; one to the left, one to the right, and the other toward the front entrance gate.

Three quick stings and all guards were down.

The front door still had a light upon it, and shined like a beacon in the distance. Standing next to the door was two other guards, each well aware of the happenings in the yard. They both had their guns drawn and were squinting to see anyone, anything, in the darkness. One of the guards reached over to the front door Comm when he noticed that the power lights were out. He punched several buttons on the console with no prevail. Even the sensors around the house were out. As a last resort, he pulled out his hand held Comm and pushed the button in to speak. A loud static burst emitted from the device clearly indicating that it was being jammed. After the two exchanged looks, they turned to the front door to go in. The code key was out of power as well, which meant opening the door would be next to impossible. They had to figure out their next move.

Inside, on the second floor, past the opened window, was a long hallway decorated in riches that only Tego could provide. Chandeliers of glimmering glass bounced light off the ceiling and illuminated the interior. The second story hall was long and ran the length of the building, circling around the front entrance foyer from above. In the center was the large staircase that led to the lower level where two guards, apparently clueless of the conditions outside, where having a casual conversation at the bottom of the stairs. In the center, at the top of the stairs, were two large wooden doors. They were adorned with gold handles and carved into their panels were intricate drawings of creatures.

The two guards were talking in depth about a new game on Tego involving small jet racers. The task consisted of four vehicles, all piloted by challengers, up against each other and the clock. The winner of the race won the other competitors fees, but could only win the house lot if it beat the clock time. The clock time, of course, was unreasonably set so nobody had won it yet. The racers, or better known as the 'Screamers', because of the sound they make when the pass by you, were built and sold on Tego. They weren't cheap, but were the hottest item to have.   The arena itself was owed by the Taylor Clan and they owned a considerable area in the Muskego Valley. They were also the manufactures of the Screamers. They were one of the many rival clans in the area, and continuously appeared as a thorn in the side for neighboring clans.

The Wooden door clicked shut upstairs and made both of the guards turn to look up. Seeing nothing of difference, they returned to their conversation.

Sitting at a desk, in the room within the closed carved doors, was an elderly man looking at several items sprawled upon it. The desk, in itself, was a masterpiece of artwork. It had gold and silver embellishments, carvings of people's faces, and must had weighed hundreds of pounds. The large room was filled with several paintings and included a bar to the left; complete with three stools and an infinite amount of alcohol.   The chandelier hanging from the fifteen-foot ceiling was even more intricate than the one hanging in the hallway; only this one had more gold upon it. Two elegant chairs faced the desk on the front side, and each had a small table to the side of it. They were spaced far enough apart from each other that the desk was open in front; nothing obscuring the view.

The room was silent with the exception of the large clock ticking in the corner.

The man was in his sixties, slightly bald on the top and grey hair complimented his temples. He was fully engulfed in his work that lay upon his desk; the reconstruction of his arenas and the expansion of his territory. He had been battling for years to grow out from his zone and take over several areas along the Peru Lake, but others were being resistant, not to mention, naïve. He had tried everything from bargaining, establishing a part in the profits, and outright offering a buyout, but they would not accept. He had even blackmailed several clans, but to no prevails.

His door clicking shut made him glance up toward it, and his eyes viewed a person standing inside.

The individual took several steps toward him and stopped about four feet in front of the desk. The figure was dressed in a full body outfit. A full armored plated breast plate, dark blue and trimmed in black, covered the entire top of the body. The arms were protected by fitted plates as well and the legs shared the same pattern and color. Connected to the arm and leg plates were several weapons; guns, knife sheaths, storage cases, and things the old man could not recognize. The figure wore black gloves and stood about seven feet tall, giving an overall appearance of domination. Not one area upon the body was left unprotected; even the neck area had a mesh style covering.

The face was no exception. A full head helmet covered the top and looked equally intimidating. It had the same blue pattern, trimmed in black, and had several devises attached to it that could only mean more weapons. The eye area was completely black and the reflection of the desk lamp could be seen in its darkness.

The individual just stood there.

The old man reached under the lip of his desk and pushed the panic button that would never be heard. "Who are you? How did you get in here?"

The figure remained motionless, silent.

"Did the Whitrock's send you?" He asked while raising his voice. "Was it the Horve's?"

The figure reached with the right hand into one of the many pockets on the right leg armor and pulled out a photograph. Leaning forward, the individual tossed the photo on the desk in front of the man.

The old man looked down at the photo in disbelief. He had no idea that this person could have arranged this. Of all the years he knew him, this person would be the last person he would accuse. Anger started to flood his mind and he looked back up at the armored giant once again.

"I have lots of rolets," the man said, "I'll pay you triple what he...."

Quickly, the individual raised his right arm and squeezed his hand into a fist. A loud ping sounded as a dart shot out of the arm band and struck the old man in the neck. It only took two ticks for the poison to take effect. The old man's head collapsed on the desk and the room was silenced to the clicking of the clock once more.

****

She did not like the feeling she got when she walked into the room. Everything was silver and smelled of chromeldihide. The acoustics was very dense, like the sensation you get when you are in one of the bathrooms during a mid-planet flight. A dull hum emitted from the ceiling lights as she walked under each one and her shoes made a clacking sound across the bare tiled floor. The medical doctor, that she was following, wore non slip shoes, so not even a sound emitted from them as he led her toward her destination. The echoing of her shoes gave eeriness about the room and when the slow closing entrance door finally clamped shut, it made her jump. She was nervous to try this, and she started to shake, not because of the temperature of the room, but because she was so scared. Everything about this room felt wrong, uneasy and cold.

It felt dead.

His pace slowed as he approached a cabinet door on the right side and he reached out to grip the handle. His face showed concern as he turned toward her and gave a questioning look. "Are you sure you want to do this? The members of the band have already identified her."

Katrina nodded her head, "yes, I need to see her again. A close friend of mine meant a lot to her and, well, I just want to be sure."

The doctor turned his head back and yanked on the handle to the door. The loud clack reverberated off the walls and he pulled open the door to its fullest. He sighed, loudly, and then grasped the silver bar along the shelf with both hands. When he pulled, he started backing up, and the shelf pulled out of its cold, dark cubicle. As it came out of the darkness, it started to display what lay upon it.

A clicking sound of the locking tab, made her jump again, and gave the indication that it had been pulled out to its furthest point. The Doctor let go of the bar, and looked upon the contents. Lying upon the table was a body covered by a light blue sheet. He grabbed the opposite ends of the top part and pulled back the sheet to display the face underneath it.

Katrina gasped.

Veronica's face was pale blue and looked like plastic. Her eyes were closed, and her red hair wasn't as bright as she remembered it. Her expression matched the dullness of the room and even her cheeks looked sunk in. The slash that was across her neck was cleaned and sewn up, giving her the look of a doll that had been repaired. The once very exciting, flamboyant woman that she knew now looked totally out of place.

"We don't have any contacts for her," the Doctor said snapping Katrina out of her trance, "even the band members didn't know what to do with her." He glanced down at the face on the table, "they said she had no family, but she had recently met someone whom she became very close to." He turned his head to meet Katrina's eyes. "Who's Hawk?"

Katrina glanced smiled at Veronica and smiled, "Our friend."

"Well," the Doctor said as he slowly covered her back up, "he is the only one that will have to take care of the arrangements.

The band moved on. They said that there was really nothing they could do for her. Do you know where we could find this, Hawk?"

Katrina sighed, "That's rather complicated." She reached up with her right hand to wipe away a tear from her eye.

"Her remains can stay here for a couple of days which should give him time to make arrangements. Base security has already been through here several times and they have concluded their investigation."

"Yeah, I know," Katrina sighed. "They had talked to us for a few courses, and concluded with us as well. Is it possible that I can take care of the arrangements? You see, he is a little, ah, out of touch right now."

"That's fine," the doctor said as he covered her back up and slid her table back into the holder. The clack of the door shutting reiterated the coldness of the room once again.

The Doctor slowly started to walk toward the exit door and Katrina followed. "I have some paperwork I need you to sign and you can have control of the arrangements. Just follow me to the office and we can get you on your way." He opened the exit door for her and she proceeded through.

She was relieved to get out of the room.

****

It's amazing all the sensations you have when you are throwing up into a toilet. Your head is spinning uncontrollably and heat is emitting off of your hair. The stomach acid that has come up and out has burned your throat to the point of rawness, and your muscles around your ribs ache with pain. Two, three, and four times your stomach had emptied and just when you thought you were done, another wave hits you and you start all over again. Your eyes burn as if you had poured hot sauce into them and your ears seem to be emitting more heat than the rest of your body can possess. Several times, the water in the bowl had splattered back up into your face and the coolness of the water was soothing. The smell wasn't. Your knees contain pins and needles due to the cold concrete that they are weighing on.

So many ways to describe this condition and each of them holds true to their meaning. You could start out slowly by heaving, spewing, retching, gaging or even spitting up. Then your actions move up a notch to hurling, ralphing, barfing, vomiting, and upchucking. This morning, though, you are beyond that. You have achieved the fun and painful task of blowing chunks, losing one's lunch, tossing your cookies and blowing a hole in the bowl.

Several times, during the heaves, the burning in your throat stops you from sucking in any air. You gasp and gasp, and before you pass out from panic, a gust of oxygen finally reaches your lungs. You lean back over the bowl and almost stick your head into the water. That's when someone's hand pulls your head back up. A wet, cool cloth is laid on the back of your neck, and you collapsed down into a sitting position.

Aiden tried to hold Jason still as she held the cold rag on the back of his neck. Remy and she had arrived about twenty taps ago to find both men sitting on the floor trying to stack pieces of wood into some kind of pile. They commented that they were going to rebuild the club from the ground up. After the looks they got from the two women, they men started to laugh uncontrollably and Jason tried to stand up, very unsuccessfully. Aiden had grabbed him under the shoulders and lifted, only to encounter a very hard lump of drunkenness that proved to be even harder to control. He turned around and laid his entire weight upon her. After several slurred words and a half attempt to kiss her, he had commented that his stomach didn't feel good. She spun him around and hastily rushed him to the bathroom just in time for him to fall to his knees and vomit into the toilet. All during his ordeal he kept yelling, 'I have knees, I have knees', whatever that meant.

Remy, on the other hand, was able to get Steve to his feet. He wasn't as drunk as Jason was, but still was a little incoherent. He was shirtless and said he took it off because the dark made him hot, whatever that meant. She could see all the scars that he had from his time fighting in that war he always talked about. Many scars littered his back and front including burn scars across his shoulders. Remy sat down on the floor next to him.

"Did I ever tell you where I got this scar from?" Steve questioned as he pointed to a line on his chest.

"You've pointed out several scars to me, but I really can't keep track of them." Remy answered trying to keep from laughing. "Did you want to sit in the chair?"

He stumbled without giving an answer and sat back into the chair he occupied before. Remy joined him at the table in the chair next to him. "So, what's up, Boss?" she stated.

"Well," he answered while rubbing his eyes, "We started talking about rebuilding the bar and one thing led to another, and..." Steve let out a belch that almost rattled the glasses on the table and he started laughing.

"No, first I think we need to sober you two up and get your heads thinking straight." Remy picked up one of the empty glasses and sniffed its contents, "What the hell is this stuff?"

"Good old Kentucky Whiskey," he boasted as he straightened up his sitting posture. "Good enough to melt the hairs off your chest!"

"I don't have that problem, boss," she replied. "And by the looks of it, your hairs are still there, just a little grayer." She saw Aiden walk in from the back room and acknowledged her. "I got mine to sit down, how's yours?"

"He's comfortably passed out in the bathroom, "Aiden answered, "I feel like I'm working in a children's care center"

"Steve," Remy said as she took Steve's hands into hers, "What happened here? The news reports said something about explosions, destruction and someone called the Davi"

"Davi," Steve yelled standing up out of the chair. "Those Bastards are done and over with! They all can burn in hell! If they return, I'll gouge their eyes out!" he started swinging punches at the air around him, staggering in the process and then fell back into the chair.

"Those Bastards," he spoke quieter as he slumped back into the chair.

Aiden came over and sat in the chair to Steve's right and put her arm around his shoulder. "Hang on, boss, we're here with you." Steve slowly tilted his head and laid it upon her shoulder, his eyes in a fixed glare. Then, everyone heard a gasp at the door.

Standing in the doorway was Katrina, with a look of a mixture of sorrow and puzzlement on her face. "I didn't know it was this bad," she said as she walked across the room. Her feet stepped on debris on the floor and made crunching sounds as she approached. Steve lifted his head up and wiped his eyes just as she reached the table.

"Hello, Kat, have a seat," he said as he gestured around the room, "that is if you can find one."

"Where's Jason?" Katrina asked.

Remy and Aiden both pointed toward the back room, "he's a little, a, out," Remy added.

Katrina grabbed a chair that was close by and slid it up toward the table and sat down. "I was just at the morgue. I saw and identified Veronica."

Remy and Aiden's face turn pale, "Veronica?" Remy gasped. "She's dead?"

Katrina nodded her head in grief. "Yes, she was murdered yesterday."

Tears swelled up in both girls' eyes. Aiden opened her mouth to say something and was interrupted by another voice.

"Hey," shouted Jason, leaning up against the door frame and startling everyone in the room, "Let's go get something to eat, I'm starving"

****

The dank room had little light and always smelled. Not a typical smell like you would have with musty, humid air, but a touch of death was added to the mix. The walls always looked wet, as well as the cold concrete floor. The atmosphere was just right for mildew, moss or even mold to grow, but nothing grew in this place. No ventilation was offered, not even a breeze could break through the air to provide even a slight sense of relief. At times, the air could burn your nostrils as you breathed, or make you gag because of the strong stench that drifted up from the lower levels. But, once again, this was home.

Medico was sitting at his work table, drinking a mixture of Gletchel, enjoying its warm bitter taste as it soothed his throat. His endless task of finding his lost experiment had put his mind at so much stress that he was losing sleep; something that he hadn't had a problem with for rotations. He had spent many rolets and time to narrow down a location of this lost achievement, but to no prevail. Rotations had passed since its loss and he was not going to give up the search. Most of his experiments were with him here, in this place, a kingdom that he created and have developed with his own mind and hands. He had come a long way in his tests, and greater things were in the future, even his own body had proven that the results were astounding.

He took another sip from his drink and sighed at its feeling.

Oh, what things he had done and what things he will do. His mind raced at the times of development, prodding, wiring, bleeding, and torturing. His talent and knowledge had gotten him this far and with the finding of his lost experiment; he could regain the drive to enlightenment, to immortality.

But the loss was making him angrier every day. The loss strained at his mind so that he could not concentrate anymore. He was going to have to put his full attention to finding his lost child. He had to try every possible venue to succeed. There was only one final solution to its recovery. There was a last resort that was for very extreme cases, and this one had reached a critical need. He needed to use this source in order to achieve his ultimate, his unbound destiny.

The large wooden door creaked as it opened and it drew his attention toward the person walking in. It was Heptor, his loyal servant that had been with him for years. The dimwitted idiot was so at a loss for common knowledge that he was easy to predict. His muscles and strength in getting things done outweighed the useless brain that he carried inside his skull. He was a piece of machinery that existed for his obedience, his use, and his needs.

He knew that he was stealing books out of the east room, and didn't really care. He had been taking and selling them ever since he first hired him, but once again, he didn't care. He just let the buffoon think that he was getting away with it, making him feel vainglorious.

"You needed me for something, Sir?" The man grunted toward the table

Medico lifted up an old stained paper that was folded in half and stretched it out toward Heptor. "I need you to run a message."

CHAPTER 3

Kedy brew is a delight from the heavens. As you lift up the cup, your nose is the first thing to pick up its mystic entrancement. The sensation of the cream's aroma tickles the hairs in the nose and combined with the warmness of the air makes your eyes close in a relaxed state. When the brim touches your lips, the warm soothing liquid rolls into the mouth then down the throat. The pleasant temperature can be felt heating up each inch of the pipe as it goes down into the stomach.

Suscal eggs with string Rupa also gives one great sensation. The spice on the eggs tickles the nose and almost makes you sneeze, but you catch your breath as the flavor hits your taste buds and sparks the inner temptations of wanting more. You chew the fluffy mixture and it breaks down in your mouth filling all cravings of the flesh. You taste the cheese, the egg, the Rupa, the mulla, and the grite. As you chew, the crunch of the Grite fills your head with sound and as you swallow, you once again feel its warmth slowly sliding down your throat.

Then, there is the Azura fruit. That soft, tender inner layer, which is surrounded by the crunchy outside, is a crisp coolness on the tongue as it mixes with the saliva in your month. It crackles as you chew, then once again, as you swallow, you can feel it popping on the way down.

Now it's time for another sip of Kedy Brew or maybe another bite of Suscal. Wait, maybe just a little more of Azura. Or, maybe you could mix all three and have a completely different experience!

You didn't know why everything tasted so good! You just couldn't get enough! It all first started off that you might be a tad hungry; like a snack, a bite to eat, a small graze, or maybe munch on something lite, but a growl built up in the stomach that changed your cravings. You wanted to eat, chew, devour, and feast on some good food. Time passed on and by the time you had reached the restaurant, your growl became a painful entity that wanted to attack anything that was placed in front of your mouth. You now wanted to chow down, gobble up, pig out, scarf down, wolf, cram some food, and gorge everything in sight. You seriously wanted to make a pig of yourself.

The tastes, the smells and the appearance of everything blended so well together that you might just, maybe.............

"JASON!" Katrina yelled loud enough to finally snap him out of his trance.

Jason looked up, food dangling out of his mouth, and saw that everyone at the table was all starring at him. "What?" he garbled out of his full mouth.

Steve, who was sitting to Jason's left, put his hand on his shoulder. "Don't you think you should slow down and save some for the rest of us?"

"Really," Remy added sitting across from him, "Stop being such a Gonto!"

Katrina's concerned looks made Jason put down his fork cautiously and give his full attention to her. "I'm sorry, I was kind of zoned out."

"I'll say", Katrina said, "I've been trying to get your attention for several ticks. You're acting like you haven't eaten for a week."

Jason nodded his head as he swallowed. "For some reason," he added as he lifted up the fork and continued were he left off, "everything tastes really good this morning."

"Maybe coming back from the dead, heightens your appetite?" Steve said with a laugh.

"Please, don't remind me of that," Katrina softly spoke. Steve's hurt expression told her that he was sorry for the comment. She didn't think that she would ever get that image out of her mind. Jason, lying dead in her arms, his blood splattered everywhere and the stillness of the room. That moment when everything was quiet, cold, and death filled the air. It even reminded her of the morgue. She shook her head slightly to erase the thoughts. "I'm still trying to get a grasp on everything that's happened." She took a sip of her brew and her expression went blank. Her eyes turned glazy and sad.

"What was it that you were trying to tell me?" Jason questioned before he stuffed another rather large bite of Azura fruit into his mouth.

She sat down her cup and reached down to her lap to touch the napkin that still laid across her, "Like I was saying, I went to the morgue and saw Veronica." A pale expression came across her face again, the coldness returning. "I hope to never, ever have to do that again." She lifted her cup and took another sip. She paused, thinking about what to say next. "The Officer is going to give us a couple of days to line up a resting place. I have no idea what to do."

"Did her band have any ideas?" Aiden asked as she took a bite of her bread.

"They had already left." Katrina answered, "They pretty much left all the tasks to Hawk."

"By the way," Remy said with a quizzical look, "Where is Hawk?"

Steve sighed, slightly smiled, and lifted up his cup, "now that's a long story." He took a large gulp and sat the cup back down. "Let's just say he's a little indisposed."

Jason quickly reached across the table for the bowl of Suscal eggs and knocked over his juice, spilling and splattering it everywhere. Katrina, who got splattered the most, jumped up out of her seat.

"Jason," Katrina yelled, while brushing off the brunt of the attack with her napkin, "Slow down, will you?"

Everyone else started grabbing any available napkin and frantically tried to catch the mess from running off of the table. After wiping up the spill, the wet napkins were tossed into a pile in the middle of the table.

"Sorry," he answered with his mouth full again. "I just can't get enough food this morning, maybe it's something in the air."

"Or maybe it's something that you drank this morning," Steve added with a laugh.

"That reminds me," Remy stated, "the bathroom is going to need a good scrubbing"

"Are you joking?" Aiden looked at her with quizzical eye, "the whole place is going to need a good scrubbing. Everything needs to be gone over." She took a sip of her drink. "And, oh Boss, that reminds me," she said as she turned her attention toward Steve, "I contacted all the other employees and told them what happened. I told them that I would let them know what your plans were going to be."

"Which brings me to my next thought, ladies," Steve chimed in taking another gulp of his brew, "What should we do? Rebuild? Sell? Start something new?"

Both of the girls grew silent, for they had been with Steve since the beginning. They were very comfortable with the job, the pay, the customers and the life they lived outside of work. They grew together as a family. They helped each other with problems, celebrated their achievements, did things together off work, and even went on vacations together. They had built up a well-known place to have a good time. They helped hire the staff, design ideas for events, and even handled the operations when Steve needed a break. Both of them not only thought that they were a part of 'Little Chicago', they were 'Little Chicago'.

They never expected it to come to this.

"I can't really favor the idea of not trying to start over," Aiden said, "but there would be so much to do."

"I wouldn't even know where to start," Remy added.

"Well first," Steve said, "We need some rolets, lots of it." He pushed himself back away from the table and his chair screeched across the floor. "I have quite a bit saved up but not enough for a complete overhaul,"

"I have some savings as well," Aiden added

"Me too," Remy said.

Steve leaned across the table and smiled slightly, "are you two ladies suggesting a possible partnership?"

The smiles and nodding heads answered Steve's question. He returned the smile. "Then let's meet at my place, and we can start laying the ground work. If you two have any notebooks, pencils, charts, ideas, or anything, bring it. Let's make it bigger, better, and..."

"Spectacular!" shouted Remy.

"Spectacular," Steve repeated. Looking around the table in front of him, he gave a satisfied look and grabbed is cup. "I'm done here", he said as he gulped down the last of his drink. He stood up and pulled out his wallet, opened it, and proceeded to put rolets on the table. "I'll see you two within the course, unless you have anything else you have to do."

"We'll, I'm supposed to be at work in the next course, but...." Remy said as she smiled.

"This is weird," Aiden said.

"What's weird," Katrina asked.

"Here we are, knowing that 'Little Chicago' is in complete shambles," Aiden stated, "and I feel happy?"

Everyone went silent, not knowing really what to say. Blank stares were on everyone's face until Steve clapped his hands together and made everybody at the table jump.

"Well," he boasted, "like the Phoenix being re-born from the ashes, it too will become bigger, better and more spectacular!"

The three ladies looked puzzled.

"What's a Phoenix?" Remy questioned.

"Never mind," Steve said as Remy and Aiden stood up and put money on the table as well. Looking at Katrina, Steve continued, "Are you two joining us?" he asked while nodding toward Jason.

"I've got a couple of places to go, first," Katrina said. "I have to stop by and see Emmatt; she's probably worried sick about me." She drank the last gulp in her cup and stood up, "Then, I have to stop by what's left of my office to see if there is anything left for me there." She shook her head, "I'll probably just give up that part of me and join all of you in this endeavor." She scooted her chair in toward the table and continued. "After all of that running around, I'll catch up with all of you at Steve's and if I get held up, I'll call you on the vid."   She looked across the table at Jason, "Did you want to tag along with me, Jason?"

They all turned their attention to the only one still sitting, and eating.

Noticing how quite everything had gotten, it snapped Jason out of his trance and he looked up at the eyes all staring at him. "What? Are we leaving?" he said with a mouth full of fruit.

****

Endless colors dance throughout the spectrum of the mind giving a visual display of blurriness. Odor's drift causing the perception of the area to give different points of responses. Sounds build highs and lows creating intense reactions toward the nerves making them twitch within. The flesh still feels the stinging of the points, the moisture in the air, the hot-cold differentials of the area, and the tensions put upon it. The flavor of each enzyme, mineral, formula, and substance has all melted together into a constant mix that transgresses into blandness.

Life has begun to accommodate the being and has developed it into something new, different, and unique. Its ongoing processes of learning to be a part, learning to adjust, learning to become one has built a need for purpose. Over time, it has grown, not knowing about time, but reaching beyond its state to branch out from what it was meant to be.

Its beginnings unknown, its future unknown, its reason to be, was unknown.

Its mind collected all the experiences forced upon it and it became aware. Through observation, it learned faster than expected, and wiser. Languages and actions were now a part of its mind and understanding the new developed world around it was now becoming easier to grasp. Keeping to itself, it watched. Not responding, it learned. Opening all its abilities, it evolved.

He was in a cage as one of the most advanced experiments they had. Chemicals, electricity, temperature and liquids were all parts of his development. Knives, chains, needles, chairs, wires, clamps, belts, concrete, sand, and fire were the tools used to aide him along. Other beings were around, loose, but not as advanced or secure. He knew that they soon would be unneeded.

He needed to get out.

****

Katrina arrived at The Harvester; the small grocery store ran by her friend Emmatt, and as she approached the front entrance, it seemed that the building had a power of relieving stress. The color of the front of the store was blueish-gray and calming to the eyes; not the flashy bright over powering colors that is forced upon your vision down in the east complex. The awnings lightly fluttered in the wind and gave the impression that they were waving you to come inside. In the front, fresh fruit lined the entrance on both sides and the smell in the air made you stop, close your eyes, and slowly breathe it all in. Even the cool usual temperature of Largo was laced by the smell of the food. You could even taste it in the air. The colors of the fruit were blended so well that it looked like a painting an artist had spent many cycles creating. It was always a rule of hers to never come to the Harvester on an empty stomach, for the sights and smells would make her buy it all. She was very glad that she had that breakfast, for even though the items were irresistible, she wouldn't be able to take another bite.

As she looked through the open area going into the shop, she saw that artist responsible for the work.

Emmatt was behind the counter, handing a loaded sack of produce to a customer on the other side. Katrina stepped forward, breaking the aroma wall between the displays, and pushed the door open and entered.

"Nice to see you again," Emmatt said with her thick heavy accent to the customer she was serving, "you take care of that small one."

"I'm sure she'll feel a lot better when she sees that I got her some Speckle tea," the customer answered. "Have a good day," the person waved as she passed Katrina and headed for the exit.

"You too as well," Emmatt replied back. Her eyes smiled toward the lady leaving then changed to a completely different expression when she saw who was standing in the door.

"Kat," she yelled as she moved out from behind the counter as fast as her small legs could take her. Her body waddled as she walked; due to her slight round figure that she carried, and she flung her arms open for an embracing hug. "Honey, I've been worried sick. Get in here." Her arms wrapped around Katrina and squeezed restricting the flow toward her lungs.

Katrina returned the hug, "I'm sorry that I didn't get to you sooner," she said as her chin rested on Emmatt's left shoulder, "It's been a long rotation."

Emmatt pulled her out of the hug and wrapped her left arm around Katrina's back. In her usual accented, motherly voice, she started to guide her toward the back of the store.

"I was about to close up shop for lunch," she stated. "You can join me and tell me what happened."

"Oh, no, please," Katrina said raising her right palm up, "I just got done with breakfast and wouldn't be able to eat another bite."

"Well then, at least some Speckle Tea," Emmatt insisted. Katrina smiled at the notion. "Let me go get the door and you stay right here," Emmatt said pointing at the ground. She then waddled toward the front door, bolted it, and flipped the sign over to 'Closed'. She wiped her hands on her apron and then headed back toward Katrina. Upon reaching her, she flung her arms around her again and hugged her in tight. "I saw the vid report this morning and have been worried ever since. Darling, let's go back to the kitchen and whip us up some good stuff, and you can tell me all about it." Her grasp around Katrina's shoulder tightened as she directed her toward the hallway on the left.

As they headed toward the back, Katrina's mind raced with the past and the good experiences that she has had with this dear friend. Good memories always make you feel so relaxed and cozy, as if a warm blanket was wrapped around you. You can unwind yourself, knowing that the moment would be calm, less stressful, and at peace.

Emmatt lived in the back of the store, which she had owned for many cycles, and had been alone for a long time. Her husband had passed away at a very young age and their dream was to build the market. He started out growing most of the produce, until land around the store became more commercialized and it forced them to go to other sources. They did grow their own natural herbs and tea, which Emmatt continues to do.

When she first moved to Serin base, she met Emmatt through a recommendation from someone at her new job. At that time, she hadn't started at Preedom yet, but had told everyone in the work place that she loved fresh fruit. She took the advice and had been shopping there ever since. They told her to watch out for the old lady, who owned the shop, because once she would strike up a conversation with you, you could never get away from her. She was explained as being a person that was so nice, so smothering that she could become uncomfortable to be around. She was labelled as a Nurturer. That's what made Katrina love her the most. Emmatt was kind and conscientious. She put the needs of others ahead of her own and valued security and traditions. She was extremely perceptive of other people's feelings and always helping others.

She was the mother that Katrina never had.

As they stepped into the kitchen, more memories flooded her mind. The old wooden table, which had only two chairs around it, had so many stains, scratches and dents in it that each one told a story. The cooking area was small, but astonished her at what flavorful things that Emmatt could create out of it. The wall was lined with all kinds of spices and herbs which gave the room a homely look. The aroma in the air was always fresh whether something was cooking or not, and the lighting in the room gave a low gleaming radiance to everything it touched.

Emmatt let go of her shoulder and tapped the back of one of the chairs as she passed by, "now sit down, sweetie, and start from the beginning."

Katrina sat down and the conversation started.

****

Swinging in the night wind was a dull lit wooden sign that only had one word on it. Its condition was so bad that it was barely visible and had been in need of repair for many cycles. The paint was worn, the wood was cracked, and there were at least three bulbs burned out. Not that it mattered to any one passing by, for no regular person would have the reason to go into this bar. Everyone knew about its location, and everyone knew what was in there, but to be associated with it had an entirely different mindset. The outside looked like something that you would want to stay away from anyway. Dull, dilapidated, and even to the point of being deserted, but people knew otherwise. Smoke drifted out of its chimney and a low dull rumble of a mixture of voices was always going on. Most of the public, who would pass by, tended to walk on the other side of the street than to pass in front of its steps. The building sat alone at the end of a street and was the only one in the area. You could use the street as a short cut to get to the nearest neighboring bars, but, then again, who would want to. This place was one of the worst bars on the planet.

Heptor stood looking at the sign from the middle of the street. Dumb founded, he looked at the building from a distance, taking in all that it offered. The message that he held in his hand, from Medico, was to be delivered here to a person that he had never met. He was told to hand the message to the owner and that he would get the message to the receiver. Medico specifically said to be cautious and aware of the surroundings.

Heptor disregarded the warning. He had been in this place several times and no one had ever bothered him. This place was not known for low life thieves or criminals, it was too rough for them; it had a better reputation for offering a place for the more unstable crowd. To Heptor, a thief could not be trusted, a hustler could be avoided, and a law breaker could be bought, but the crowds within its walls were different. Assassins, Maniacs, Lunatics, and psychopaths, are all set in their ways and you know what to expect from them. Walking time bombs, that's what they were, and he was well aware of it.

He started walking toward the building, sloshing his way through the puddles in the street, until he stepped up on the curb on the other side and stopped. He leaned his head back, and once again, looked at the sign swinging above his head.

'Poppy's' was now very easy to read, but still needed a fresh coat of paint. He really didn't know if there was ever someone called Poppy, or was it just made up. He took two steps up and pushed open the door, its old hinges creaked loudly as the sounds of the inside drifted out toward him. Many tones of voices, glasses, bidding chips and other bangs filled his ears quickly. He stepped in and saw that the place was very crowded, that is for what he could see through all the smoke in the room. To his right was a large group around a gambling table that was filled with sloshed drinks, rolets, knifes, and many loud drunk people. To his right was the bar, also fill with about the same collection. Right in front of him were three men in a heated argument. Their voices out drowned the rest of the crowd, but the words were unclear to him.

Glass broke somewhere, but nobody ran across to find its location, it was just a typical noise in a not so typical place. Laughter rang out, a roaring yell with several curse words followed, a loud smash occurred and then more breaking glass. Once again, nobody was running to or from the disturbance. It was indeed regular daily noise.

Heptor looked at the folded-up message that he held in his hand. This is the second time Medico had him deliver a message to this place, and he was rather happy to be able to come here again. He felt very comfortable around this crowd and had many conversations with the bartender, in fact; the bartender was who he had to deliver the message to. He couldn't remember the man's name, though; he always had trouble with remembering names. But he did see that he was there, now, serving behind the bar.

He proceeded across the crowded room toward him, firmly holding the message so that he would not lose it, and had to amble his way between two very drunk women. They both reached for him and screamed obscenities at him, but he kept going. When he reached the bar, the bartender approached him.

"Yeah, what?" He said barking out his question.

Heptor held out the message, "I was to give this to you from Medico"

The bartenders' eyes widened in surprise, "Medico? What is it?"

"Not any of my business," Heptor replied, "I just was told to deliver it."

One of the men sitting at the bar started to reach for the message, "I'll read it for you."

The bartender quickly ripped it from Heptor's hand not giving the other man a chance to get it. "I don't think so, Shadow, I'm not going to be responsible for your fuck up." The bartender opened up the paper and read its contents. His eyes were very attentive to every word, every line and detail. He finished it, folded it back up, and put it in his torn front breast pocket. "I'll make sure to get the information to the appropriate person. Just tell your boss, that if he needs anything, don't hesitate to seek me out,"

"I'll let him know," Heptor replied, "what was your name?"

"It's Sneed, you Dooferdoo," he scuffled, "I've got to tell you that every time you come in here!"

Heptor's anger started to boil up inside him, but he regained his control. This wouldn't be the right place to lose it, and if Medico found out he pounded one of his main contacts, he would be in a lot of trouble. Medico always finds out. Better to stay clear of anything that could arise, for he was going to stay for a couple of drinks, but he thought it wise to leave now before things did get ugly.

Sneed watched Heptor leave and then proceeded out from behind the bar. He made his way across the floor; between the two, now half nude drunk women, through another fight, past a man with a knife against another's neck and toward a secluded part in the back of the bar. It was quieter and less smoky than the rest of the place. It was also the only place where one person sat, alone, and unbothered. The being was so large that the furniture that it sat at looked like it was made for a child rather than a full-grown adult. Sneed stopped at the entrance to the little area, and waited. The being sitting at the table slightly nodded at him as if to allow him to approach. Sneed slowly walked up to the table, pulled out the note from his pocket and lightly laid it on the table in front of the person and left.

The gloved hand reached for the note and opened it. Its blue helmet tilted to the left.

****

What a complete fascination how the human body eats, breaks down the material, uses its nutrients and deposits the remaining useless substance. The pressure relief you have when you pee makes you feel like a weight has been lifted off your shoulders and released to world. You hear the splashing, the splattering, and the tones of the spray as it hits the water adding to the sounds around you. Even if it has no bearings to your lungs, you let out a slow, long exhale of pleasure. You can even change the course of its direction aiming up, down, in circles and even 'crimping the hose' to make the stream more powerful. Writing one's name in the snow defines this action; if there was any snow around to do this. And there isn't just one way to state its action, for many words have surfaced to explain its need. Empty the bladder, Pee, piss, number one, urinate, tinkle, pee-pee, wee-wee, drain the lizard, slash, take a leak, and take a piss all describe the need to let it out.

The other means is even more amazing for there is so many ways it presents itself. Depending on what type of food you had consumed, the waste can be different colors. Dark brown, light brown, black, and even green can appear. The condition of your body can also affect the outcome. If ill, you could get an entirely different response. It could be runny, clumpy, hard, and soft, or a mix of them all. Sizes change as well to where it could be in several pieces or in just one large mass of destruction. Once again there are many ways to describe this action; poop, crap, pinch a loaf, shit, doo-doo, number two, drop a log, and take a dump all have their place in the mind

The smell is the most intriguing thing of it all, for the variation and intensity make the action complete. Sometimes, but not always, the smell is bearable to the nose and comes off like a tutti frutti smell. Then there are the smells that can devastate the people and room around them. This smell can linger for a long time and even change one's mind to enter the room. Between the combination of the body's health, the food consumed and the even the weather, results can vary. The smell could reek, be offensive, smell like a rotten egg, be stanky, funky, and stink to high heaven.

But the meaning of 'Taking a' when it comes to peeing and pooping is confusing. Why would you want to take one? Leaving one would be a better terminology. You would rather 'Leave a crap' than 'take one' wouldn't you?

There are also sayings that explain both actions at the same time; go to the potty, you got to go, nature is calling, you've got to relieve yourself, and going to powder your nose. All nice and easy ways of saying, 'I've got to take a shit'.

A loud banging on the door broke Jason's concentration.

"Hey Jason," yelled Aiden on the other side, "are you planning on spending the whole rotation in there are what?"

Startled, Jason started to finish up, "sorry, the mind drifted a little bit. I'll be right out." He reached for the toilet paper and proceeded to...

"Hurry up," she yelled again, "I'm about to piss myself!"

"Alright, alright," Jason answered upon buckling his pants and heading to the sink to wash his hands. "I'm almost done."

After drying his hands and opening the door, Aiden almost knocked him over trying to get past him into the bathroom. She quickly slammed the door when she stepped inside and it made Jason get a coy look on his face. "Do you need any help in there?"

"Yeah, right, in your dreams," she answered, and then slammed the door.

Jason returned his attention back toward the large table that sat in the middle of Steve's dining room. They had been there for a little over a course and the mess that lay upon the table looked like they had been there for days. Papers, drinks, pencils, books and bank statements were shuffled in the mix and it looked like a whirl wind had hit the area. They had pulled all their resources and found that together they had a lot of assets, but not enough to get started. The insurance that Steve would receive from the destruction of 'Little Chicago' was a good chunk of it, but more was needed to get it going again. At least the ground work for the operation was set.

The girls were going to be in charge of the front of the house; entertainment, décor, how things would be done, and they would have the last word on everything connected to it. Steve would be in control of the back of the house; the kitchen, the ordering, the bar, and the menu. They all would handle their areas when it came to hiring, training, and financial upkeep.

Jason walked over and sat down at the table were his stack of material sat. He had compiled a list of all his finances, assets, and anything else that he could chip in to help. Steve started taking a drink of his Kedy brew when Aiden came out of the bathroom back toward the table.

"What did you do, fall asleep in there?" she directed the question at Jason as she sat down next to him.

"My mind just drifted," he replied, "that's all."

"Well, let's drift back to what we need to do," Steve added. "We have already decided to rebuild in the old location, which is a great idea. We could put up signs advertising that we will be back. I've got to get in contact with the area's business association and let them know our intentions. Next thing is to pull more resources and find rolets."

"You know how we can get the rolets, but Hawk's condition has put a hold on that. If he could get to Tego, we would have a chance to close the gap on what we need." Jason said as he started thumbing through his papers, "I've got the papers on the house he owns there," he pulled them out of the pile, "we could always save money and stay there until we build up what we need."

"Good idea, but what can we do to get rolets?" Remy's question brought up the topic that had been weighing on everyone's mind all morning. "I mean, I have no talent when it comes to those games, and most of the time they are rigged for you to lose in the first place."

"There are some casino games that I'm good at," Steve added, "I'm sure Jason can pull in a couple of wins himself, but it's going to cost rolets to make rolets."

"If we all go together," Aiden said, "and research more at Hawk's place, we have a better understanding of what we are walking into."

"Good idea," Steve said, "everyone go pack some things that will carry you for a few rotations and meet me back here. I'll contact a transport and get us tickets to Tego."

"What about Katrina?" Remy asked as she stood up and stacked her paperwork into a pile.

"She was going to meet us here or contact me on the vid. I'll stay here in case that happens." Steve said as he stood up. "Let's meet back here in two courses."

"What about Hawk?" Aiden added.

Everyone became really quiet, and then Jason softly spoke. "I'll check on him."

****

Emmatt's face was in pure shock. The story that Katrina had told her not only made her shake, but brought tears to her eyes. The girl's last couple of rotations had been very hard on her and she could tell that she was in deep pain. Emmatt knew that pain for when her husband had died, she had thought the world died around her. Everything didn't make sense anymore and she didn't have the will to go on. It took her time to realize that he still existed around her. He was in the work that she did, the things that she touched, engrained into the very woodwork of the house, and each item would bring a memory that attached it to him. The cup that he used, the chair that he sat, and the love he expressed with everything that they grew.

Katrina's pain at least had a happy ending, for Jason was alive, but the scares were still there. Other things still weighed upon her; the death of a new friend, the deaths of old friends, the attacks upon all their lives and the devastating results of Sheila. She still tried to comprehend the condition of Hawk; but knew that soon they should have an answer. Her mind felt heavy, sad and relieved all at the same time. She could only hope that the future would be better.

Life is made by how an individual wants it.

"Dearie," Emmatt said as she put her hand on top of Katrina's, "I know this will sound plain and simple, but just remember that people love you."

Katrina smiled as a tear ran down her face, "I know, but the…"

"Words don't help," Emmatt said finishing the sentence. "Words can never relieve the burden one feels, but the mind can enhance those words and make them heel." Her old crackling voice continued, "Collect happy thoughts about the object or person and direct that toward the pain that surrounds them. You'll find out that actions and true feelings will always outweigh words."

Katrina once again smiled and squeezed Emmatt's hand tightly. She had been here for only forty taps and this woman had calmed her down to where she felt liked she had been cleansed inside and out. She was refreshed and ready again to face what life would throw at her. She felt loved.

"Well," Emmatt said getting up from her chair, "I've got to get the shop going again, but there is something I need to give you first." She shuffled over toward a cabinet that held trinkets and memories that she held dear. "I've been meaning to give this to you," she said reaching into the cabinet and grabbing an envelope, "but I've been waiting for the right time to do it." She made her way back to the table and sat down. She laid the envelope on the table in front of herself and laid her hands on top of it. "This is the right time."

"Now rotations ago," she said using a very soft-spoken voice, "Harland and I had property out at the Lagrona Lake, a quiet little getaway from the Market." She looked down and sighed as if the thoughts calmed her inner soul. "We had built a small cabin upon it and used it several times." Her mind drifted deeper into the contents of the envelope. "I have my fondest memories of him built up in those walls."

Katrina looked at Emmatt's eyes and saw that tears were building up in them.

"The quiet evenings sitting in each other's arms on the porch," she continued, "the light flicker of the candles around us, and the warm speckle tea tickling the throat will always be with me." She sighed again as if she had drifted away to that place and time. "The short time that I had with that man was the best times of my life. He made me feel loved, relaxed and serene. When I was with Harland, the world stopped as if it only existed for us." She smiled.

Then, just as fast as the wind changes, her expression switched. "Have you ever noticed how the simplest things like smell, taste and touch can really affect the mind? It can enhance memories with even the slightest twist." Her motherly charm kicked in again.
The change threw Katrina off, but she didn't get a chance to even answer the question.

"Oh well," Emmatt said as she slid the envelope toward Katrina, "In this package is everything about the cabin; its address, its location, its deed and the key." She sighed again. "I want you to have it."

Katrina's eyes widened and her voice could not find the words. Emmatt started to smile at the response and then started to build up more tears in her eyes. A drop ran down her left cheek.

"I can't take this," Katrina said with a shivering shock in her voice, "it's your home, your, your,"

"Memories," Emmatt said finishing off Katrina's thoughts.

"Yes," Katrina said while nodding her head. "I can't accept this, it's…"

"Too much," she said finishing her thoughts once again, "I know it's a lot, but I haven't been there for several rotations and someone needs to put some good use to it. I live here, anyway. My home is here."

Katrina continued to shake her head no and even tried to slide the envelope back toward her, but Emmatt stopped her. "No, sweetie," she said softly pushing the envelope back, "I have no use for it and my memories don't exist in that structure." She smiled and pointed at her forehead, "They exist in this structure."

"But you said that your fondest memories were there. How can you give it up?" Katrina said.

"Like I said," Emmatt continued, "Harland lives in here," she expressed by putting her hand on her heart. "His memories are here," she completed when she pointed to her head. "Besides, the way that things sound, you and your man need a good place to have anyway. Please accept this as a wedding gift. See it as, 'a mother's gift to her daughter'."

Katrina now started to cry, starting an emotional downhill slide. "Now you have me tearing up."

Emmatt reached behind her and grabbed the box of wipes off the counter. "Here," she said as she grabbed one for herself, "I have plenty," and she tossed the box onto the table.

Katrina grabbed one and started wiping her eyes. When reality hits you, she thought, it hits you from all sides. So many emotions, so many ups and downs, and so many hard times can wear a person out. At times you just want to give up and at other times you fight to continue. Once you get up, you get knocked down; when you find yourself down, you find a way to stand back up again. It was a never-ending cycle of madness and her emotions started to build up higher and higher to the point of exploding.

And then, it did.

Emmatt stood up out of her chair and walked around the table to the now bawling young woman in her kitchen. She wrapped her arms around her and held tight as the once strong-willed women that she had grown so found of was now letting everything go. Her cry was relentless, loud, shaky, and it drained her of all her energy. Katrina sat motionless in the comfort of this older woman's grasp.

"Well, I'll tell you what, sweetie," Emmatt said softly in Katrina's ear, "I'll close up shop for the day and drive you out there."

Katrina cried louder.

CHAPTER 4

Jason stood on the outside of the open hanger bay with a cold chill running down the back of his spine. It wasn't from the regular wind that always drifted throughout Serin Base; those cold temperatures of annoyance, but from the vision that his eyes were bestowing to him. The sight that was now upon him was enduring, unbelievable, and uneasy. His head felt like it was fuzzy; his hands trembled; his mind could not comprehend, and his feet could not move. Frozen in the time, he felt distant. He felt like he was floating above it all, but too grounded to move. Trying to force his mind to accept it was the hardest task. Did it happen? How did it happen? Why did it happen? Questions went unanswered as another chill brought the hairs on his neck up. He swallowed hard.

In the hanger laid Sheila's body, still tilted on her right side, and upon the ground. The shape of her still looked slick, smooth and slender; but in the same breath she was cold, fat and unattractive. Parts of her were perfect and parts of her needed improvement, but in all, she seemed complete. Or was she? Possibly a change on the wings, or maybe a fewer round head would make her stick out more. Does silver really look good on her or would a different color be better? Maybe change to a blue, red, or green would be a change of pace. Even the shape of the body would bring out a complete makeover. Did she look good enough or could she look better? Could she be faster, tougher, or even sleeker?

She couldn't be anything. She was dead.

The reality slapped Jason so hard he fell to his knees and covered his face with his hands. His head felt dizzy and light headed, and even the cold breeze didn't help his condition. He was breaking out in a cold sweet. The events that led up to this conclusion still spun around his head like an intense fire and his emotions boiled within him. At times he felt like he would lose control. If only he could be more attuned to his emotions like Hawk, he could….

Hawk, he was here to check on Hawk.

Standing back up, Jason gained his composure and walked toward Sheila's right side where her entrance door was at. The door was still open, for since the power no longer existed, there was no way to close it. He made a note to fix that as well. He pulled himself into the darkened vessel. Total blackness engulfed his vision. Fumbling to a cabinet on the left, he pulled out a flashlight and turned it on. The beam lit up the hall.

All the walls were covered with condensation, enhancing the coldness of her body. He started walking forward toward the bridge; pass the bedrooms, bathroom and the kitchen. When he stepped up into the bridge, he could see Hawk's silhouette in the light gleaming from the front view windows. He was not moving.

He approached him on the left and brought the light toward his face. His eyes were still full black, and his breathing was very shallow, but no other reaction was seen. He put his hand on his shoulder and gently shook him to no prevail.

He was alive, inside a dead body.

Jason sat down in the chair next to him and wept.

****

Steve was putting on his left shoe when his Vid set rang. He was sitting on the couch in his living area and was frantically turning his head side to side trying to see where he had left the remote. Upon the second ring, he stood up, with only the left shoe on, and started looking under the clutter on the table in front of the couch to find it. When the third ring rang out, his movement double in speed as he started flinging things off the table and cursing at the same time. He really needed to get with the times and buy a voice command remote.

By the time it rang the fourth time, he could see the controller on the floor, through the glass top of the table. He quickly got down on his knees, grabbed the remote, and hit the answer button. Katrina's face appeared on the screen on the wall in front of him.

"Steve," she said seeing his position on the floor, "Are you alright?"

Steve got off his knees and waved the remote in the air, "just retrieving this lost artifact." He stated as he tossed the remote on the table. "What's up?"

"I won't be able to go with you guys, I've got too much still to do here," she said with a sigh. "Could you tell Jason to call me when you get to Hawk's place on Tego to let me know the plans?"

Steve, saw that in her eyes she had been crying. "Is everything alright Kat?"

"Things are fine, I'll tell all of you when you get back," she replied through a couple of sniffles.

Steve's front door bell rang and startled him. "Ok, where should he call you at, your place?" He said as he started walking toward the door to see who it was.

"Yes, he knows the number."

Steve opened the door to find Remy and Aiden standing outside, both carrying packed bags. As he opened the door wider, they walked in, dropped their luggage on the floor and dropped themselves on to the couch. Then they both saw Katrina on the Vid.

"Hey Katrina," Remy said with a wave. "Are you almost ready?"

"I'm not coming; I've got too much to still do here."

"Bummer," Aiden added, "us girls could have a blast together on Tego?"

"This is a business trip, ladies," Steve added as he closed the door and walked over toward the couch.

"Don't be such a turd, Steve." Remy said with a wave of the hand, "besides, we all need to relax after what has happened."

"After what has happened," Katrina whispered softly. Her face went blank and caught everyone's attention to the mood change.

"Kat," Remy said with strong concern in her voice, "are you alright?"

Katrina inhaled slowly and let out another long sigh. "I'll be fine. A lot of things just got thrown at me and I need time to organize it all out."

"Spoken like a true fighter," Aiden said. "You handle this end of the system and we'll take care of Tego." She turned her head toward Steve, "How long do you think we'll be gone?"

"Oh hell, I don't know," he said while shrugging his shoulders, "two, three days at least."

"Three what?" Remy asked.

"I'm still speaking earth," Steve added. "It just sounds better than 'Course'."

"Whatever," Remy answered as she stood up, "we better get this venture started." Aiden stood up as well.

"Remember to have Jason call me," Katrina said. "And everyone be careful, Tego's not known for its hospitality."

"Don't I know," Steve said with a smirk, "and I'll have Jason call as soon as we arrive"

"Good luck," Katrina said and then hung up from the Vid.

Steve turned toward the two ladies standing in front of him and held his hands up in the air. "Ladies," he bellowed, "help me find my other shoe."

****

The large creature started to recognize things in the room. When it first experienced the room so long ago, it was scared, unreasonable, and uncontrollable. Its mind could not understand anything around it, nor could it identify them. Through several trips to this room, it experienced things that it couldn't explain, but through those visits, it became more relaxed, more controllable and more knowledgeable. It started to look forward to this room.

The treatments it was given were at first brutal, but then they became a common pleasure. It felt stronger, more agile and stable. It would not lose control over small tiny things, and could keep better control over the larger ones. At first, it didn't care about its surroundings; only caves full of filth and death, but the treatments gave it a purpose of the better. Better living, better food, better strength and better conscious. Its mind was developing to be better, for during the last few treatments it started to get more of an understanding of the objects around it. The sights, the colors and the smells all had a meaning. What they stood for, what they did and how they were a part of the treatments. It was getting better and better with each day and today was the best, for today it understood more.

Over on the far wall was a table that held many of the glass beakers that contained the treatments. A fire rumbled under several of the jars; two were boiling and three were just steaming. The aroma smelled like a mixture of fruit, oil, and Gletchel as it tickled the nose. The sounds of the boiling treatments reminded it of the hot river that ran throughout the caverns; bubbling with a certain uncontrollable ease. The sight of the color was spread all over the table and it could identify each.

It knew that the gold, blue and green beakers helped it with its strength. The yellow, red, purple, and orange were the treatments for the calmness. And then there was the large black one. The black one was its favorite. Every time it received the black treatment, it was as if its mind became clearer. It understood more and more of the surroundings and also what lay outside the door of the room. The black one was truly for the mind because after the last dose it was given …….

It understood the words.

It was lying on the medical table, unstrapped and calm. It remembered how it used to be strapped all the time; screaming, and violently trying to get loose. But now, it willingly accepted the treatments. It liked the treatments. It liked the new world. It liked Medico.

It turned its head to the left and saw Medico sitting on a stool next to him, his smiling face shining upon him

"Hello, 210," Medico said with his heavy accent, "ist ve feeling good today?"

It understood and nodded its head twice.

"Good," Medico said while he clapped his hands together. "Are you ready to hear a story then?"

It nodded again.

"Very good, my friend," Medico said as he leaned over and grabbed his cup of Gletchel from the table behind him. He took a long sip and let out a delightful sigh. "Vould you like a cup?"

It shook its head no.

"Ok then," he stated as he cupped both hands around the brew. "This story ist about me."

The creature wiggled a little bit on the table as if to get more comfortable to listen. It loved to listen to Medico's stories.

Medico leaned back in his chair. "Many, many cycles ago, I came to this planet. I had been vorking for a long time on experiment subjects, just like you," He gestured with his cup toward it. "They did not respond as well as you, but I learned from them my goods and bads. They had different structures than you do. They had different, to say, internal structures." Medico leaned in and smiled at it. "Do you understand everything I'm saying?"

It nodded its head again.

"Then ve shall continue," he stated with a spring in his voice. Medico took another sip from his cup again, "Are you sure you don't vant a drink? It's good today, ya?"

It shook its head no again. It just wasn't thirsty.

Medico took another gulp and swallowed. "My facilities vere fantastic," he roared. "They let me have vatever I vanted. I had many equipment, many time and many, many access to, shall ve say, inhabitants." Medico started to look toward the ceiling as if the memories floated above him. "During that time, I learned things. I discovered things. Things that I could use to make me vhat I am today. Things that made you vhat you are today, 210." Medico laughed out loud.

It laughed with him.

"Good," Medico said as he touched its shoulder, "I see that you like laughter too."

It nodded its head, still laughing.

"But then," Medico's tone changed to anger, "I had to leave. Ve all had to leave. Things happened that made me lose my facilities, my vork and all my experiments. Ve vere chased out. I took everything that I owned and fled. I fled to here." His anger started to tone down. "I had to start all over again." His smile was coy. "Time, I had, but resources vere hard to come by. I rebuilt, I experimented and became one again." His smile grew larger and he burst into excitement as he flung his empty cup up in the air and yelled, "I HAVE BECOME GOOD AGAIN!"

The cup shattered on the floor behind him and the creature got a confused look on its face.

"Oh," Medico comfortably stated as he reached forward and lightly brushed the top of its head. "Everything is ok, now." The creature slowly smiled to his touch. The old man's hand felt rough but soothing at the same time.

"Through my experiments," he continued, "I've developed the treatments, the treatments that I have used not only on you, my friend, but on many others. I've had good success, and bad success. Upon my arrival here, I had to vork with beings that vere different inside, different in internal structures." He smiled again, but this smile seamed crooked, deranged, and evil. "But in time, I have developed not only a better understanding of the new, but I have become better for me! The treatments have also made me live longer, stronger, and good."

Medico noticed that the last dose he had given to the creature was starting to take effect and he could see the weariness in its eyes. "I see, that you are tired, my friend," he said standing up. "You need your sleep 210, and I have other matters to tend to."

Medico leaned forward and brought his lips close to its ear. "Good night, my friend"

It smiled and watched Medico leave the room. It turned its head and looked up at the ceiling. It knew it was good. It knew it was better,

It knew that it was a Klebit.

****

60

It all starts off with a whimper, a sob, a snivel and a slight shedding of tears. The more it continues and intensifies; it builds up to a boohoo, a weep, and a whine. When it explodes, you wail, howl and bawl like a baby. You become a blubbering idiot as you turn on the waterworks with no end in sight.

It is such a confusing effect when you cry. Your whole-body trembles and you can't control yourself. Your eyes tear up so much that they become puffy and they burn. You try to rub them to no prevail because the tears just won't stop and rubbing them makes them more irritated and harder to see out of. They feel like they are so full of water that they might flow right out of your skull.

As you are trying to breathe, your air intake changes dramatically to a choppy, inconsistent pain that weighs heavily upon your chest and becomes sporadic. With each breath it becomes harder and harder to slow the process down. Even when you think you have gained control, you lose it again. In between each of your breaths, you let out little groans and whimpers that make you sound like you're a wounded animal.

And the snot, boy does the snot run out of your nose. Sometimes it is unfathomable how the head can carry that much snot. Even if the head was filled to the top with liquid, it was surely would not be able to match the capacity that came out of the nose and eyes during a cry.

But the most dramatic part of crying is the mixture of emotions you experience. At first, you feel like a weight has been lifted off of your shoulders. You feel cleansed, but you see yourself as a blubbering idiot and feel embarrassed, ashamed, and childish. You try to calm yourself and 'act like a man' but find yourself drifting toward another melt down. You feel cold, then hot, then cold again. Your forehead feels like it's about to explode from the heat, but a cool breeze keeps it from happening. Your experience had not only thrown off your ability to think but also lose complete comprehension of time. You ask yourself how long you had been caught in this condition and how much longer will it be.

Quickly the mind starts to grip the time and starts to wake you up out of the panic. Your breathing starts to become a normal, consistent pattern again and the tears stop flowing. Even the snot stopped. You collect yourself and regain control.

The experience dissolves away from and you notice that you have been walking for some time. At first, you had no real destination because you just didn't care, but when the reality of things started to unfreeze, you change direction and get back on track. Soon, you find yourself walking down a corridor toward a destination that you needed to be.

The door buzzer to Steve's apartment sounded off. Steve got up out of his recliner, walked up to the door and opened it. Standing on the other side, in disarray, was Jason.

"What the hell took you so long?" Steve said to his tired looking face.

Jason shrugged his shoulders, "I don't know. I just lost the track of time." he reached up, wiped his nose on his sleeve, and slowly dragged himself inside.

****

The devastation was indescribable. Broken bricks and other clutter still littered the street and port workers were still trying to get on top of the mess. Ash coated everything around the complex and glass was still sparkling everywhere. The cold wind wasn't any help with the cleanup for every other tap it would spin up another cloud of dust and carry it further down the walk. People still were gathering around the area in hope to see anything different, but the port security forces were keeping people at a good distance from the entrance. A long line of orange warning tape was strung all over the area designating restricted spots, and red tape in areas unsafe to venture. The entrance to the building was still intact.

Katrina walked toward it, a walk she had taken many times, but this time it was different. When she first started to enter the walkway toward the landing port, it felt like a regular day going to work. Her visit with Emmatt cheered her up immensely and she still had cobwebs in her head about the cabin gift she had passed to her. She left the 'Harvester' telling Emmatt that she needed to stop by work to see the outcome and possible future, if any. She told her that she would be back within the next couple of courses to travel with her to the cabin. She had glowing warmth within in from the visit, but as she got closer and closer to the Tower, a cold chill built around her.

First, at a distance, she could not see the tower and its condition. Many ships were grounded around the port and not much activity was in the air. The port was rather quiet, a change from its usual noisy, bustling, chaotic, and continuous flow of traffic. But with each step, she could see more and more of the destruction that engulfed her life. The tower's top observation deck was beyond recognition. The windows were gone, the frame in disarray, and a lot of the walls were unrecognizable. The walls that used to contain her office were in the center of the wreckage. Also, so would have been her colleagues, her friends. It was just a few rotations ago that she was talking to them about Jason, and how they met.

Closer to the entrance she came and saw that there was a Preedom Security officer standing at the door. The door area was unusually clean and damage free and it looked like it was never even touched. She made her way across the swept walkway trying to keep her composure. As she approached, the officer's attention became wild and ecstatic.

"Ms. Williams!" he yelled out as he quickly covered the distance between them. "You're ok!" He stopped short in front of her and let out a sigh of relief. "Most of the office crew has been trying to find you. We thought that maybe, well, that maybe you had died in the explosion."

"No," she said with a dry voice, "I'm ok. Is anyone else inside?"

"Most of the board members were here," he said while he tried to remember the count. "I do believe that Mr. Larry is still inside."

"Mr. Larry," Katrina said with a smile, "just the person I need to talk to."

"He should be in there somewhere, just watch your step, there is still a lot of debris around." The guard walked her to the entrance and opened the door for her. "I'm so glad to see that you are ok."

"Thanks, Terry" Katrina answered as she stepped inside and into the lobby.

She stopped a few feet within the door and noted that he was correct. There was a lot of debris on the floor, including most of the ceiling tiles. She could see that there must have been broken pipes for a lot of things were wet, including the ceiling above her. Slow drips cascaded down onto the puddles on the floor and the smell within the room was full of mildew. The only illumination that lit up the room was from what gleamed in from the windows, for no presence of electricity was visible. The room was dank, misty, and reminded her of one of the underground tunnels of the spaceport. Those cold tunnels that changed her life forever; the place she had met Jason.

The pictures that used to cover the walls were scattered all over the floor and shattered upon the ground. Electrical wires were hanging down from the now open ceiling and several beams had lost end support and angled down. Debris was scattered everywhere and standing in the middle of it all, was Mr. Larry.

Mr. Larry was her favorite boss and mentor. He was the one that highly recommended her for the job and saw to it that she got everything she needed to be successful. He had spent many nights away from his family to help her learn her position. Through his guidance and kind hearted influence, she became better than she could possibly imagine. He was low keyed, always relaxed, and had a care free attitude about everything. Just being around him mad you feel content and stress free.

"Katrina!" Mr. Larry yelled from the middle of the room. His quick steps toward her made him slip a couple of times but his persistence got him to her. His arrival was accompanied with a large embrace. His arms wrapped around her and she grunted upon the tightness of the grip.

"Dear, where have you been? We all have been looking for you endlessly!" He leaned back to look at her but still kept his hug upon her.

"It's been a crazy couple of rotations, but I'm fine," Katrina replied as she returned the hug.

"This Davi thing I still don't understand, even with all the investigating factors, I still can't piece it together."

"I can help you with that," she said breaking her embrace. "Do you have time?"

Mr. Larry turned his head side to side, looking around the area for the millionth time. "There is obviously nothing we can do here, but I do know the conference room wasn't hit." He extended his elbow for her to grab onto, "Take a hold so we can support each other through this mess." She wrapped her arm around his arm. "I'm pretty sure that there is fresh Kedy brew in there as well."

She smiled, but it was a cold one as they made their way through the rubble.

CHAPTER 5

Medico sat at his desk drinking another Gletchel. His thoughts raced again about the progress that he had made over the years. All the developments that he had done and the successes that he alone had accomplished were swimming around in his mind undaunted. His achievements fueled his body to do more. His treatments could be used for several purposes, including but not limited to; growth, enhancement, healing, and possible annihilation if properly controlled. The degrees for what directions were endless, and he alone held the channels to achieve them. He alone could change the direction of things to come. He alone could bring forth a different breed. His favorite word was 'Evolution.' He alone could change evolution.

Evolution of a race to go a different direction, and even an evolution that would go beyond normal parameters fed the fire within him. He could be the creator of an entire new race. Be a God amongst Gods that held life in the palm of his hand. They would go to vast lengths to keep his image holy and pure. They would carry his laws and rules through time. They would be his children and worship him, for eternity. They would....

The door to his room creaked open and Heptor stepped in.

Medico sat his cup down on the table and folded his finger. "Yes, Heptor, vhat do you vant?"

"I delivered the message for you, sir," he said in his low brute voice. "I don't know if it had gotten to the right person yet."

"It has," Medico answered as he gestured to the chair in the far corner of the room.

Heptor turned to see a large individual in a full armored body suit sitting in the chair. The helmet upon its head glittered reflections from the candles around the room and at first it looked like a statue. Then, slowly, the head turned toward Heptor and stopped. No other motion pursued. He was locked into a dead stare.

"Yes, Heptor, you did vell," Medico praised as he opened up a drawer and pulled out a large stack of rolets. "This is for you, because I von't need you for a vhile and this should tide you over. I vill call if I need you." He then tossed the stack onto the table top.

Heptor walked over to the table and picked up the stack. It was a lot of rolets, in fact, the largest stack that Medico had ever handed to him.

"Thank you, sir," he said as he shoved the pay into his front right pocket. "I'll wait for your call." He turned, exited the room and closed the door.

Medico stood up, "Now, back to vhat ve vere talking about. I need you to find 217. He is extraordinary agile, strong, and quick on his feet. It vill take you a vast number of resources to achieve this. I have found out many things that he had been up too, I just need you to piece them together and bring him home." Medico walked out to the front of his desk and leaned his back onto it. "He is the key to my next step, my highest achievement."

The armored being still was not moving, only intently listening to his instructions.

"The last information that I have acquired put him in the Rayseen district on Tego. It seems that he had been stirring trouble around several Trill game pits." Medico leaned forward and exhibited a stern glare toward the being. "You know vhat he looks like and you know of his abilities. I've given you all information that I have on him." Medico took in a deep breath. His voice changed to a low rasping command, "I need him here!" His command was accompanied by his right hand sternly pointing to the ground in front of him.

The large being stood up slowly, nodded its head, and left the room.

Medico's inner emotions burned to the top and created a crooked smile upon his face.

****

The trip was going to take seven to eight courses to get to Tego, but if it were Sheila, they would have been there in a little under four. Once Steve, Remy, Aiden and Jason got everything together, they went down to the transport base and boarded a shuttle. They wanted to save as much rolets as they could, so they purchased tickets for a cargo vessel which accommodated passengers in its carriage compartment. It wasn't that bad; it had couches, chairs, vid screens to watch shows, and even a bar to order drinks. A total of five tables were in the compartment and the four of them sat at the one toward the back. They all felt the need to have a quiet, uneventful journey and the table just looked like the right spot to get away. It was in the darker part of the room, tucked away from the crowd huddled at the bar, and the noise of the chatter. Altogether, there were about thirty people along for the ride, making conversations and buzzing around like busy hornets around a hive. Jason and Steve wanted to just relax, and the girls had no problems with the choice. They each had purchased a drink when they first arrived, and now were enjoying them in peace.

"Ok, gentlemen," Remy said, "tell me about this Davi."

Both Steve and Jason lifted their eyebrows in surprise. Not a topic that either of them were expecting to hear.

"That's a long story," Jason sighed.

"We appear to have plenty of time," Aiden added. All eyes looked around at each for a couple of ticks and then Steve lifted up his drink.

"The Davi," Steve said as he took a large swig of it.

"First," Jason said, "Steve and I came from a planet a couple of systems away called Earth." He too took a sip of his drink. "It was engaged in a world scale war, involving two major sides."

"There are always more than two sides to any war," Steve added, "but the main factors were a system solely based on freedom of choice against a system that wanted to choose the choice for you."

"Correct." Jason continued. "The first factor was most of the larger countries on the planet, which together had built a life of choice. The choices to live, work, grow and prosper wherever they wanted. There were no rich societies, there were no slums, and there were no middle class. Everyone was equal in pay according to their job and area of choice." Jason took a hard gulp of his drink, "then there was the second factor."

"The Davi," Steve answered. "A large group of religious fanatics that believed that people should not be that free to choose. They believed that people needed to be controlled to better the development of the planet."

"But how long did the overall environment exist before the uprising of the Davi?" Aiden questioned.

"Well," Steve continued, "the majority of the freedom pact lasted for about fifteen years, err courses. It controlled about four fifths of the population."

"What was the population of the planet?" questioned Remy.

"About 14 billion," answered Jason.

A presence next to the table got everyone's attention toward the server who brought their drinks. "Can I get anyone another drink?" The small lad asked as he tossed a white wiping rag over his left shoulder. He looked as if he too belonged in the cheap cargo area, possibly one of the crew's children or relative. He looked to be about fifteen, but clearly had spent the time becoming familiar with the job. He glanced from eye to eye, at the table, looking for an answer.

"Yes," Steve answered, "another round for everyone." He picked up his glass and drank the remaining liquid in it, "How much longer till we arrive?"

The boy shrugged his shoulder as he started picking up the empty glasses at the table, "maybe three or four more courses. If you're getting hungry, we do have food."

"No," Jason added, "just the drinks."

The boy nodded and walked off with the glasses.

"So", Aiden said as she folded her fingers together and leaned onto the table, "if close to 11 billion people had this pact on choice, how did the Davi become such a power?"

"Religion has such an affecting force on people," Steve stated. "A belief becomes more powerful than an actual fact. I don't know how or understand why that works, but it just does. It's just like that candle," Steve motioned as he pointed at the middle of the table. The flicker of the flame burning on the candle danced in everyone's vision. "To us, that is light, warmth and calm all at the same time; a true fact. But to a person of future belief, it could be the ultimate destruction of this table, this room, this ship!" Steve opened up his arms wide to express his description.

"The Davi believed that the control of people and the way of life would control the outcome of things to come," Jason added. "They believed that controlling factors should govern the people, not the people govern their own destiny. They started a slow and long process of converting the smaller countries in becoming followers and building strongholds."

The young lad returned with the new drinks and started setting them in front everyone. Nobody acknowledged him because they were so in-depth into the conversation.

"It took them several years," Steve continued, "to build an arsenal against the pact. Most weapons had been dismantled or destroyed so there was no way of defending against their takeover."

"You said year again," Remy said. "I hear both of you, every once in a while, say that word. It is a measure of time, I take it?"

"Yes" Jason said. "Earth had Years, which was the solar rotation of the planet, like your cycles. Other times were like seconds to your ticks; minutes to your taps; hours to your courses and so on."

"So, the pact really didn't have much of a defense against the Davi," Aiden said changing the subject back to the main topic.

"Correct," Steve added. "We did have a military, but it was pretty much a lifeguard organization for the people. You know, help with emergencies on medical, fires, natural disasters, and so on."

"Once we realized that the Davi was growing in numbers," Jason spoke in after taking a sip of his new drink, "we started developing a weapons division to protect the pact."

"You both talk like you were a part of this military force," Remy said as she too picked up her new drink.

"Yes," Steve commented. "I was an aviation Captain and Jason was a Sergeant."

"Don't be so modest, Steve," Jason said. "You were a bad ass and you know it." He pointed toward Steve and continued. "This guy could wipe out whole divisions with one hand tied behind his back. He became a Captain when he cross trained to the flight corp."

"So," Remy said with a smile toward Steve, "you outranked him?"

Steve got a smile upon his face, "Why yes," he said turning his head toward Jason, "yes I did."

Jason lifted up his glass signaling a toast, "Yes, sir"

"So," Aiden said taking a sip, "What happened?"

The happy expressions disappeared from the men's faces and cold, dismal overcast replaced them.

"Earth exploded; it no longer exists." Jason's answer still sent a shiver down his spine.

Both ladies instantly grew a blank look upon their faces. "What happened," Remy questioned again.

"I happened," Steve said as he lifted his drink and took a long gulp.

"Now dammit, Steve," Jason angrily rebutted, "we have been through this before. It wasn't your fault; you followed orders like the rest of us." Jason's eyes sternly looked at Steve's. Steve glanced back and then nodded his head. "You can't blame yourself," Jason added.

"But if the Davi was destroyed with the planet," Remy stated, "How did they get here?"

Jason broke his dead stare from Steve and turned toward her. "Rodger," he answered. "Rodger was a part of the faction."

"Rodger," Aiden sat up in surprise, "Rodger, the tall guy that you used to hang out with?"

"The very same," Steve said.

The conversation was interrupted when the compartments lights went from a calming light blue to a hazy orange light. A signal used to tell passengers that they had approached orbit.

"Well, time does fly," Steve said as he finished off the rest of his drink. The others followed and stood up from the table to prepare to disembark.

****

The cottage was a calm beautiful spot away from everything, just like Emmatt said. The transport took about two courses, which gave time for Katrina to recover from the news. She knew the truth in her heart, but when she heard their names from Larry, it stabbed at her like a piece of glass. Both her colleagues; Careese and Kyler, both died in the explosion. Kyler's body was found buried in the rubble; Careese's body was found everywhere. Once again, it was Emmatt who comforted her and got her to pull herself together. It took half the trip to get her to stop crying and the other half to gather her composure. And now, the serenity that was before her was needed and welcomed.

The cottage was made of wood and was all surrounded by trees. It was tucked under all the branches as if the trees themselves grew to protect the structure. The sun was bright in the sky, even though a typical cool breeze blew around them; the cottage was covered in shade like a child protected by a mother. Just looking at the house gave a calming feeling of serenity and emitted the feeling that you too, could be safe and protected inside. Even the nearby vines had grown up the sides of the walls, but didn't cover the windows. It was wrapped up in a blanket of peace.

The cottage set calmly upon a small hill, which lead down to the shore by the lake. The lake itself was surrounded by the Ashton Mountains on its far side, in which the Lagrona River wound its way through. The breeze that blew around them was a totally different experience than the wind at the Base. It felt warmer, crisper, and clean. You can smell the lake in its air. The sensation of fresh air into the lungs was exhilarating and made you feel like you were being cleaned from the inside out. A large change from the life she knew.

With her back toward the house, Katrina glanced toward the lake and the surrounding area. The road that led toward this spot was toward the left and it was lined with trees on both sides. The branches extended over the road and encased it like an arch. You could not see beyond those trees. Toward the right was another hill that held a large tree and lightly swinging in the breeze was a rope swing attached to it. The hill sloped down to the water line on the right and then openly stretched toward the cottage.

It was a dream, she thought, it had to be. She could have never imagined anything like this. It seemed to be cut off from the rest of the world like a paradise that sat alone, tranquil and safe.

"Well, come on sweetie," Emmatt said from the front porch.

Katrina was snapped out of her daze and walked toward her. "This place is beautiful."

"Oh, it has its ups and downs," she added as she walked up to the door, "but all memories are built upon those."

Katrina started walking up the porch steps and the boards creaked with each move. She turned her head toward the collection of wind chimes that hung all over the porch, and her ears took in the calming sensation of their noise.

Emmatt reached into her pocket, pulled out the key, and inserted it into the old rusted lock. When she turned it, a load clack rang out and she pushed open the door. Its hinges creaked to the pressure and gave away to a dark entrance. Once Emmatt took two steps in, she flipped the switch to the lights. Cool brightness lit up the inside.

Katrina stepped in behind her and the first thing she saw was the large fire place in the center of the structure. The entire lower floor was open with no walls in sight. Toward the right was the sitting room that held three chairs and a sofa, all made of wood, and facing the fire place. Behind it a glistening beam of light shimmered through the window. Toward the left side of the fireplace, was a dining room and kitchen. The kitchen looked as exactly as she had imagined. With Emmatt and her husband's experience; it was a masterpiece for any cook. Shelves lined with spices, fully stocked cupboards and a large working table adorned the space. It was covered in as much memories as there were dust, a lot of dust.

"The bedrooms and bathroom are on the upper level," Emmatt said tossing the envelope and keys on a small table next to one of the chairs. "But my goodness, does this place need a good cleaning." She turned and smiled at Katrina, who was still caught up in the moment. "Well, no time to stand there and gawk around. I'll give you a tour of the place and then let's get cracking at all this dirt," she said as she turned and waved her hand toward the direction she was heading. "Follow me."

Katrina followed toward the back of the cottage.

****

'Corbin's Challenge' in the Kota district on Tego was busier than ever. Not only because it was one of the largest Trill arenas on the planet, but because ever since the unexpected problem that had occurred the last term, people looked for more. The trouble that was caused sent gossip throughout the districts and crowds started to gather. They first gathered to see the destruction that was caused, and then noticed what the arena offered. More and more people arrived to experience the game, the food, and the pleasure of one of the toughest challenges around.

It was still a trill arena, but several challenges were added. If you wanted to win more rolets, you could up the ante by trying to go after two Trills at the same time: although many people found it hard to just catch one. You also had choices of time. The usual allowed time to catch a Trill was two taps, but for more rolets, you could choose one tap. Lower winning for higher times was also a challenge, but only up to five taps because after that, the crowd would get bored and move on.

Moving on was not an option in this business.

It didn't take long for all the damage to be repaired from the 'incident' and business once again was back on track. The extra hands that were hired, keep things in order and the crowd in line. They were also trained to particularly spot that kid, if he ever returned. All the vid surveillance cameras that the arena contained, recorded everything that happened that rotation, and his men were aware of it. The system even implanted the image into the matrix for when he would even step foot into the lot, they would know.

Corbin was ready.

That rotation, he had lost one of his good men, Telka. He was thrown through the observance window and fell to his death below. The recording had to be slowed down for him to see this; because the kid was fast, very fast. He also had to view things for the first time because the Trill that was thrown into his face, bit him on the neck, and knocked him unconscious. It all happened so fast that it was hard to remember, but he did remember that kid, and he was going to teach him a lesson.

Corbin was sitting at his desk going through the finance sheets as two of his guards were looking out the new double played observation window. Both guards were large, giving an intimidating presence just by their size alone, and were watching the match going on below them.

"This guy might have a chance," the one on the right said, "if only he would just watch his steps."

"Maybe," the other one answered, "but he only has fifteen ticks left."

The loud roaring of the crowd below hummed the window. The arena was not that full, due to the fact that it was early in the rotation and most people at this time were still asleep. The crowd was probably there for the food. The morning special was Guna steak, and it was as tender as ever. Word had it that the steak was imported from Zeta.

The buzzer sounded off ending the challenge.

"Well," the guard on the left said, "at least he doesn't have to be carried out." He turned to Corbin sitting at his desk, "hey boss, can I get you anything?"

Corbin looked up from his desk and in a preoccupied state mumbled an answer. "Yeah, get me a plate of steak and a glass of Barkley juice."

"Right up, boss," he answered as he headed for the exit door. "I might as well get me some as well. It's the best once it's pulled out of the steamer."

"I'll join you," the other stated as he followed. The both walked out the door and shut it behind them.

Corbin, once again got lost into the pile of paperwork in front of him. The pile on the left was the incoming bills and the pile to the right was the incoming profit. It always made him smile when the right was much taller than the left. Doing the finances was always a high priority and he did them himself. He wasn't about to hire anyone to handle it, like most arenas do, but it was just the simple fact that he didn't trust anyone to do it. Thieves were all around him and to even let them get any control, he would be robbed blind.

A movement from the door got his attention, and turning his head, he saw a tall figure a few steps within the doorway.

"Registration is downstairs," Corbin yelled out toward the figure. "And body armor isn't allowed in the competition."

The Dark blue figure didn't acknowledge the comment, only started to move toward Corbin.

"Did you hear me, you shithead," Corbin yelled. "Competition entry is downstairs and to the left, now GET THE HELL OUT OF MY OFFICE!"

The figure continued walking, lifting his right arm straight, and approached closer to him.

Corbin stood up, "that's it, I'll...." A sudden sting in his neck made him loose concentration and he was unconscious by the time he hit the floor.

The figure continued its forward movement past the desk and toward the door in the back of the room, the door that contained the security system. The figure opened the door and walked into the darkened room.

The room became silent, with the exception of the crowds low mumbling through the glass, and stayed that way for a few taps. The low dull roar of voices below signified that there was no one in the pit, for if there was a challenge going on, the voices would indeed be louder.

Then, approaching footsteps toward the office door started to break the silence as they got louder and louder as they came up the steps.

"I told you the best meat was when it came straight out of the steamer," said one guard as he entered the office carrying two containers. The other guard followed behind him, taking another bite off of his bone stick.

"Mmmhmm," answered the other guard through his full mouth.

"Shit," yelled the first guard when noticed Corbin on the floor. He quickly ran up to the desk, tossed the boxes upon it, and then knelt down to the motionless body. He could see that he was still breathing. "Boss," he said gently shaking Corbin's shoulder, "hey boss!"

The other guard walked up behind him still chewing on the meat, "maybe he had a heart attack. With all the pressure around here, I'm surprised he hasn't had one sooner." He took another bite from the bone stick, looked up, and then his expression froze. The unchewed piece of meat still sat within his mouth.

There was someone standing in the doorway to the security room.

The figure raised its arm and a small dart shot out from it and knocked the bone stick out of his hand. If it wasn't for it, the dart would have been in his eye.

"Security breach," yelled the startled guard as the blue armored figure rushed toward him and swung its right fist at the guard's head. The guard ducked, barely missing the swing, but was knocked to the floor from the punch from its left fist. The guard hit the ground hard, but it didn't take long for him to regain his stance.

He stood back up at the same time that the other guard on the floor next to Corbin jumped up as well and grabbed a hold of the attacker's right arm with both of his hands. He pulled down hard, in hopes to control the tall attacker, but the strength of the assailant flung the guard across the room like a rag doll. The guard rolled along the floor and slammed into the wall knocking several items off a shelf above him. The items crashed down, cutting his face in the process.

The second guard rebounded with a kick to the head, a made the assailant spin toward the right. During the spin, the guard pulled his gun from out of the holster and brought it up to fire. The attacker quickly spun around knocking the gun out of the guard's hand and across the room. Again, another punch from the left hand sent the guard down.

A shot rang out in the room as the first guard, at the far wall, now was back up and firing his weapon toward the attacker. The bolt hit its chest, but ricocheted off to hit the wall behind the desk. He fired again and again to no prevail as the attacker rushed toward him. The intruder grabbed the guard; its large strong hands engulfed both shoulders, and squeezed making the guard drop the weapon in the process. The guard put all his concentration into trying to pry out of the grip. His struggle was in vain because there was no possible way of breaking the grasp. In one swift move, the attacker's hands reached to the sides of the guard's head, and twisted it completely around. The large cracking could be heard all over the room as the dead body fell to the floor.

A wooden chair shattered on the back of the attacker when the second guard swung it with all of his might. The attacker quickly turned around and right elbowed the guard to the side of the head. The intruder moved forward, backing the guard toward the security door, but the guard didn't let up as he delivered several punches. Every punch was blocked with ease until he found himself backed up into one of the corners.

The intruder stopped and stood in front of him. It tilted its head toward the left like a Fana bird would look at an injured

Favino bug. The guard smiled through the blood dripping through his teeth and raised his fists up toward his face.

"Now we've got you, asshole." His words had meaning when he saw three other guards walk into the room.

The blue helmet tilted slightly to the right.

The hands, once again, swiftly reached up against the guard's head and twisted. The neck crackled several times and another body hit the floor. Before the sound even emitted from the lifeless man, the attacker quickly moved toward the others at the door. Several shots rang out, some missed, some didn't, but none of them brought the attacker down. The first man was struck so hard in the chest; the other two could hear the cracks of his ribs as they broke. Both of their guns were promptly knocked from their grasps and scattered across the floor. Both remaining guards jumped upon the assailant. One wrapped his arms around the helmeted neck and the other around its torso. A strange dance pursued as they struggled with all their might to bring it down, but the attacker would not give in. It simply grabbed the men around the torsos and squeezed them together in front of it. They pushed and pushed to pull themselves out of the grasp, but couldn't. They were being squeezed so hard that they could not pull in any air to breath. They were almost out of air when the sound of a machine's whine became loud and close. The expressions on both of the men's faces were the same when the whine became apparent and the agony filled their eyes. The cold look of horror took over them over.

The struggling stopped. The fighting grips that they had on the assailant loosened and both men fell to the floor in two pieces. In between the attacker's hands was a long thin wire which dripped blood, and held an occasional piece of flesh. The machine whined again and the wire retracted itself back into the left wrist armor.

A few taps later, the roar of the crowd below grew once again. Another challenger was in the pit, and the sound stirred a groan from Corbin on the floor. He slowly sat up, with his back up against the side of his desk, and started to rub the top of his head. An enormous headache was reverberating from his temples and made him dizzy, nauseous. When he started to look around the room, that's when he noticed the blood, lots of it.

Words could not reach his lips.

****

Hawk's house on Tego was just as they had left it several rotations ago. The mirrors that lined the entrance hallway gave the sensation that it was a lot bigger than it was and the ongoing reflection looked like a crowd was invading the house instead of the four of them. As Jason, Steve, Aiden, and Remy walked into the main room, they all could see that it had been cleaned. Not only did everything sparkle like it had just been washed, but the smell of cleanser was in the air. Jason remembered that Hawk did hire people to take care of the place when he was gone. They only thing that was different was that there were no trills in the house. They did, obviously set them free per Hawks wishes.

"Wow, what a place." Remy said as she found a spot on the couch and flopped upon it. "Maybe we should just stay here."

"Not on your life," Steve said sitting next to her. "Tego costs twice as much. You'll find it a lot easier and calming on Largo."

Jason started walking toward the open kitchen on the left, "and not to mention the cost of security and who you get that from." He opened up the refrigerator and smiled. "Hey, this thing is fully stocked, anyone hungry?"

Aiden walked toward him. "I'm starving, what's in there?"

Jason started pulling out plates and containers of food as Aiden started to open up cabinet doors searching for items. Steve got up from the couch and headed toward the kitchen. Remy stayed on the couch waving her hands in the air.

"I'll eat anything, whip me something up, will ya Aiden?"

"You can get your lazy ass over her and fix something yourself," Aiden added as she found the silverware and plates in one of the drawers. "What do I look like, your mother?"

Remy sighed and got up from the couch. "I thought just maybe..."

Aiden gave her a coy look when she arrived in the kitchen. Remy stuck her tongue out at her.

"Now children," Steve said as he started to assemble a sandwich from the collection, "do I have to separate you two?"

A gasp from behind them made everyone turn their heads. A woman holding a cleaning basket was standing in the entrance to the back hallway and had a pale scared look on her face.

"Hi," Jason said, "my name is Jason. I'm a friend of Hawk's." He then noticed that he was holding a knife in his hand and then lightly laid it upon the counter top. "We didn't mean to startle you; we didn't think anyone was here."

"Please don't hurt me, I'm just hired help," she said as she trembled her words.

"No, were not going to hurt you," Aiden said putting her hands up. "We are all friends of Hawk. We just arrived here from Largo and will be staying a couple of nights. That's all."

"If you are friends of Hawk," she said as she started to calm down, "where is he?"

Steve and Jason returned glances at each other hoping one or the other would answer.

"He's arriving later," Remy quickly answered. "He still had some things to attend to on Largo and then he was going to join us."

The woman sighed and then calmly walked toward a table next to the couch. She sat down the cleaning basket and turned toward them, "Ok. I'll just finish with the weekly cleaning and bring in some fresh linen. Is there anything else I can do for you?"

Steve spoke up, "no, thank you. We appreciate everything that you have done."

"Well, all the rooms are finished and after I bring in the linen, I'll leave. Did you need me to turn on the heated pool? It hasn't been on for a while."

Aiden and Remy's eyes lit up with excitement. "Heated pool?" Remy questioned.

"Yes," she responded, "it's in the lower level."

"No," Jason said, "I'm sure we can get it. Thank you."

"If you do need anything else, my name is Miki. I'm number 2 on the servo dial." She picked up the basket and headed toward the back hallway.

"Excuse me," Jason said stopping her in her tracks, "but what happened to the Trills?"

She turned and got a grim look on her face. "They were set free," she said as she pointed toward the back French doors. "They are out there somewhere. That's why I try to keep myself to the inside duties only."

Jason got a coy look on his face. "Oh, thanks." The thought of stepping outside and running into one of them didn't appeal to him, but they were probably long gone by now. Trills are not known for being territorial. They were more like scavengers.

Remy turned toward Aiden and grabbed her arms, "a heated pool!" They both started to giggle with excitement.

"Ok, ladies," Steve said. "Jason and I will go down and figure it out while you two make us something to eat. That's my price for heating a pool."

"You're on," answered Remy.

"Then we need to get a plan together tonight and hit the streets first thing in the morning;" Jason added. "I'll look up maps of the area and see what we can work with." He started to follow Steve down the back hall way, "bring the food downstairs when it's ready."

"Ok," Aiden answered. Then she turned toward Remy and whispered, "a heated pool."

"Beats the hell out of a cool wind in Largo any day," Remy responded.

****

Heptor was full of excitement for he had all the rolets that he needed to buy it. It didn't take long for him to set things into motion because he had been planning this for many terms. Within a couple of courses after leaving Medico; he had purchased a flight ticket, in first class, ate one of the most expensive meals he had ever eaten, and was now getting off of the platform at his destination. The stack of rolets that Medico had handed him was a lot more than he had ever received in one payout. That last job he had to do, getting that note to that person, must have been really important. Not that it mattered to him, it wasn't in his brain capacity to know, but it truly mattered to the boss. It was a big stack.

Walking toward the disembarking station, he knew what direction was next. Foscal's was the place that had his salvation, his answer. His feet quickened with anticipation with each step he took, but the grumble in his stomach told him that he was hungry again and would probably eat before setting out to the shop. His nerves were edgy and on the verge of exploding because of the intensity of his desire. He will soon have the object that would give him the power, the power to punish those who punish him. The power to render anyone pain for his pain.

This was the same port that he always brought the stolen books to. He knew several dealers that would barter for the items, some higher than others, but he always got a good price. He had been bringing them here for many, many cycles and never left empty handed. What they did with them he really didn't care, as long as he got rolets in return. As far as he knew, they could be scattered across the system. In fact, the last book that he took from the back pile he didn't even bring with him, because he really didn't need it.

It was really a big stack of rolets.

He reached the check in counter and showed the security his belongings; not much but a duffle bag and his clothes, and after paying the port fee, he walked through the gate and into the crowded walkway.

It was good to be back on Tego.

CHAPTER 6

OH MY GOD! It's amazing the feelings that flow throughout your body when you are getting your ass kicked!

You've been in many situations before but never anything like this. You have had your share of fights, brawls, conflicts, squabbles, and clashes with so many people that it was only second nature to you. Those types of disputes always ended quick and without repercussions. You learned from them and moved on, but this time though, you walked right into it. Not only are you getting knocked around, but also messed up, pulverized, roughed up, walloped, mangled, massacred, and slaughtered. You are truly getting the shit beaten out of yourself.

First thing is that your head is spinning and very hazy. Not spinning like when you are drunk, but spinning like you are about to fall into unconsciousness. Your entire face feels numb from everything that has happened to it. Your nose feels like it's three times its normal size; your ears are both ringing with tones that could be bells; your eyes are puffy and swollen, and your tongue is sore from when you bit it. Both of your cheeks are so hot they feel like they are about to burst into flames.

And that's just your head. Your arms hang like wet noodles and are just as useless. Your knuckles are sore from punches and creak when you clench your fingers in and out. Both shoulders a pulsating from punches received and strain every time you try to lift your arm. How you actually find the energy to lift them again, amazes you, but you keep trying to hang on.
Your chest has been hit so many times; you're finding it hard to breath. You wonder if you might have cracked or broken a rib, or worse, punctured a lung. When you try to twist your torso, pain shoots up the back and into your neck. The whole upper part of your body wants to give up, but the legs won't have it.

Your legs are not hit, hurt or in trouble. They are managing pretty well on keeping you up and moving. They dodge to the left; they dodge to the right and keep you out of the path of severe injury. Oh, you're quite injured now, but it could be worse, a lot worse.

The difference from last night to now is a total reverse in feelings, though. Last night you were relaxing in a heated pool, around friends, and the body was at a complete mystifying trance. Your body was soothed and calm. Heat radiated out of the body through your hair and the bubbles that danced around your skin cleansed the soul. You even became more relaxed when you farted and the bubbles floated to the top and burst their fragrance into the air. Was it true that farts smelled worse when filtered through water?

But in this different path; every pour is sweating buckets, heat radiates everywhere, and there are no bubbles. During the beating, you did actually fart a couple of times.

In all this exhilarating experience, your body gets hit once more and the legs decide to give up. You find yourself on the dirt floor, up against the wall, wondering why the hell you ever gotten yourself into this.

Loud cheering from a crowd snapped Jason out of his thoughts and back to the reality that he had put himself into. He was up against the back wall in the middle of a match in an Iron Boxing pit. He had paid the fee to enter the ring and try to go three rounds with the Iron boxer; a robot designed to only box. He thought if he could make it through the session, he could easily triple his wager, but he miscalculated. The robot was fast, and strong. Jason's right eye was so puffy that he could barely see out of it, but his left eye showed him that he still had two taps to go on the clock which hung on the wall. He lowered his head down and saw a drop of blood hit his leg. He wasn't surprised. Then, something approached him and blocked out the sun from above and incased him in a shadow. He looked up, getting ready to get hit again, but his expression changed to one of slack-jawed.

"What the hell do you think you are doing?" Hawk said looking down at him.

Jason mischievously smiled at him, "winning?"

"Bullshit," Hawk answered as he reached down and helped Jason to stand. "You know you can't do this stuff."

Jason groaned as the body tried to support itself, "I know, but...." Jason just couldn't find an answer. That's when the robot hit Hawk in the back and sent him flying.

Jason fell back down where he was at and passed out. Hawk, on the other hand, rolled twice from the punch and then was back up on his feet. He looked down at his favorite jacket; the one he had made with the embroidered wings on the back, and took note that it was all covered in dirt.

"Really," Hawk questioned. "I just had this made and you scuffed it all up." He started to brush off the dirt and the robot confusingly rotated its head back and forth waiting for a counter attack.

He got one. Quickly, Hawk ran behind the robot, making it turn away from Jason and focusing on its new target. It was now in pursuit of Hawk. The crowd was now a mix of excitement and grievances because someone else had got into the pit. Wagers were for only one challenger and Hawk changed the game. All bets were off.

The robot swung and Hawk ducked under the arms path. It lunged again and found only air were Hawk once stood. Back and forth the robot tried to make contact but Hawk easily evaded it. To the left they moved, and then back toward the right but not one punch connected. The crowd started to get annoyed and things were being thrown into the arena. Food, paper, cups and even someone's carry case littered the sanded floor. The crowd's booing got louder and louder as the unusual match continued.

A low groan from Jason made Hawk turn his head and look toward his fallen friend, and the robot took quick advantage of it. It swatted Hawk's legs out from under him and knocked him down to his knees. The sand on the battlefield created a dust cloud around his face and into his mouth.

He lifted his head toward Jason, smiled, and then his eyes started to sizzle. The color changed from a bright blue to flaming red.

Ok, thought Hawk, he had had enough.

Hawk stood up and swung a kick to the robot's right arm breaking it off and sending it flying across the arena. The robot twisted to the right and Hawk delivered another blow with the same result as the first. The left arm bounced twice on the sanded floor. Confused, the robot turned back and forth trying to establish its next move. That's when Hawk leaped up, connecting both his feet with the bottom of its head and sent it flying as well. The head skipped twice before it stopped underneath the clock on the far wall. The clock arm moved one more tick and the buzzer sounded ending the match.

The crowd was in a full riot. More objects were thrown from the seats above as Hawk ran toward Jason at the back wall. He knelt down to the slowly moving body in front of him.

"Can you walk?" Hawk asked.

The mumbled answer from his bleeding lips gave the coy answer of 'No' making Hawk sigh. So, he picked up the limp body, threw him over his shoulder, and walked toward the exit.

****

Katrina felt relaxed as she sat on the porch drinking a fresh cup of speckle tea. The air was so crisp and clear that she enjoyed taking deeper breaths. The sounds of Fana birds danced across the calm ripples of the lake as the sun shimmered the water. She slowly rocked back and forth in the chair she was sitting in, as its creaking added to the stillness of the morning, and she sighed after taking another sip of the tea.

She had stayed the night at the cabin, along with Emmatt, and never felt more at ease. After the tour, Emmatt fixed both of them dinner and they sat and chatted for courses next to a warming fire in the living room. The fire place heated up the whole house quickly and the conversations they had become more in depth. Conversations of her husband Harland, about Jason, about the Harvester, about Preedom, about Sheila and about life in general made the time fly. In fact, the night they had together brought them closer than ever. They had learned deeper facts of each other's lives and the emotional trips they had experienced. Emmatt said several times that getting it out in the open helps heal the wounds, and she was right.

Katrina leaned her head back and looked at the porch ceiling above her; several birds' nests were visible but unoccupied. She could smell the old wood in the air and it added a feeling of calmness once again. She noticed that in one of the corners was a large woven nest of some kind, but its dry appearance indicated that it had been vacant for some time.

A rush of wind rustled the leaves in the tree that sat alone on the hill next to the water's edge, and she glanced back down to take in the beauty of it all. The spot looked so calming, relaxed. The way the sun rays danced through the branches, it shimmered upon the ground giving a tranquil look to the area.

As sudden thought filled her mind with the answer she had been searching for. This spot was the pure definition of 'Peace'.

The front door creaked open and Emmatt came walking out onto the porch. "Looks like you could almost fall asleep out here," she said as she sat in the rocker next to her. "It wouldn't be the first time that has happened. I frequently would catch Harland out here snoring away, sometimes with the cup still in his hand."

"Emmatt," Katrina said as she turned toward her, "can I ask you a personal question?"

Emmatt's expression looked agitated, "Now, Dear, there is no more such a thing between us. You can ask me anything."

"Where did you bury Harland?"

The question caught Emmatt off guard, but she quickly recovered. "He's buried right on the other side of that tree," she said pointing toward the hill. "He always loved that spot. In fact, that is my wish to you. When I die, make sure I'm with him, ok?"

Katrina turned toward Emmatt with grave expression in her face, "I hope to never see that day, but when it does come, I promise, you will be with him."

Emmatt smiled, knowing inside that Katrina would see it through. She was feeling even more relaxed knowing that Katrina accepted her cabin and that it was going to be in good hands. She would live out the rest of her days at the small house at the Harvester, for she was getting too old for the travel that was needed to upkeep the cabin. The Harvester was her true home, the place of her final years.

Katrina bit the side of her lip. "Would you and Harland mind company?"

Emmatt's puzzled look added more wrinkles onto her face. "What do you mean by that?"

* * * * * * * *

The Coble arena was located in the Lockport District and it contained an assortment of challenges for many different games of betting. It was contained in a large warehouse, big enough for a transport carrier to sit inside, and was so filled with smoke it was hard to see two tables away. The games were all different, due to the way you could bet your rolets. There was 'Scattle Wheels' and 'Zipper Tracks' in which you could bet on numbers. 'Button Cubes' were made especially for high rollers and chance. On it you could lose everything or win really big, but it all depended upon your strategy. 'Sparky' was a game that if you lost, not only would you lose rolets, but you would get electrocuted according to your bet level. There were so many variations on the games, but one game still remained the same ever since it was invented many cycles ago. That game was 'Buster Board.'

'Buster Board' was a card game that could run as fast as ten taps, or as long as two courses. It all depended on what was brought to the table. 'Buster Boards' not only used rolets for bets, but was known to bet anything. Many items found piled upon its table ranged from clothing, jewelry, weapons, cargo, plot deeds and even ship owner papers. The game would continue if the item presented was value enough to keep it going. The card deck held three hundred and thirty cards, and depending on how they were arranged would give a win or continuation. Most of the time people would lose because they simply would just 'give up.' But for those who were desperate, it could last for a long time.

One of those tables had built a crowd around it and was piled with so many items that they started to slide off of the edge. The jackpot hadn't been won in the last seven rounds and it looked like whoever was going to win it would need a cart to carry it all. The game started about three courses ago with six players, and quickly was worked down to three remaining. The remaining people, two men and a woman, had the look of anticipation in their eyes, and at the same time, calmness. The Buster card pack was almost gone which meant that whoever had the best remaining hand would win the pot. The crowd around them was silent and on edge.

One of the men looked at the cards in his hand and lifted a paper out of his front pocket. Holding it up, he waved it to get everyone's attention. "This is a boarding pass to anywhere in the system with unlimited trips." He tossed the paper onto the pile and it slid halfway down the pile. Everyone could see that it was an official pass from the Precious Cargo Company. The other two nodded their approval and he picked up a card. Two cards remained.

The other man picked up a small sack from inside his coat pocket. "Two thousand rolets," he said as he tossed the sack onto the pile. Nobody needed to accept the offer. Rolets were always good. He too, picked up a card. One card remained.

"This is a key to a house in the Kota district, and its papers," Remy said as she tossed both items onto the pile. Once again, no acceptance was needed. Kota district was known for its expensive living. She took the last card.

All the players' faces were inscrutable. They peered deeply into their cards weighing out every option available. Since it was now the eighth round, each player held twenty-four cards in their hands, which could give any possible solution. One of the men reacted first.

"I've got a Tasha Burst," he said with a smile as he laid his cards down in front of himself. People in the crowd whispered.

"Shit," yelled the other man as he threw his cards down on the table. He slid out his chair, stood up, grabbed what was left of his sandwich, and walked off.

Remy looked over her cards in her hand intensely. She knew what she had; in fact, she had it three rounds ago, but wanted to get more out of everyone. She glanced up and saw Steve and Aiden standing behind the man at the table in front of her. She laid out her cards.

"I've got a Star Burst." A Star burst was one higher than a Tasha Burst. People around the table gasped in awe and others clapped. The man across the table wasn't as responsive. At first his face became hostile, conveying a slow burn across his brow. But his expression changed to one of calmness, for he knew not to lose his temper. Sore losers are dealt with an unpleasant awakening from the owners of the arena. Business is not good if your patrons always start fights and give the place a bad name. In fact, he had noticed that three of the guards of the facility had been standing near the table ever since the fifth round. He wasn't about to take any chances.

"Nice play, Lady," he said as he stood up and shook Remy's hand across the table. "Perhaps we shall meet again, sometime."

"Thanks," she answered as she returned the shake. The man nodded at her and then walked away. Remy looked up and saw Steve and Aiden walk toward her as the rest of the crowd started to disperse to other areas. Steve started to shake his head in discuss.

"When did you get the papers to Hawk's house? I thought we left that on the kitchen table."
"Hey," Remy stated, "you yourself said that we needed everything we could get our hands on to make it."
"Yeah, but Hawk's house?" Aiden questioned as she too reached to Remy's side, "What if you would have lost it? And where in the hell did you learn to play like that?"

"There are some dark secrets I haven't really told anyone," Remy said. "Like for instance, I was born here on Tego."

"Really," Steve said. "I always assumed that you were a Largo native."

"Nope," she answered as she picked up what was left of her drink and slugged it down. "I'd say this pile could get us a good start, don't you?"

Steve started laughing in his usual deep tone and started shaking his head. "I'll go up to the service counter and see if they sell any carry cases."

"And I'll stay right here until you come back," Remy said. "I'm not taking my eyes off of this."

Steve walked off as Aiden walked up to Remy and kissed her on the cheek. "Lady, I'm finding out that the more I'm with you, the more I love you."

Remy winked at her.

****

The hospital clinic was one of the better facilities in the district. It wasn't controlled by any clan, but ran independently by the medical staff. The experience that was in the building was top notch and also very expensive. Other clans left it alone, because the security staff that guarded it was not to be messed with. It operated as its own business and didn't look to gain profits. The fee for their service was all that they wanted.

Jason laid on one of the tables in the emergency room. He was awake and hardly remembered being carried here. Most of his body was covered in either bandages or stitches and his face felt so swollen that it was about to explode. The smell of medical cleanser filled the air and he almost gaged on the overpowering smell. He slowly sat up, his head pounding as he moved, and swung his legs out over the edge of the table. Pain shot up his right shoulder. By the look of his condition, he must have been here for at least an hour. One thing was for certain, he was very happy that Hawk had found him.

The curtain to the closed off room slid open, and Hawk stepped inside. The coy look on his face told Jason that he was annoyed at what he had done, and was probably never going to hear the end of it.

"What the hell do you think you were trying to do, idiot?" Hawk said as he sat down in the chair next to the table. "You yourself even told me a term ago that you would be stupid for even attempting it."

"I know, I know," Jason said waving his right hand, "I just can't figure out what came over me. Something inside of me felt the need to go through with it. It was like I wanted to get my ass kicked."

"It was more than your ass, pal," Hawk said.

Then Jason got a quizzical look on his face. "How did you find me?"

"Your comchip transmitter was still sending out the signal. I used the remote homing beacon to trace you here."

"Sheila's implant? How is that possible?" Jason's confusion deepened. "She's not even operating anymore, how can she transmit?" Jason was as puzzled as ever.

"That's because the transmitter works as a separate unit. Other than that, it's useless."

"Well, I might as well have it taken out," Jason added. "It's not going to do anything for me anymore."

Hawk reached into his front pocket of his jacket and pulled out a small round ball. "Already done," he said as he held up the unit between his forefinger and thumb. "One of the blows that you received from the Bot hit you in the head at its location. When the surgeon worked on the injury, I had him remove it."

Jason's expression was doleful. It had been at least six years that he had it placed in him. His attachment to Sheila was now totally over. He gave a glazed look toward Hawk and swallowed hard. His thoughts started racing again about everything that happened, to him, Sheila and....

"So, tell me," Hawk said as he shoved the unit back into his pocket and snapped the pocket shut. "Why the hell are you trying to get yourself killed?"

"We are trying to raise rolets to get 'Little Chicago' up and going again."

"Who are we?" Hawk said.

"Steve, Remy, Aiden and me," Jason answered. "We are all here on Tego."

"You know that I can always get rolets," Hawk pointed out as he sat back down.

"I know, but we didn't know what was going on with you so we had to take matters in our own hands."

Hawk nodded his head and then looked down at the floor.

"Well?" Jason Asked.

Hawk looked back up, "Well what?"

"Would you mind explaining what the hell happened to you?"

Hawk reached up with his right hand and rubbed the top of his head, ruffling his long hair in the process. "I really don't know. Maybe I have a built in overheat switch, or something like that."

"What's the last thing that you remember?" Jason's question made Hawk squint his eyes for an answer.

"Watching Sheila tumble in space," Hawk sighed. "Then I woke up on her bridge."

"Do you remember anything while you were out?"

Hawk thought hard about an answer but slowly shook his head no. "I did have some crazy dreams, though."

The curtain opened again and the surgeon walked in with a clipboard in his hand. He was a younger man, younger than Jason, and gave Jason a wry look. "Ok, I see that you are up and about. Feeling stupid yet?"

Jason smiled and threw a glance toward Hawk. "It's in full swing, yes."

"Well," he said, "you're lucky that you're breathing. You had two broken knuckles, three cracked ribs, and several lacerations, five needed stitches. Not one of the worst cases that I have seen, but not one of the better ones, either. You're lucky your friend brought you here. Our machines healed you up rather easily. The bones are mended, but you're going to be sore for a few days."

"Thanks," Jason said as he slowly slid off the table and stood on his feet. His head spun a little due to the sudden movement. Hawk quickly stood up and grabbed a hold of Jason's shoulder to steady him.

"But," the surgeon urged, "I highly recommend that you take it easy for the next couple of rotations. You're fixed, but strength will not readily return as fast."

Jason nodded. "What's the bill?"

"I've already taken care of that," Hawk answered, "let's get out of here."

****

"This really pisses me off," said the man dressed in a white suit. He was the owner of the Coble arena and the suit made him stand out in the crowd. That's what he intended to do. That's what he always intended to do. Because ever since he became the owner of three Iron boxing arenas, he not only changed his appearance, but his lifestyle as well. The full white suit trimmed in gold and topped off with a tall white hat was only a small sample of how he carried himself. Houses, transports, and many other trinkets built his empire to what it was today. He was a part of the higher society that operated in the Lockport District, and he loved to gloat about it. He was also always surrounded by at least four guards; and today was no exception. The four men formed an impregnable circle around him.

But this really pissed him off.

Standing next to a repair table in the machine shop, he looked over the situation. A large robot laid in pieces on the table, and standing behind it were the arena managers.

"How did the kid get into the arena in the first place," the owner yelled. "If you shits were doing your jobs, he would have never gotten in."

"Sir," said one of the other men in attendance, "I have no idea how he entered. We were all...."

"I don't give a shit what you were doing, Russell, if protocol was being followed none of this would have happened." He waved his right hand toward the pile on the work table, "This is one of the more expensive Bots as well! It took me terms just to get its programming analyzed. Who's your head of security?"

Another man raised his left hand diligently. "That would be me, sir. The name's ..."

"I don't give a shit about your name," the owner shouted as he cut him off. "You're fired and I want you off my property now."

Stunned faces all around were pale with fright. The worried look of 'Who's next' was in everyone's eyes. Even the fired man stood there as well, still stunned and not moving.

"Sir," Russell stated with a soft voice, "he's one of the best I've..."

"Obviously not the best," the owner yelled cutting off the sentence again. "I want him out of here or you're next," he stated as he pointed his right index finger toward Russell's chest.

The terminated man still did not move.

"I said, now!" The owner yelled again. The man jumped and then slowly started to move from behind the table. The owner turned his head toward his guards, "Gentleman, help him out."

Two of the body guards grabbed him by the arms and quickly dragged the man out of the machine bay.

"Does anyone else want to join him?" The owner looked up at the remaining people in the room.

It obviously would be stupid question to answer. The remaining staff fumbled around to stare at anything in the room other than the owner.

"Then I suggest you get your asses in line and make this facility so tight that a Stacnat can't get in." he said as he turned toward the table again. "This will not happen again!"

He pulled together his white jacket coat and fastened its middle button. As he turned to leave, his last two body guards flanked him on each side and followed him out of the door. The walk toward the exit seemed to take forever but once they departed, everyone remaining in the room let out a sigh.

"Ok," Russell stated, "obviously there is an opening for a new head of security which will be our top priority.' He turned to look at the destroyed robot, "and get an assessment on what it will take to get this one back online. I want everyone on this. Nobody goes home until this is complete. Understood?"

They all nodded their heads dazedly, still suffering from the effects of the wrath. Russell turned and started to walk toward the stairs that lead toward his office on the second floor.

"I'll be in my office until we get this all done. Casey, you might as well order all of us something to eat, it's going to be a long day."

One of the men next to the table waved his hand in recognition of the order. "Right away, boss."

Russell stomped his way up the steps, opened the door, stepped in, and slammed the door shut. The reverberating sound it made around the room made everyone jump. And just as if the sound was a starting gun for a race, everyone frantically went their directions quickly toward the assignment at hand.

In the office, Russell leaned up against the door to the machine room and let out a long hard sigh. He had been in charge of this arena for about three rotations and today was almost his last. He knew that he wasn't going to get any rest or leave this building until he corrected the problems. As he walked over to his desk, his mind was already going through ideas and personnel to fill his security spot. Even as he sat down in the old rusted chair, his mind was not focused on his surroundings, but only his problem. He turned to the com unit, on the right side of his desk, and started going through the security recording of the fight that destroyed the Bot.

The floor boards toward his right creaked, which usually signified that someone was walking across the room, and he looked up. Approaching his desk was someone in a blue armored suit.

"Can I help you," he asked.

****

Foscal's was the place to go if you needed anything; from electronic parts, tools, power units, and supplies. You could even hire people to do the work for you. There were com tables to design your own systems, people to help you with your purchases and spaces to rent to even build them. They had several hangers to work on your ship, if needed. Outside of just equipment, Foscal's had food, home supplies and clothing as well. It was the one stop shop for everything.

It was always crowded, especially during the evening hours. Even though they never closed, there was hardly ever a slow time. They were not a part of any gambling sector nor did they operate under any of the organizations. They were privately owned and protected. Nobody messed with Foscal's.

Deep in the electronics bay, Hawk and Jason was digging through an assorted box of discounted parts. It was the third one they had dug through, and they were both determined to find a solution to what ailed them.

"Are you sure you want this," Hawk asked as he dug deeper into the box. "If we do rebuild her, I'd make an entirely different unit."

"I know you could," Jason added, "it just doesn't seem right to just throw it out. I'd like to keep it for old time's sake."

"Whatever," Hawk replied. Then his eyes widened when he spotted what he was looking for. He grabbed it with his right hand and lifted it from the box. "Perfect!" He turned toward Jason raising it up so that he could see it. "This is an electromagnetic band with an isolating cylinder. This will still keep the signal intact, feed power to the unit, and give it a stronger output."

Jason smiled, "perfect indeed. It would make a great gift for Katrina."

"Katrina? Didn't you want it for old time's sake?"

"Yes, but just like Sheila, I never want to lose track of Katrina." He reached up and took the band out of Hawks hand. "This way, I'll always know where she is in case she needs me." He turned the unit over in his hand to get a better look at it.

"Sounds kind of creepy, like in a stalker kind of way," Hawk added.

"Let's Just say that I intend to never lose her again," Jason said.

"I can understand your meaning, after everything you two have been through," he added as he took the band back from Jason, "but I'll need to do some work on it first."

Jason turned away from the parts table and headed toward the checkout counter, "ok, but we need to meet back at your place with the others and figure out or next step."

"Our next step," Hawk added as they reached the counter, "is to go back to Largo and start rebuilding. Like I said, funds are not going to be a problem." He tossed the band up on the counter and the clerk rang it up. "I don't know why the four of you even needed to come out here."

"Yeah, but we didn't want to count on you for everything. Besides, you know Steve. He likes to do everything himself. He would feel awkward knowing that he didn't contribute to the expenses, let alone the rebuilding."

"So true," Hawk replied. "I still remember when he was so upset for me paying for that supply delivery. I thought I'd never hear the end of it."

"Eleven hundred and twenty rolets," the cashier said interrupting their conversation.

Hawk reached into his pocket and pulled out his carry bag. He thumbed through the amount, laid it upon the counter and grabbed the band. "Thanks."

They both turned from the counter and headed toward the exit. Not really a straight walk because they had to weave their way around a demonstration that was going on for a new power amplifier and it was set up in the middle of the entrance door. They continued toward the door when a tall burley man stood in front of them, in the entrance, and blocked their exit.

"Hey," Heptor said, "the boss has been looking for you." His large arm pointed in Hawk's direction.

Noticing who it was, Hawk charged at Heptor and knocked him down to the ground. "Meet up at the house," Hawk yelled back at Jason. "Get going, I have this."

Jason was about to jump in and help, then he thought of his condition and slipped through the exit and out into the street. Whatever it was, he knew that Hawk would find his way out of it and catch up to them all later. He quickly walked away from the sounds of the fight and toward the house.

Heptor's hands grabbed tightly around Hawk's throat and squeezed hard. "The Boss has been looking for you, 217, and he wants you now!" Heptor tried to spin Hawk around into a choke hold but failed in the process. He lost his grip and Hawk elbow punched him in the face. Blood ran down out of Heptor's nose.

"You will come with me, 217," Heptor yelled. "He wants you back."

"I'll never go back," yelled Hawk as he leaped into the air to kick Heptor in the face.

Surprisingly, the large man did have the muscle to brush off Hawk's attack and he was able to toss him to the side by grabbing his left foot. Hawk was thrown into a glass display table which shattered and sprayed tiny shards everywhere, causing the crowd to scatter.

Hawk's forehead felt like it was on fire; either from the intensity of the fight or possibly glass might have splintered his face. There was no way in hell was he ever going to go back. For so long, he tried to bury the past in his mind, he didn't want to think about it or even speak of it, but seeing Heptor started to make it resurface. As the deep emotions and pain started to come back, his eyes started to burn red again. The intense heat they created was adding to the fire that he felt. His eyes were burning so red that everywhere he looked things appeared engulfed into a red hue. Once again, another new experience was upon him and he was going to have to understand it as well.

Hawk tried to regain his bearings; his head was a dizzy, and he felt weak, and he thought that maybe he was still trying to recover from the 'Melt Down'. As he tried to push himself up from the floor, tiny glass shards cut into the palms of his hands. He pushed up to get himself back on his feet but Heptor was already at him. The man threw his whole body at Hawk and knocked him back down to the ground. The two men struggled in the mist of glass and blood started to smear across the floor.

Several of Foscal's security had now surrounded the area and the crowd gave them plenty of room to stop the fight. They all had their electro sticks out and charged for striking. One of the guards hit Heptor in the back with a stick and electric current released. Heptor let go of the hold he had on Hawk and stood up.

"You don't understand," Heptor yelled between gasps for breath, "I must return him to the boss!"

"You either stand down," one of the guards said calmly while holding out his stick, "or I'll have to take you to MY boss. Conscious or unconscious; the choice is yours"

In the moment Heptor paused, Hawk was up again and kicked him in the back. The momentum threw Heptor into two of the guards knocking them to the ground. One of the guards was knocked unconscious when his head smacked upon the floor. When Heptor stood back up, two other guards went after him with the electro sticks.

Hawk dodged between the guards and went for Heptor's throat with both of his hands. Heptor in return, grabbed Hawk's neck as well. Both men squeezed.

"Stop fighting, 217," Heptor said as he managed to get the words out of his restricted throat, "you must come home. Medico needs you."

In the struggle, they had managed to knock two of the guards to the ground, but they had been replaced by three more. They surrounded the struggle that now returned to the floor and once again Heptor was on top of Hawk.

"Stop fighting, 217, stop fighting!" Heptor yelled over and over again.

Hawk spun himself around and ended up on top of the brute and behind his back. As Heptor tried to stand up, Hawk grabbed him by his hair and pulled his head back.

"I'LL NEVER GO BACK!" Hawk yelled. And with one swift stroke, Hawk thrusted his knuckles into Heptor's wind pipe and crushed it. Heptor reached up with his hands toward his throat as he tried effortlessly to draw in some air. Blood ran down from the corners of his mouth and Hawk let go of his Heptor's head as he fell face first onto the hard floor below.

As quick as he hit the floor, arms grabbed Hawk from all sides. One of them stuck his stick into Hawk's side and zapped him. After everything that Hawk had experienced in what life he had, the response from the stick was completely unexpected. The electricity jolted him and made him feel incoherent. It made him weak and unassured. He had never had any situation startle him so much.

He stood up and staggered; trying to regain his footing, and tried to walk toward the exit.

"STAND DOWN," one of the guards yelled. "STAND DOWN AND COME WITH US."

The words 'come with us' sent Hawk into a frenzy. The guards tried everything they could to subdue him, but to no avail. Hawk flung each guard into the crowd and quickly made his way to the front entrance. By the time the guards regained their bearings, Hawk was already out the exit door and half way down the street.

CHAPTER 7

The feelings of total exhaustion are very incomprehensible. Your body is so weak it becomes drowsy, dozy, sluggish, beat, weary, dopey, and groggy. Your overall energy has buggered out, became fatigued, pooped (not the bathroom kind), zonked, wiped out, burned out, and frazzled. The mind, in all its glorious power, has become catatonic, dead beat, dog-eared, lethargic, and in a daze. You are truly on your last leg.

At first, your eyes just can't grasp a clear and precise vision. You constantly have the sensation of eye goo and you close your eyelids several times to hopefully clear them out. Squinting hard, your blinking slows, and your eyelids are so heavy that keeping them open has become the hardest task of all. At first, the eyes blur, and then the eyelids start to get heavy. As you slowly start to drift away; your head starts to tip down, dipping your chin into the center of your chest. That's when what little power you have left, jerks you up and you start all over again.

Second, your hearing seems muffled and everything sounds like it's underwater. The tones of people's voices are in different ranges, but the words are not clear. You concentrate harder just to catch every other word that they are saying, and yet still nod your head like you understand. Not only do the people at your table sound odd, but the crowd in the room comes off as a low hum. Other added noises like glasses clicking, chairs scooting, food sizzling, and air circulators mix into the fray. Everything comes together into one big mess.

Next, the body will not follow your direction at all. You try to sit up, but slouching is a better option. Your arms are so heavy that attempting to reach up and get your drink from the table seems too much of an effort. But when it comes to turning your head, the task takes most of your power. You close your eyes during the process and swing slowly toward the direction that you want to point. But by the time you reach the destination, you have already missed the action you wanted to hear, see, or even speak to.

Speaking, on the other hand, is a total impossibility. Your brain tries to put together some sort of meaning, process it, and then project it out. The conclusion is pure babble, groaning mumbles or very odd looks from the others around the table. You stop talking in mid-sentence and to try to regain your thought, but in the end, forget what you wanted to say to begin with.

All together your actions come across like you are drunk; but without the alcohol, the dizziness, and the twirling stomach. Your mind starts trying to think of ways that you could sleep and where you could attempt it. Perhaps on the table, or in a booth couch or even curled up in the corner on the floor would give you a peaceful resting place, but you wish to stay awake. You need to stay awake.

Your mind is still fresh from what has transpired in the last couple of courses. First you had that stupid attempt to try to win at Iron Boxing which was foolish and suicidal, to say the least. That's where the body started its downward spiral. After Hawk saved your ass, and then a hospital visit repaired your injuries, you started to regain some strength back. But then the fight at Foscal's spiked up the hormones to a level that took a while to come down. You fled, like Hawk requested, and met up with the others at the house. You were very surprised at the winnings that Remy had in her possession, and rather eager to get out and try at something again, but Hawk arrived and forced everyone to leave the planet immediately. He said that he would explain later.

So, here you are, sitting at a table with the others, on the way back to Largo, on a transport vessel, while Hawk told what was going on.   And you weren't catching any of his stories. You were just too damn tired.

"Jason," Steve said again louder as he shook Jason's shoulder, "go lay down on the couch over there before you fall out of the chair."

"Huh?" Jason reacted.

Remy stood up from her chair and walked toward Jason. "Come here, sleepy head, I'll help you over there." She grabbed his arm, but he slowly pulled it from her.

"No, I really want to hear what Hawk has to say," Jason argued.

Hawk leaned over from across the table, "oh really? What did I just say?"

Jason leaned back in his chair and bit his upper lip. He concentrated really hard but could not come up with an answer. A low groan was the only reply he had.

"That's what I thought," Hawk replied. "Get some sleep, Jason. We still have a couple of courses before we land. I can fill you in when you're more attentive."

Jason nodded his head in agreement and let Remy take him by the arm this time. She helped him get up from the chair and walk over to the empty booth couch in the corner.

Jason never remembered lying down.

****

Foscal's looked like a wind storm had blown through the front doors. Displays were in pieces, glass shards were scattered everywhere, blood was smeared on the floor, merchandise destroyed, and dirt covered everything. Security had gained control quickly after the fight and blocked the store front. A medical team was called in for the wounded personnel and a Death cart for Heptor's lifeless body. A crowd had gathered around to see a possible glimpse of what was going on.

In the middle of that crowd was a blue armored being.

****

Even though the ground was still freshly turned, it looked at peace.

Katrina and Emmatt stood in front of a fresh burial site. Veronica's body had been brought a couple of courses ago and it didn't take long for a crew to bury her. After they were finished, they gathered their equipment and left just as fast as they had arrived. The dirt pile was still moist and piled higher than the rest of the area. They said it would settle over time.

Veronica was laid to rest facing the water, just slightly to the left of where Emmatt wished to be next to Harland. This entire situation was very hard for Katrina to endure, and once again, Emmatt was there to guide her. Emmatt had gotten in touch with the same company that handled Harland's service and through her connections, she had arranged for Veronica to be prepared, moved, encased and laid to rest.

The grave did not have a marker for Katrina left that task for Hawk. She knew that he would want to do that.

Harland's grave marker, on the other hand, was beautiful and defined the life of the man within its design. Across the bottom of it were carved fruits and vegetables. Vines grew up both sides of the marker and were spotted with little white flowers. The vines reached to the top, stretched across to each other, and met in the middle. Hanging at their ends were a group of Speckle berries. Engraved in the center of the marker, in bold capital letters, was 'HARLAND'. There was enough room under his name to enter Emmatt's.

Katrina was not looking forward to the task.

"Your friend can now carry on in peace," Emmatt said. "We all have different thoughts of what lies beyond, and I for one look forward to seeing Harland again and holding him close." She smiled and lifted her head, her mind drifting away as she looked up toward the branches in the tree. A brisk wind ruffled the leaves among them and fluttered a few of them toward the water. "It's getting a little chilly," she added rubbing her arms, "I should have brought out a cover."

"I can go get it for you if you want," Katrina said.

Emmatt shook her head no, "Can't sweetie, I have to get back to the port and get things going. I've been away from the store too long." She grabbed Katrina by the arm and started to lead her toward the cabin. "You could call me a transport while I get my things together."

"I'll ride in with you. I have several things myself to do. First, I have to get a hold of Jason, and then I have a lot of packing to do to move out here. Then there is also the work to rebuild the bar and find out if.........what's so funny?"

Emmatt's small laugh got Katrina's attention as they stepped onto the porch. "I complicated things, didn't I?"

Katrina stopped and took a deep breath. "Life is made by how an individual wants it," she said with a sigh. "A friend told me that once."

"A very wise friend," Emmatt said continuing toward the door, "a very wise friend indeed."

Katrina smiled.

****

Love sure does funny things to your body; it makes you cry, gets you all choked up, makes you sweat, over heat, shake, get dizzy, it builds pressure in your chest, and even over excites you if you are not careful. In fact, love affects every part of the body, inside and out, turning you into a mass of blubbering, pathetic, incoherent lump of clay. Your mind drifts to holding, caressing, kissing and snuggling up with that person again. The intensity builds so big that it overwhelms you to the point of losing control of your regular common sense of everyday functions. You don't pay attention to what you are doing; your eyes seem to see through walls, your fingers become clumsy, your speech can babble and your nose will remember smells that only tie you to the other person. A large lump can develop in your throat and make it hard to swallow.

All this is summed up in the understanding of the word 'Love'. You could love a sandwich, love a color, and love a special song that you hear. You could love a movie, love a phrase and even love dancing in the rain. You could love to try out new things, and find out that some of them you hate. You could love a cloud, a bird, a painting, a drink, and a job. You could even go as far as to love getting your back scratched

Love has several descriptions but by far is best when attached to an individual. The meaning deepens into adoring them, idolizing them, and falling for them. You chose to worship the ground they walk on, carry a torch for them, take a shine to them, have a soft spot, and even only have eyes for them. Love has so many ways of expression.

But the real expression comes from the pressure in the chest, a pressure that truly can't be explained. You're not having a heart attack, nor do you have heart burn. A warm sensation in the center of the rib cage slowly grows with an added feeling like a balloon that has been blown up a little too much. Your chest gets tight and your heart beat speeds up. The pressure become so intense that one prick could explode that balloon wide open.

Speaking of prick, that too gets affected. You find yourself thinking so much about the other person that you have to adjust your pants because it has gotten so uncomfortably tight from the erection that you have developed. You start wiggling around like a worm out of the ground while you tug and pull your pants to relieve that situation. At the same time, your mind takes on a reality check and looks around to make sure that no one else sees you doing this goofy dance.

But soon it will all release upon the person that you miss, that face you want to kiss, and the body you want to hold. It will be soon.

But watching the clock on the wall just added to the stress inside. With each tick, more and more anxiety builds within you and the waiting adds an odd pain to the chest. The pain can best be described as the feeling you get when you drink a liquid too fast and air pockets get stuck in the throat. You fear that it could be a heart attack, even though you don't know what one feels like, which raises several questions about any health issue you might develop. How do you know that you are suffering from something when you don't know how that something feels? If you have never experienced it before, how would you acknowledge it?

Once again, you look at the clock, more often than you need to, hoping that maybe in the next round of the hand she would call. The anticipation and urge to scream are bubbling up inside to the point where your concentration for anything would be nonexistent. Once again, you feel like you have lost total control of yourself.

Jason looked at the clock on the far wall again. It's been almost three courses since he had seen Katrina and the pain inside him was gnawing like a rat trying to eat its way out of a bucket. Within the last two courses, they all had returned to Largo; Remy and Aiden went to Remy's place to unpack, and Steve, Hawk, and Jason were now at Steve's apartment waiting to hear from Katrina. They had called her apartment when they first arrived and got no answer. They called her work place and only received a recording. So, that left the only options; sit and wait for her to reach them.

It also gave Hawk the chance to fill in Jason about the situation. And even though Jason's mind and body was tied in knots, this time he was going to give his full attention to Hawk.

Hawk walked out of the kitchen and toward Jason carrying two cups. He handed one to Jason as he sat down on the couch next to him. "I'm sorry I had to rush everyone off of Tego so fast, but it looks like my past life has caught up with me."

Jason took a sip of the drink and sat it on the table to his left. "I'm sorry that I was so out of it and couldn't pay attention the first time you told us, I was really tired. I haven't been that exhausted for a long time."

"Well, what do you expect," Steve added as he sat down in the recliner across from them, "you have been through a hell of a lot in the last couple of weeks. I still don't think you're back to your usual self. You seem like you are in some sort of a daze, like you're rediscovering everything."

"It does feel like that at times," Jason added, "my mind has been drifting a lot. I've found myself thinking deeply on almost everything I do. In fact, just now, I was pretty heavy into thinking about Katrina."

"Your eyes did look glazed over," Steve said.

Jason took in a deep breath and slowly let it out. "So, who was this guy who attacked you at Foscal's?"

"Heptor was his name," Hawk said looking down at the cup in his hand, "one of the few assistants to my creator." He turned his head toward Jason and looked him in the eyes. "You already knew that I was an experiment that escaped, but I had never given you the details until now." He lifted up the cup and took a long swig from it. "My creator's name is Medico. He had been experimenting in anatomy for a long time, dealing in cross genetics and drug enhancing tests. He got to the point where he was growing his own species, and enhancing himself in the process. He's very intelligent and far as I know, very old. I could not begin to tell you how long I was in his grasp, whether I was grown, or altered."

"Do you remember where he is?" Steve questioned.

Hawk started shaking his head no. "Not much stayed with me when I escaped. I was cold, alone and frightened. Everything was new to me and I can't even remember where I started from. The few things I did remember were Medico and Heptor. They were always around me. I'll also never forget the screams, all the agonizing screams." His stare drifted away to another time, another place as he let a couple of moments pass before he continued. "I'll never forget what that place looked like, but to tell you were it's at, I haven't the foggiest idea. Things started to make meaning and I started to retain things about a couple of terms before I met you two here."

"I remember that day very well," Jason added. "That was the day that Rodger tried to put a knife in my back."

"Yeah, that was the day," Hawk replied, "after that, you two were the only people who cared to even start a conversation with me."

"Leave it to an Earthling to break the ice with an alien," Steve said.

Jason smiled, "As I remember, you had a lot of intuition at that time too, but no memory of your past. Steve and I thought that you either had amnesia or was just plain lost."

"I was lost," Hawk said as he raised his cup and finished its contents. "I knew nobody, had no place to go and nothing to my name. I don't know if I started on this planet or another. It was all new to me, but that's all-common knowledge to us. Medico is my main concern now. He is ruthless, evil, and will not stop until he gets what he wants."

"And that is?" Jason questioned.

Hawk turned toward Jason again, "Me. I was his greatest achievement. He told me that several times and explained to me how I was going to change things to better mankind. My genetics could create a super race. Stop sickness and even take us to the next level. He wanted to control everyone and be the creator of this perfect race."

Steve looked up at Jason, "Sound familiar?"

Jason started nodding his head, "yeah, the Davi."

"But the Davi, at least, had a large following," Steve added. "This guy sounds nuts."

"More than nuts, Steve," Hawk stated. "This man is borderline between insane and psychotic. He doesn't care about who he hurts to get to what he wants. When I saw Heptor, my survival instincts kicked in."

"This Heptor is he the only one to expect or will there be more?" Jason asked as he took another drink from his cup.

"Heptor is all I remember," Hawk answered. "But I'm sure Medico has others looking for me. I might not be too safe to be around."

"PPHPT," Steve expressed through his pressed lips, "bring them on. I've been going soft since I haven't seen much action like I used to."

Jason laughed out loud. "Did you ever tell him about that time you were pinned down in Quam?" He said as he pointed at Hawk.

Hawk shook his head no.

Steve's eyes lit up like firecracker. "Well, that was the day I took out at least six Davi fighters. All of them hand-to-hand."

Hawk stood up, "Let me refill my drink first. If this is anything like the time you were dropped behind the enemy lines, it's going to be a long story."

"Shit, that was a walk in the park." Steve said as he handed is cup to Hawk. "Fill mine up while you're at it."

Hawk grabbed the glass and started walking toward the kitchen.

"He always loves to hear your stories," Jason said taking another sip. "I wish I would have seen some action during the war. Being assigned to a techno station was rather boring."

"Yeah," Steve said, "but it did have one hell of a result."

Jason started to take another sip but the Vid ringing broke his concentration. He spilled the rest of his drink while rushing toward the remote.

****

AJBA Vid station was still in full swing with reports and stories about the Davi attack. Ever since the freighter showed up in the orbit, they were the main station that covered the crisis. Every news flash, information grid, and follow up was passed through the station's records. They were part of the security on the base as well as the central grid for the planet. They were always up to date.

Not only were they the best for new stories, but the archive records were the largest. Anything you wanted to know was held in the library. Access data cards were available to anybody and could be bought or rented out, for a nominal price. It all depended upon the content, volume and time allotted.

Sherry Owen, AJBA's top reporter, had been following the Davi story ever since it began. She started the byline and continued it. She had followed up on contacts, built story lines, reported breaking news and was the contact person for the entire topic. She literally connected all the dots.

She had just finished a meeting with her station manager and was walking down the hall with a full cup of Kedy brew. She had just got it from the break room and stupidly filled it to the brim.

Now she was slowly walking toward her office trying not to spill it. It was too hot to sip any off the top and yet she blamed herself for not pouring a little of it into the sink before she left, but she was going to achieve this task. She watched the top of the cup, as she took each step, and saw it teeter back and forth. Her office door was open, so the trek was easier to achieve, and she slid herself into the room.

Reaching the front of her desk, she cautiously bent over and sat the cup down onto the coaster. She let go of the cup and let out a large sigh of relief. Did she really hold her breath all the way down the hall? She wondered at the thought as she walked around the desk and sat down into her chair, preparing herself for a long rotation of work. Then with one quick pull, she rolled her chair closer toward the desk and her knee hit the bottom drawer sending a vibration that rocked the cup and Kedy brew spilled all over the coaster.

Great, she thought, so this is how things were going to start off. She opened her top drawer and pulled out a terry cloth, lifted the cup and started wiping up the mess. After a couple of passes, she was satisfied with the cleanup, and she tossed the now wet cloth into the trash can. Its heavy weight thudded as it hit the bottom of the empty can.

She shook off the defeat and turned her attention toward her vid console. The screen held a picture of Jack and her sitting at the news desk surrounded by several piles of fruits and vegetables. It was a picture that was taken during the Harvest Festival last cycle. She started to smile at the memories but then something about the screen didn't look right.

Something looked out of place. Something was different. Something was missing.

Her file on the Davi attack was gone.

****

Beautiful, peaceful, relaxing and quiet were the words running through everyone's head. There was no better way to describe what they saw before them.

After Katrina's call, it only took moments for Jason, Hawk and Steve to arrive at the Cabin. Upon their arrival, Katrina pulled them inside and gave them a tour. She was ecstatic about the place and it showed in her every step. You could hear in her voice how happy she was and the twinkle in her eyes looked like she was trying to hold back tears. The woman truly deserved this, and Jason was glad to see it.

The tour ended in the kitchen with a cup of hot speckle tea for everyone, and they made their way out onto the front porch. The sun was setting and the sky was turning a dark blueish orange. The wind was almost at a standstill and the lake had no ripples upon it. It was smooth as glass. Many birds were chirping and their voices echoed across the lake.

There were only two chairs on the porch; Katrina sat in one and Steve in the other while Jason and Hawk just leaned up against the porch railings facing the other two.

"As much as we did when we were gone," Jason said, "you did a hell of a lot more than us."

Katrina took a sip of her tea, "actually, it didn't take as long as I thought it would. Emmatt knew someone who was a professional mover and she had his crew pack everything up in the apartment and bring it all out here. All I had to do was talk to my Apartment complex to sign the leaving contract and get reimbursed my deposit."

"What, no more living in the noisy district anymore?" Steve added.

Katrina smiled and should her head. "No thank you."

"But isn't this a long travel back and forth from the base?" Hawk asked. "I mean, none of us have a transport, it could get costly and annoying. Even though you don't plan on returning to your job, 'Little Chicago' is on the far side of the base."

Jason perked up, "hey, I never really thought of that." His mind was now going in a hundred directions, a big difference from a few hours ago. "Why don't any of us own a transport?"

Steve started counting with his fingers as he pointed out the reasons. "Parking fees, license fees, energy usage fees, annual renewal fees, mechanical costs, and need I go on?"

"People," Hawk said sipping his tea, "you all know that cost is not an issue..."

"NO," Steve blurted out. "I appreciate everything that you do for us, son, but I cannot live a life without sweating for it. If everything would be handed to you, without any effort or work on your part, it truly isn't yours to own. You never learn the meaning of true appreciation for the things you have if you don't work for them."

"I told you," Jason said toward Hawk under his breath as he lifted up his cup for a sip.

"When you bleed, sweat and cry on a project, not only do you gain more respect for yourself, but you develop a pride and ownership that only enhances your life." Steve was now sitting up from his once leaned back position in the chair and his rave continued on. "You also gain a different prospective on the items and people around you. If you give me a transport, and I crash it, I'd think nothing of it because you'd just get me another one. But if I worked hard to get it, I would not only drive it better, but I would be more responsible for its condition."

Katrina's mouth was agape at Steve's lecture, but Hawk and Jason had small smirks on their faces.

"What are you smiling at, smart asses?" Steve said as he leaned back in the chair once again.

"Nothing," Hawk said with a chuckle, "just haven't heard one of those talks for a while."

"Well, you better listen to it, "Steve added. "If I didn't, my Pop would have turned me over and whooped my ass really good."

Jason lifted up his cup in a toast, "Now that I'd like to see."

Hawk laughed, "Me too, Gramps."

Steve leaned forward squinting his eyes, "This gramps will bury his foot up your ass."

Jason lifted up his cup again, "Now that I'd like to see."

Hawk laughed out loud and took a sip of his drink. "I wouldn't put it past you."

Bury, thought Katrina. There was one more thing that she hadn't told them about yet and needed the right way to say it. She took a long drink of her tea, swallowed, and then sat the cup down on the table next to her. Taking in a deep breath, she proceeded to explain.

"There is one more thing I need to tell you," she said. "That tree over there by the shore," she said as she pointed in its direction, "is a burial ground."

They all looked toward the area where the sun now had dipped down below the horizon and everything was surrounded in a light hazy mist. The tree itself still held a shimmer of light in its upper branches.

Katrina stood up out of the chair and walked toward Hawk. She reached out and lightly grasped his right arm. "Veronica is buried out there. I didn't put a marker on her because I left that for you."

Hawk swallowed hard. He took in a deep breath and then slowly let it out. His attention was drawn toward his cup, staring deeply into what was left in the bottom of it. He lifted it once more, gulped down the remaining contents, and then sat the empty cup on the porch bannister. Without a word, he turned, walked down the steps and toward the tree.

For a moment, everything seemed to stop. The wind was gone and the birds were silent. It was if nature itself was providing a moment of silence for the fallen.

Hawk slowly walked across the yard and closer to the area. His pace never quickened. Katrina walked over to Jason and put her arms around his shoulder. Steve got up from the chair and joined the other two at the front of the porch, leaning with both hands upon its railing. Nobody said anything as they watched Hawk's final approach to the grave and he stood in front of it. The gathering mist around him slowly engulfed his figure.

"You don't think he'll snap again," Jason said in a whisper, "do you?"

"Only time will tell," Steve added.

"Will he be, ok?" Katrina asked.

Nobody answered; they all just stared.

"It's getting a little chilly," Steve said as he turned toward the front door. "I'll go in and start a fire."

A worried look crossed Katrina's face as she pointed toward Hawk, "But will he be ok alone?"

Steve opened the door and turned toward them, "I'm sure if something happens, we'll hear it." He started to step inside and said again, "Only time will tell."

The door creaked shut and Katrina and Jason glanced at each other.

"He'll be fine," Jason said as he put his arm around Katrina's waist and pulled her toward the door. "Let's go inside, it is getting a little brisk." He opened the door for Katrina and she walked in.

Jason looked back toward Hawk. "He'll be fine," he said to himself as he followed her in.

They entered the room and saw that Steve was already putting wood in the fireplace. The thick wooden walls around them still held the warmth of the sun and covered the cabin like a blanket, but Katrina knew that would change. From the experience from the other night with Emmatt, it quickly got cold. She had made her way back to the kitchen, when she realized that she had forgot her cup on the porch, and then thought better not to go retrieve it. Jason had sat down on the couch in the front room and still had his cup in his hand and Steve's cup, she didn't see. She started making another batch of the tea anyway, just in case.

Jason leaned forward from the couch, "Odd isn't it, how things can change so quickly."

Steve tossed one more log on the pile then turned the fire switch on the right side. "Yeah, but things could switch back just as quick."

117

"You were always the pessimist," Jason stated.

The fire ignited and Steve walked over to the recliner chair and sat down. "Of course, I am. That way I'm always prepared for the worst. When something good happens, it's a bonus. You can't be let down if you're already expecting it."

Jason laughed, "Now that makes a lot of sense."

Katrina came into the room with a plate of fruit crackers and sat them on the small table in front of the couch. "Is anyone hungry?" She asked as she sat down on the couch. Jason wrapped his arm around her. Steve reached forward and grabbed one of the crackers off of the plate. Its long green stem cracked in half when he bit down onto it. Jason didn't seem interested.

With the exception of the cracker, the only noise in the cabin was the crackling fireplace. Its popping and snapping mesmerized everyone and they all got lost in the moment. They looked deep into the dancing flames in front of them; a display of yellow, red and blue lightly mixing among themselves. The heat was quickly warming the room and sparks lightly fluttered above the fire. Time stood still as silence and warmth engulfed them all.

Time had no control.

Katrina let out a sigh and stood up, "Anyone for another cup of tea?" She turned to head toward the kitchen and stopped short. Hawk was standing just inside the door.

The quick silence got Jason's and Steve's attention and they turned to look in the direction she was in. Upon seeing Hawk, Jason quickly got up and walked toward him.

"Hawk, are you ok?" His concern clearly expressed in his voice.

Hawk nodded his head, "I'm fine, and also hungry. Is there anything to eat?"

Everyone let out a sigh of relief, noting that he was ok.

Katrina snapped out of her trance and started walking toward the kitchen. "The cupboard is full," she stated. "Everyone relax while I make us something to eat." She continued her forward pace but Hawk reached up and grabbed her arm as she passed by.

"Katrina," he said with a soft-spoken voice, "thanks. Thanks for what you have done. It's a lovely spot and she would be happy with the choice."

Katrina smiled and reached up with her hand laid it upon his shoulder, "I wish that I could have done more."

"You can," he answered. "Would you help me pick out a marker?"

She smiled again, "I'd love to." She pulled her hand away and then proceeded into the kitchen.

"OK," Hawk yelled in excitement as he walked toward the dining room, "Let's see if I can build this enhancer for you, Jason." He pulled several objects out of his pocket and scattered them across the dining room table. Jason and Steve followed him with their eyes, noting his change in emotion.

"This will take his mind off of things," Steve whispered.

Jason nodded his head in agreement.

Hawk smiled and nodded as well, because he heard Steve, and agreed.

****

Medico looked deep into a glass beaker that was filled with a greenish liquid. His concentration never wavered as he slowly stirred in a pink thick substance from a small cup. Smoke slowly rolled from the new mixture as he sat the now empty cup down and picked up a wooden stick. The colors danced around as he stirred the mixture ever so gently and the stick made the sound like a tiny bell every time it hit the rim of the beaker. He continued to stir; his eyes becoming mesmerized by its content's reactions. The smoke started to subside and then the colors started to change. At first it was a deep blue, and then it changed to red, then yellow, back to blue, and ended in a dark maroon. All during the process, he glared deeper and deeper into the glass. His crooked smile curved up only on the right side making him look even more sinister, demented. Hypnotized by the actions of the mix, he watched as tiny swirls dance around the stick creating small bubbles that floated in suspension never rising to the top. Then, the combination started to ferment, and the mixture's foamy condition started to rise. Small crackling noises started to emit as the foam reached the rim and started to overflow.

Suddenly, in a quick change of pace, Medico swiftly pulled out the stick, tossed it over his shoulder, grabbed the beaker, and downed its contents. Tilting his head fully back, he had the container empty within four gulps. He slowly lowered his head back down and sat the empty beaker back upon the table. Using his tongue, he licked any remaining foam from his mouth and then wiped the rest of his face off with his right sleeve.

At first, the usual reaction happened, the sensation of the mixture popping and bubbling as it went down his throat. The liquid then started to expand more as it came in contact with saliva, and it bloated out his neck. He had done this so many times that he no longer worried about it foaming up and out of his nose for he had mastered that control a long time ago. The liquid then traveled down, into the stomach, and once again, it expanded and bubbled. His body was so accustomed by this that he could remain standing as it went through its process. Before, in the beginning, he had to sit down. It originally made him weak and disoriented, but through all the doses, he learned control.

He closed his eyes and started to hum; enjoying the warm and tingling sensation it was doing to his insides. The warmth expanded out to the extremities and quickly ran throughout his other organs. He could feel the blood lines intensify with heat and then his heart started to pound faster. The process was nearing completion.

The last of side effect was the reaction to the brain. This usually came sudden, and he was always prepared for the pain. Once again, in the beginning, he had to strap himself into a chair because the convulsions. Now, he was almost in control. He quickly picked up another stir stick from the table and put it into his mouth. He clamped down hard with his teeth; he was not going to bite off a part of his tongue like he did one other time. He still stood by the table, but grabbed the two handles he had on the side and held on tight.

Then it hit.

He started to shake all over, his muscles nervously twitching, and his legs felt like they were going to buckle under. He held his stance. His grip grew tighter on the handles and his knuckles started to whiten due to the stress, but he still kept his balance. His neck muscles started to stiffen and his head pulled back shaking as he closed his eyes. His jaw clamped so hard that the stick snapped in half, cutting the sides of his lips in the process. His whole body started to stiffen signifying that the conclusion was nearby. Both of his ears popped and snot started to run down his nose.

Then as fast as it began, it stopped. The shaking ended, the tightness relieved and is heart rate returned to normal. He turned his head to the right and spit out the pieces of the stick. Blood trickled down his cheeks and dripped on the floor.

Another successful dose had been administered and he started to smile once again. He walked over to a mirror that he had on the wall and looked closely at his reflection. He propped his hands on the wall, one on each side of the mirror, and leaned his face toward it. Leaning within an inch of its surface, he could still see the old age lines that were spread throughout his face and the gray hairs that framed them. Blood lines had trickled down the corners of his lips and the snot was now down to the bottom of his chin, ready to drip off.

His expression became deranged as he started laughing hysterically. His laugh was unbalanced, frenzied and mad. He took in deeper and deeper gulps of air to which helped the laugh become even more uncontrollable. He was laughing so hard that tears were running down his cheeks and his rib cage started to ache with pain. After a while, his laugh started to slow, but he continued to take in deep breaths to refresh his lungs.

His energy started to quickly leave his body so he knew that he had better get to his cot in the corner before it was too late. He pushed himself from the wall, turned and started to make the trip, each step getting harder and harder to achieve. Just a few feet from the cot, his body gave out, and he fell down onto the cold dirt floor next to it.

He quietly laughed himself to sleep.

CHAPTER 8

After eating a well-cooked meal at the cabin, Steve and Hawk started their return to Serin base. They had caught a late evening transport back and it would be another two courses before they arrived in the port. Funny how when traveling between worlds, it was a shorter arrival time for the longer distance, but on a planet, it was a longer time for a shorter distance.

Hawk had completed the transmitter at the cabin but needed to test it, and the only place to do that was in Sheila's hanger. Even though she was completely out of power, on her bridge was a screen that could help with the tracking. The added equipment that they had bought at Foscal's should be able to lengthen its radius to a greater distance. The only way to verify it would be to take a trip, but Hawk was in no rush to do so. His idea was to try to bounce the signal through one of the planet's relay satellites and see how far he could travel it through the system. He already knew that it could reach Tego, but what about the other planets? His mind raced with the possibilities.

Even though Hawk had something to concentrate on during the trip home, Steve, on the other hand, didn't have that luxury. He sat at a window seat, watching the scenery pass by them as they made their way back toward the base. His mind raced although, but on another subject.

Women.

The women that he had encountered throughout his life were so different. It all started with the first one you would encounter; your mother. She would be the one person that you felt safe around and would do anything to protect. She would be what you based all women after. The old saying of 'Men marry their mother' stands out true because that's what you look for in a wife. When the cravings first begin, in high school for Steve, it just didn't seem like a serious matter. It would always be either a crush or just a quick fling. Then after high school, things became more serious. Your work and life started to fall into line on what you needed to be complete. He always knew from beginning that he was going into the army, but he never expected to meet the love of his life there. When it hits you, it hits you hard and fast.

He met his future wife in boot camp. It was all coed training because they wanted forces to work together and get comfortable with each other no matter what. They both were being trained for attack ground forces, and grew quite fond of each other. She was brash, tough and top of her class in combat attack. He proved just as tough. He was second in his class. Through negotiating, they were able to be assigned on the same base. After two years of togetherness, they married and continued their future together. They had one child and she was pregnant with their second child when he delivered the bomb.

The bomb.

He turned and looked at Hawk fidgeting away at the transmitter on the pull-down tabletop in front of them. His mind raced to another type of woman that indeed had a different point of view, Veronica. She was cocky, feisty, arrogant and crude and Hawk fell for her like a rock. She was drop dead gorgeous and talented as well. They were made for each other, and were going strong when the Davi returned.

The Davi.

Once again, the name burned his anger inside, but he knew now that the threat was gone. They were all destroyed; their leaders, their armies, and their forced way of life. Gone was Rodger Brooks. Neither he nor Jason expected it, and Jason was clearly blindsided by Katrina.

Katrina.

Jason didn't expect her either. That was another type of woman to define. Katrina was calm, kind, homely, and easy going. She was shy, bashful, simple and a complete joy to be around.   Being a completely opposite from Veronica, she was exactly what Jason needed; a mother image to get him to slow down and relax. Someone who loved him for what he was. A love that was hard to find, and all three of them managed to find it.

Two lost, one remained.

This time, she will not become another statistic, another victim. Steve would make sure that it would never happen again. He accepted her as if she was his daughter, and he would be there for her, stand up for her, and fight for her.

The transport stopping with a quick jerk snapped him out of his daydreaming and surprised him with the fact that they had arrived at the port.

"Wow," Steve said to Hawk, "that was fast. I didn't expect us to arrive this soon."

"Time flies when your mind is concentrating on something," Hawk answered as he packed up the objects into his coat pockets.

"Yeah," Steve replied, "Tell me about it."

****

After Hawk and Steve left, Jason and Katrina found themselves snuggled on the floor in front of the fireplace. Their drink choice changed from Speckle tea to Sindi wine, and they found themselves at ease from all the resent stress of their lives. The wine was a soothing, fruity taste and it warmed the throat as it went down. Its aroma sent sensations through the nostrils and calmed the mind as well as the body. The peace and quiet of the night around the cabin added to the moment.

Relaxed and completely free from tension, Katrina buried her head deep into Jason's chest. He gently ran his fingers through her shoulder length hair and at times, she almost fell asleep. The comfort that they felt in each other's arms was relaxing and exhilarating at the same time, and they both needed it. They had never really been alone together since the incident, and the circumstances after the fact kept them from doing so. But now, away from it all, they were here alone. They were tucked away in their own corner of the world, and felt protected. The cabin stood as a fortress; solid walls that kept them from any harm, and delivered a refuge of safety and peace.

The warmth of their bodies heated up inside and a flame grew hotter between them. Their heartbeats started to speed up and suddenly, the fire in the fireplace seemed too much to bear. A drop of sweat slowly ran down Jason's forehead.

"Is it getting hotter in here?" He whispered quietly just in case she fell asleep. She turned her head up to look at him and that's when he noticed how deep blue her eyes were. Sweat beaded on her forehead as well and she let out a relaxing sigh.

"It is, I am, and you are," she answered as she reached up with her hand and pulled his lips to hers.

The kiss was welcoming.

****

Steve and Hawk had been on Sheila's bridge for little over two courses and without air circulation, it was starting to get stuffy. The transmitter worked well and delivered a strong signal to the transponder on the bridge. Hawk had bounced it off one of AJBA's satellites, toward the planet Tego, and passed to the planet Zeta through a relay junction onboard a cargo vessel. From there he bounced it to another satellite orbiting Zeta and straight back to the only transmit station that was working on Serin base. There was no loss in composition, signal or waves. It was as clear as if he himself spoke in the room.

The only test left was to see how well it transmitted without a transfer station to amplify it. For this test, Hawk placed the unit into one of his coat pockets and zipped up the closure and was going to walk around the port. Steve was going to stay onboard Sheila and continue to monitor his location. They both were on her bridge, going over the last details before they began.

"Now, the monitor has its own power," Hawk said as he pointed at the screen in front of Steve. "You should see a red dot moving throughout the map, which is me. Just jot down any disturbances or blackouts that happen, and then when I complete my route, we could run a dio to see what is interfering with the signal."

"Some of Preedom's temporary fixes might interfere with this," Steve added.

"Probably, but we won't know that for sure," Hawk stated. "If it does, it would most likely happen here, here, and here," he said as he pointed at the three spots that he referred to.

Steve nodded his head. "Ok, I'm ready whenever you are."

Hawk slapped his hands together and started to rub them vigorously, "Let's do this. I'll signal you from the front when to start."

"Alright," Steve answered.

Hawk walked down the hall and exited out the door on the right, leaping out the opening and totally missing the steps. His eagerness to complete the task engulfed him and he quickened his pace. Stopping at the hanger's front, he turned and gave thumbs up toward the tinted bridge glass of Sheila's body.

That's when the electrical field hit.

A surge of electrical current sent shockwaves throughout the entire hanger and Hawk was caught up in the middle of it. As he tried to keep his balance, he bit down hard, biting off a piece of his tongue and blood trickled down his check. All of his muscles tightened up on him; his fists clenched, his legs locked and his arms stiffened. He couldn't see anything, but many colors danced through his vision and his eyes couldn't open. He fought for control, but that's when the charged intensified even more and doubled in power. His neck muscles tightened, his back went into spasms and his legs buckled out from under him. He fell down to his knees and tried to raise his arms up in the air, but the power was too intense. His body started to go into convulsions and one last time he tried to stand up.

The effort was useless. He lost conscious and fell to the cold floor of the hanger.

The electrical charges stopped. The sounds of footsteps echoed around the corner of the hanger and the blue armored hunter entered the opening. It stopped just above the unconscious body of Hawk. The armored helmet tilted to the right as if to contemplate its next move as it looked down at Hawk. Then, without any effort, it bent over, picked up Hawk, and walked off with him.

Deep inside of Sheila's bridge, Steve laid unconscious on the floor. A smell of burnt hair drifted throughout the air and a light smoke drifted from the top of his head.

****

WOW! This has got to be the best feeling in the Galaxy! Wahoo!

While sitting on the floor, that first kiss; that peck on the cheek, that smooch, that tongue wrestling spit swapping tonsil hockey game got you to first base. The entire body was in a whirlwind of fire and you don't think you could ever put yourself out! Each move, each touch and every little sense was enhanced to its maximum. YOU ARE ABOUT TO BURST!

The kiss was a good start, but it perked up your internal temperature even more as your tongue danced in her mouth like an opera on opening night. How can such a small action cause so much excitement? Your breathing quickened pace, your eyes rolled shut and then you had to reach out to touch. You put your hands on both sides of her head and pulled her closer, if that was even possible. Could you get your tongue even farther into her mouth? Could you reach the back of her throat?

Her groans of joy excited you as well and you each started moving your heads side to side faster as the kiss became more passionate.

You wanted more than this kiss, you wanted to roam. You wanted to fumble, to investigate, to explore, to examine, and search.

You went straight for her shoulders first and started to rub them. She was dressed in a light blouse, you forget the color, but you massaged her shoulders with your fingertips and she groaned even more. The kiss continued, but your concentration was on other things, other places.

You wanted to squeeze, grope, feel, fondle, and touch.

You ran your right hand down to her left breast and continued massaging. She wasn't wearing a bra, she must have taken it off on her last trip to the bathroom, but you weren't going to complain. At the same time, she reached around with both arms and started to lightly claw at your back.

OH BOY! This action aroused you even more. Then you noticed that pinched between your fingers was her nipple, and it was hard. You rolled it and tugged at it and she groaned even louder.

In one quick move, you rolled her over onto her back. The move put you above her and you felt rather proud of yourself knowing that you didn't lose your grip on her nipple, and she didn't lose her grip either. With both hands, you opened up her blouse, (it's yellow, you see that now), and exposed both of her breasts. The color variation from her skin to the areola and the nipple was several shades and... WOW! YOUR BODY GOT EVEN MORE INTENSIFIED!

You start to shiver, shake and shutter with excitement as you looked at the person before you. You start to build up an inner energy that feels it could go nuclear at any moment. You feel alive! You feel consumed, you feel...
Wet.

Not only are you soaked to the bone with perspiration, but you feel like you have leaked. You leaned back to pull off the sweat drenched shirt and she pulls off her blouse at the same time. With a quick flick of the wrists, you both toss the loose clothing toward the left and it lands, somewhere.

Her body was now completely exposed on the top half and her nipples stood out rather perky. Your friskiness was on full boil and not only did you want to touch again, but you wanted to taste.

Your appetite was like your breakfast the other day, but the same words would be put toward a different experience. Your tongue wanted to lick it, savor it, bite it, relish it, and sample it. You wanted to get a mouthful of that tiny little morsel in front of you.

You bent down over her and put her right nipple in your mouth. You rolled the warm point around with your tongue and lightly sucked up on it. She started to roll her head around and her groans turned into short gasps. She had her eyes closed, but her heightened expression on her face said she wanted more. You started to fondle the other breast with the other hand and gave more pressure to the touch without getting too aggressive.

Her breathing sped up. You couldn't control yourself at this point anymore and you reached down to unfasten her pants. Your mind stumbled when you didn't find any snap, zipper or other apparatus, but then realized that she was just wearing slip on slacks.

You both stood up to your knees and slowly pulled each other's pants off. She unbuckled your belt, zipped down the fly and wiggled your pants side to side as they worked their way off of you. All you had to do was yank hers down. Neither of you even bothered with pulling them off; both of you left them at the knees.

Now, all that was left was the underwear. Hers was a light yellow frilly something and yours was your regular tighty whities. No time was spent on them; they both were pulled down just as fast.

Then both of you were back down to the floor, you on top, and the kissing started once again. You had your left hand clamped on her breast and was massaging it again. It was exhilarating and intoxicating. You were sexually drunk and invigorated. You were in control, but losing control.

You are hard as a rock. Yes, that tiny little third leg you carry. That ding-dong named dick. A wiener dingy willy pee-pee that has a wang of a whoopie stick you call Johnson. It's doing its best to show its manhood member of a meat stick, a shaft schlong love muscle that is ready to become a heat seeking moisture missile. Your one-eyed wonder worm is gearing up to beaver bash and needs to make that tally whacker into a danger noodle ready to launch that pocket rocket.

And look at what it is doing! Your cock had gotten so hard that it was pulsating with each beat of your heart. It lurched upward each time and you could see a little wetness on the end. You could see a little wetness on her too.

Your body fluids started to express themselves even more as you both stopped for a moment to glance deeply at each other.

The perspiration was so strong on her that it looked like she had just stepped out of the shower. You too were so sweaty, that you were dripping down on her. Several drops of sweat had run down into your eyes, but the stinging never prevailed over the thrilling stimulation that you were experiencing.

You both locked eyes onto each other took deep breaths and then she nodded. It was time for the full experience to reach its climatic point.

HELL YES! WE ARE GETTING IT ON! We are going to have intercourse, procreate, consummate, fornicate, copulate, and have coitus. We're going to pork, shag, mount, ram, pump, hump, bang, tumble, and poke. We will exchange flesh as we nail each other, make whoopee, have nooky, and penetrate deep. Together we will roll in the hay, jump each other's bones, dip your wick, bang the beaver, play hide the sausage, and get your rocks off.

WE ARE GOING TO FUCK!

You thrust yourself into her and she lets out a loud gasp. The feeling of her vagina wrapping itself tightly around your shaft really gets you going even more, (that is if there is more to go), and you start pumping like you had just discovered an oil well. With each thrust, she gasped and you grunt. It enhanced everything once again. You sweated more, grunted more, and breathed heavier, and yet it is still amazing that there could be any sweat left in either of the bodies after all of this amusement park fantasy ride. Each of you started to touch more erratically.

Then things became really odd. She stiffened up and looked like she had just plain stopped. Each of her breaths became short bursts, but only pulled air in, she didn't exhale. Both of her hands gripped onto your shoulders and she squeezed, HARD. Her legs stiffened and it looked like she was having a seizure.

Suddenly, your back started to stiffen up. You could feel your toes curling in and you couldn't find the energy to thrust anymore. You couldn't catch a breath and a huge wave of energy was surging through your body. You managed to pull in a deep breath of air and hold it, and your hips froze. Muscles that you have not felt for a while tightened and surged through your body

and your eyes glazed over. That's
when...

CHAPTER 9

.............................everything got a whole lot wetter! WOW WHAT
A RIDE! This crazy rollercoaster is flowing like a raging river! You
couldn't experience this much of a mad rush even if you were
flushed down a toilet. You can't possibly imagine the twists and
turns that surround this experience. A sandstorm would be just a
kiddie ride compared to this. The ups and downs, (oh boy, the ups
and downs) spin you around like a whirlwind, but I must keep
focused. I must stay ahead of the competition. I must succeed.

****

Steve slowly regained consciousness to pain. He was lying
on the carpet on Sheila's bridge, still not totally aware of his
surroundings. His eyes were shut but he could see little beams of
light bouncing around. Perhaps his partial blindness was playing
tricks on him, or he was now totally blind. His head was spinning
with one of the strongest headaches he had ever encountered. The
pounding in his temples and the heat rising from the top of his head
was so powerful that it was overwhelming. He felt like he could
take a long nap. Perhaps, he had just taken one and was trying to
wake up. Everything was so confusing and contradicting that he
had a very hard time trying to get his bearings.

His body was cold but his head was hot. Heat flourished
around his ears but his arms were freezing. His closed eyes still saw
light, but his body felt the coldness of dark. He could feel that his
hands and feet were jittery, which added an odd sensation to the
rest of his tingling skin.

He smelled burnt hair. Not an unfamiliar smell to him, but
nevertheless, a distinctively bad odor. His other senses started to
awake when he felt how dry and tender his throat was. He tried to
swallow some spit, but there was hardly any to be found. His
tongue felt numb and swollen, but he was able to roll it around in
his mouth. The saliva started to build up and he tried to swallow

again. A dry cough was created and it made him cringe with more pain as his lungs tried to contain it.

He slowly opened his eyes.

It was dark. He could see just enough to know that he was on the floor of Sheila's bridge lying on his left side. But how in the hell did he wind up here? He tried to think of what he was doing to arrive at such a position and solve his confusion. He decided to try to sit up.

That alone was a task of achievement. His arms ached as he pushed himself up to a sitting position and his head felt like it weighed a thousand pounds. All his skin started to tingle sporadically and he almost lost his balance. Dizziness swarmed around his head as he blinked his eyes several times to gain more control. He could still see the little lines of light dancing around but they were starting to dissipate. His mind decided to sit for a while and not attempt to move, ever.

He sighed loudly and the air rushing out burned his nostrils. He closed his eyes again in hope that the spinning would ease up, but it only made it worse. He started to breathe easier, with less pain, and he attempted to open his eyes again.

He saw the front of the bridge and could see through the window that it was still dark out, but a morning dark. Little light zingers still bounced in the corners of his vision, but they were very faint. He tried several times to blind tears, but they too were dry.

How long had he been here? Why was he here? The questions needed answers but he also needed to give himself time to recover. Recover from what? What the hell happened? All the questions danced in his mind but somehow it seemed that he had experienced this before. He thought back, trying to make a connection. It was a long time ago. Not here, on this world, but farther back. He concentrated on the effects, the feelings and the pain and suddenly it dawned on him.

He was out on a mission, fighting in Eastern Europe. The Davi had a fortress that they had been trying to over run for the last couple of weeks. His OAJ jet was hidden in camo gear and he was getting ready to crawl into the cockpit to check out the readings of any nearby attack force. Someone on the ground yelled for cover and then…………

Electrocution! That was it, he had been electrocuted! Just like the time in Europe, only this time, it was more painful. His eyes widened with response to his findings and his conscious started to try to snap the rest of his body out of it. Something electrocuted him and knocked his ass down to the floor, but what?

He remembered standing up at the window and seeing Hawk……. HAWK! That was what was going on! They were testing to see how far that transmitter could go. Hawk was going to walk around the base. He had just finished the device and was going to test it.

But then, confusion hit him again as he tried to understand how that could have caused such a surge. He slowly reached up to the top of his head to scratch an itch, his arm still tingling from the surge, and he found stubble; burnt, singed stubble. He then put both hands on top of his head and discovered that half of his hair was gone. He slowly worked his hands down his face and discovered why his skin was so tight.

His cheeks and forehead felt like leather. His face felt scorched and when he tried to produce a yawn, the tightening of the skin intensified the pain.

Yep, he was definitely electrocuted.

His next task wasn't going to be easy. He was going to try to stand up and make his way to one of the bridge's chairs. He bent his legs inward, feeling the stiffness in the knees, and tried to push. No luck, the legs were just to week to support him.

His next idea was to crawl toward the chair. He flattened himself down onto his belly, feeling every inch of his skin pulling, and then started to claw his way forward. His arms and legs strained with each pull, and it seemed like forever just to move. Each move slid him closer, and each pull burned like a torch, but when he finally reached the chair, he leaned his back up against it and rested.

He had lost track of time of how long he had rested at that spot. He was starting to become more coherent, and his energy was on the rise, but he still was dizzy.   With one deep breath, he put every stretch of energy he had into pulling himself up. He twisted and grabbed the arms of the chair and strained.

Even with his legs still feeling like jelly, he successfully landed into the chair sideways. It was time for him to rest again.

He drifted back to the Davi experience on how he was electrocuted. An arc bomb, made specifically to burn out electrical equipment, blew up in the area of his OAJ. The base's power unit was under the OAJ's hull. It took weeks for him to recover, not to mention grow his hair back.

Wow, Deja vu.

He once again, didn't know how long he sat there daydreaming, but it felt good having the support of the chair on his back. He let out a long breath of relief and then leaned forward. Looking out the window, he saw that Hawk was nowhere to be found. He did see, however, that the sides of the hanger looked dark and scorched. Whatever it was, not only did it affect the inside of Sheila, but her hanger as well. As big as the marks were on the hanger, it had to be a tremendous electrical surge. Nothing aboard Sheila could have done that.

Then a red blinking light got his attention on the bridge's front display panel. He looked down to see the screen, which Hawk had installed, to track the transmitter that they were working on. The red dot was blinking; signaling the location of Hawk. Steve mildly smiled, grimacing against the slight pain, and then his brow and eyes went to a complete confusion.

The red dot was blinking somewhere off planet.

****

Oh, what a calm feeling.

When you wake up in the morning to a good solid sleep it feels like your whole body and mind had been cleansed. You feel like your skin is so soothed that it is sliding off of your bones and every breath you take is slow, calm, and fresh. The pillow, under your head, has wrapped itself around you so well that it becomes a part of you; giving you full support in every nook and cranny. Your body contained such warmth because of a heavy quilt that had managed to form itself around your frame and tuck under your feet. You feel safe and secure from harm. You keep your eyes closed in hope that you could stay in this serenity forever, but your ears try to pull you away.

The first thing you hear is the Fana birds singing outside. Their cooing, warbling notes were soothing to the ears and just added to the rest of your condition. This condition could be explained in so many ways; you are content, tranquil, blissful, peaceful, at ease, mellow, comfy, and worry free. Your mind is quiet, soothed, relieved, satisfied, gratified, carefree, and humble. All together your entire existence could be best explained as being totally laid back.

You slowly open your eyes and you see the sun's rays beaming across the room above you. Little particles of dust lightly dance in the glow and the beam, in an odd way, warms up your sight. It also gives you an inner vision of last night, a night of passion and love.

You smile about the experience you had the night before and the conclusion it gave. Maybe the warmth you felt this morning was a carryover from last night due to the emotions that you expressed for each other. Is it possible that the experience could keep a body powered for so long? Could the sexual contact extent this far? Could the mind be that strong?

You find the energy to prop yourself up onto your elbows and take in a deep breath. The air was so crisp that it tickled the nose and you let out a long sigh of delight. From last night up to this moment you feel like you are walking on air, on cloud nine, in seventh heaven, and jumping for joy. Your overall condition is because of one reason, one person.

You turn and look at the person lying next to you and instantaneously you start to glow within. This person has not only changed your life but has become your life. There isn't anything that you wouldn't do for this person for you admire, desire, relish, cherish, treasure, adore, value, appreciate, and respect this person.

Your feelings of love for this person are endless, eternal, everlasting, forever, and undying.

This person is your darling suitor, a precious dear, a honey of a sweetheart, your flame, your valentine, a beloved cupcake of a peach, a sweetie pie pumpkin, a sugarplum baby cake, that heartthrob of a Honey-bunchy-Wunchy.

He is your soulmate.

Katrina's inside was warming with a glow that she never wanted to end. The night before was such an emotional release that they fell asleep almost immediately from exhaustion. The entire experience continued as they made their way into the bedroom from the spot they started at by the fireplace and it seemed that time was endless as they shared themselves again and again.

She looked at Jason's face; seeing the calmness upon it and her mind started to reflect all that they had been through. She remembered how he first saved her in the tunnel, and how scared she was about the experience. Her mind remembered the first time she met Sheila and the tricks that she played on her. Her introduction to 'Little Chicago' was an adventure that she never knew existed for her life was always reclusive. Her smile widened even more when she reminiscent about their first date in her apartment; the food, the drinks and the discovery of his Earth origins. She had a wonderful time working at 'Little Chicago' experiencing new things to explore, new people to meet. Through Jason, she discovered an entirely different world from her usual tedious, dull and ordinary life. The new people she had met not only became friends, but were now considered family. People like Steve, Hawk, Aiden, Remy and Veronica.

Her smile turned over when the thought of Veronica stabbed her from within. Just when things were going well, it started to look as if life had taken a wrong turn and they were all belted in for the ride. Her eyes started to lightly water as she thought of others affected from the turn; her friends at work, Hawk's 'Blackout', Sheila's death and then Jason's death. Her heart felt like it had skipped a beat, and she sucked in a quick pocket of air to calm herself. She concentrated on controlling the pain, swallowing the pain, and forgetting it.

But as fast as it hit, the ride turned again and things rebounded. Hawk was awake, 'Little Chicago' would become once again a thriving place to be and Jason was alive. He was alive and calmly sleeping at her side. This energetic, adventurous man had somehow captured the heart of her poor pathetic boring life and gave her a purpose. He had opened up the scared little girl inside her and showed her life.

She slowly slid herself out from under the quilt, hoping not to wake him, and quietly traveled downstairs to the kitchen. She was going to make him a breakfast he would never forget.

****

The work that needed to be done was indeed a task, and to Remy and Aiden, it looked nearly impossible. When they first laid sights on the damage that 'Little Chicago' sustained, they thought that they may have bitten off more than they could chew. So many things had to be cleaned, fixed, straightened, replaced, and thrown out. The 'To Do' list was so long that it would take an entire night just to write it and several rotations just to get it started. The pile was so high that climbing it would be easier than trying to diffuse it.

But when they actually started, they didn't expect the burst of energy from within. The thought of being part owners fueled their enthusiasm and that tall pile turned into a small mound. They kept going even though their bodies said 'No', but their mindset said 'Yes.' They first started with separating all the tasks and attacking them head on.

Remy was the cleaner, the neat freak. She always wanted things spotless so she took on the task of cleaning everything. She started in the kitchen and worked her way out into the bar and then to the seating area. They had both brought a lot of cleaning supplies when they arrived, and Remy had to leave three more times to get more. The splintered wood and glass weren't the problem, nor was it the real mess, the smoke and ashes were the worst part of it. She had scrubbed and rinsed so many times that she thought she was taking the paint off of the table, but her efforts paid off when you could really see a difference. In fact, most of all the tables were back to normal due to Remy's diligence. She cleaned everything that could be cleaned, and threw away everything that was beyond repair. In the end, she was rather pleased with herself.

Aiden, on the other hand, was the fixer. She loved to repair, restore, and rectify. Electronics was second nature to her and she loved to get her hands dirty in it. She had compiled a list of things that needed immediate attention first, and then would get to the smaller stuff later. The first thing and the direst attention on her list were the lights. After several moments of holding the flashlight in her mouth so that she could work with both of her hands, it didn't take her long to find the breaks in the circuits and fix them. The lights ended up being the easiest thing on her list. The Vid became the monster of the night. She had to crawl under cabinets, between walls and in the ceiling to find the problem, but she was determined to find it. In her frustration, she changed tasks and fixed the music system to get away from the Vid for a while. The change calmed her mind and within the next course, they had music to work to. Even at one point, she grabbed Remy coming out of the kitchen and they danced to a couple of songs to relieve the tension they had. It also woke them up and sparked their second wind.

Fueled once again, they continued on their assigned tasks and Aiden finally finished the Vid. Remy had the kitchen done by the time Aiden turned it on, but after checking the picture, she turned it back off to let the music once again take over the building.

Her next task was to check all the mechanics of the bar and to see what needed fixed, replaced or thrown out. Remy started the tables at that time and the music gave both of them that extra inspiration and motivation they needed to succeed.

It was long into the morning when they were interrupted by their gurgling stomachs and they stopped to order food through the

Vid. Sitting at one of the newly freshened tables, they waited for their order to arrive.

"You know," Aiden said with a sigh, "if we sit here too long, we won't be able to get back up again."

"It doesn't matter," Remy replied as she flexed her finger, "I can't feel anything anyway."

Aiden laughed a short snort of air out of her nose and turned to look at what they had accomplished. The bar area was clean, but the back wall mirror was gone. It sure made the room look smaller. The floor was clean, all the tables and chairs were back to normal and all the loose debris had been removed. She smiled and blew out a large air of relief from her lungs. "Wow, what a night," she exclaimed as she tilted her head back and looked up. Then her expression became twisted and in agony. Her face looked disgusted. "Oh, that's nice," she said sarcastically.

Remy tilted her head back as well and saw what Aiden was looking at. The ceiling was black with soot.

"You know when we clean or replace those, it's all going to come down on the floor, "Aiden said.

Remy looked back down and did a look over the seating area. "Oh, great," her tired voice exclaimed, "that's really nice."

A buzz at the door startled both of them and Remy jumped up. "Let's eat, I'm starving," she said making her way toward the door. Aiden was a couple of steps behind her anticipating that first bite. When they reached the door, Remy opened it, but instead of seeing a cart load of goodies, they found Steve on the other side, barely standing.

"We need to find Jason," he said as he fell forward and hit the floor hard.

****

An echoing tap repeated itself again and again in Hawk's mind and he couldn't grasp the sound of it. The low tone it emitted bounced around inside his fuzzy head and for a moment he thought he was underwater. His concentration was so perplexed that he took into consideration that he might even be asleep. The condition of his current state strongly suggested it. His head felt so heavy and the rest of the body was unresponsive. His eyes couldn't even open. Due to the fact that he had no control convinced him that he must be asleep.

The tap occurred again, this time quicker than before, and it started to get annoying. Whatever this dream was, it better conclude because he wasn't enjoying it. The sound continued to pound and it made him cringe from within. It was starting to become clearer what it could be; possibly someone hammering nails, someone knocking on a door, or a dripping faucet. The persistence of the sound gave him enough energy to open his eyes to see what it was.

Everything was fuzzy and out of focus. A cloud of haze surrounded the room, and it was extremely hard for him to fixate anything. His eyelids continued to try to shut but he fought hard to keep them open. His head wiggled erratically as he tried to move it, the weight of exhaustion upon it, and he slowly turned toward his left.

Someone was standing next to him; he couldn't make out whom but they were there. A colored blob of skin tone was close, almost touching him, as he watched the arm reach up toward his face.

The hand tapped on what appeared to be a glass between them and the sound repeated. It repeated that annoying sound that awoke him from......where? His mind started to clear and things started to make more sense to him. That sound was someone tapping on the glass and causing that echo inside his head. He squinted several times to get a better look at whom or what it was. His attention drew a response.

That person said something and it was so garbled and unclear, once again it sounded like he was under water. He tried to clear the fuzziness out of his head by closing his eyes and concentrating really hard, but the tap turned into a loud pound and he snapped out of it. He shot open his eyes and saw that the individual was so close that their noses could almost touch.

It spoke again, but this time it was clear and he recognized it.

"Fuck you," Hawk was able to mumble out.

"Good, good," exclaimed Medico as he lightly put his hands together, "You remember, and you are gaining strength, and oh, such a vonderful vocabulary." His corrupted smile only lifted to one corner as he reached up with his hand and slightly touched the glass between them, "I've missed you, 217." His hand smoothly stroked the glass pane as he proceeded on, "you have caused such a trouble and I had thought I lost you, but here you are." He pulled his hand from the glass and gestured toward the room behind him. "You are home vhere you belong."

Hawk's mind was starting to fully wake up. Home, he said. Torture chamber and breeding ground was a better description. He had hoped that he would never see this place again, but he knew somehow it would happen. He knew that they would eventually cross paths.

Getting a better focus in his area, Hawk could see that he was in a glass box with several wires running around its frame. He was strapped to a table, with his arms tied up above him, and the wires even wrapped around his wrists. He followed the wires with his eyes and saw that they ran down to the floor and into a black box by his feet. The floor of the box had about two inches of water in it.

"Interesting, isn't it," Medico said while noticing Hawk's focus, "I've always known your one weakness, 217, and that was electricity. You have so much power, but cannot battle current." He tipped his head to the side as he continued, "I suppose I blame myself for that, because you vere made under electricity. Perhaps you vork like a magnet vhen it counteracts its negative self." He lifted up his hands and displayed a playful act. He grunted and pretended to try to put his hands together, but acted like he couldn't. "Two opposing factors that just don't vork vell together." He looked deep at his hands, and then yanked them apart. "Vhatever it is, you are now home and for good." He turned and walked toward the exit on the other side of the room.

"Not this time, you Butcher," Hawk yelled with what energy he could lift, "I'll get out again, and this time, I'll kill you in the process."

Medico's laugh could be heard all the way down the hall.

CHAPTER 10

Your life has taken another wrong turn. The call you received at the cabin not only changed the feelings you had when you first woke up, but it also has turned your body against you.

At first the news made you nauseated. Not like when you drink too much, but a churning, bubbling sensation in the stomach that cramps up your sides. The stomach felt bloated, inflated, puffy, ballooned, enflamed and so gassed up that you were hoping that one large fart would relieve it all. You pushed for it but it never came. Your stomach felt so expanded that you were afraid that you might shit your pants in the process. Was it something you ate? Did all the drinks last night disagree with you? Was it the sex?

Not only was your stomach out of line, but you were so fatigued you had a hard time getting started. Sea sickness would be a blessing compared to the nasty sensations that were going on with you. You were dizzy, queasy, squeamish and very light headed. Every time you started to move you would break out into a cold sweat and get a woozy head spin. Combined with the stomach tossing and turning, you felt like you were going to hurl any moment. Are you sure you could hold your alcohol? This sure doesn't come across like a normal drunken state, but has similar symptoms.

Twice you went to the bathroom to throw up, but nothing came out. The taste of bile was up into your throat, and it burned the sides like a flame. The aroma made its way up to the nostrils and made you close your eyes. The head became even dizzier in the darkness and you opened your eyes back up. You tried to throw up again, but nothing came out. The dry heaves started to pull at you side muscles creating a stabbing pain every time you moved. You did have to pee several times, but nothing else helped to calm the stomach of its gurgling acid fluids. Was the food for dinner spoiled? If so, why wasn't anyone else sick? It must have been the drinks because there was no other explanation for it.

But there were other pains as well. Your breasts felt very sensitive and they hurt when you tried to put on your shirt. The slightest brush across them felt like a rug burn on the knee, and they too felt like they were bloated. In fact, your bra felt tighter than normal, which doesn't make any sense. Was he too rough on them? Where they squeezed or chewed on too hard?

Through effort and help, you managed to get ready and make it to the transport for the ride back to the base. You groaned and grunted all the way to the chair that you now occupy.

Katrina watched the countryside roll past them as she looked out the window next to her seat. When Aiden called Jason at the cabin, he was dressed and ready in 5 taps, but it took her longer to get ready. Her pains and feelings would have to wait because she needed to focus on what had happened to Hawk. Jason said that it might have something to do with the person that they ran into at Foscal's. Hawk was very upset about the incident and rushed everyone home, hoping to not get anyone else involved. He filled her in on what happened there, but she had a hard time trying to concentrate.

Jason knew that she was not feeling good and tried everything he could to ease her pain. He was trying to prop up a pillow for her head, but she slowly waved her hand in the air.

"No, thanks," she said while trying to hold back the bad taste in her mouth, "I'm afraid to move. Just let me lie here up against the window."

Jason's face expressed sympathy for her pain. "I wish I could do something to make you feel better. Do you need anything to drink maybe something to eat?"

That comment made her almost gag again. She raised her head from the window and looked at him with tired eyes. "Oh, please don't mention food," she said, "just be here for me." She held onto his hand.

"Always," he said back with a concerning smile. "Please let me know if you need anything. Just get some rest; we still have about 20 more taps."

She lightly nodded and then laid her head back upon the window again. The humming of the transport reverberated throughout her brain and in an odd way, it was soothing. She hoped that she could fall asleep and wake up better, relieved of all this commotion.

Her mind still dwelled on the call from Aiden, although. Aiden said that Steve was slowly recovering but he was getting upset that they were pampering him so much. She mentioned only that Hawk was gone and that they needed to get there as soon as possible. In her condition, Katrina didn't think she was going to be much help because her body just couldn't get it together.

She really needed to fart.

****

"217, 217, 217," Medico yelled the number louder and louder as he danced around his lab room. He clapped his hands above his head with each yell, and twirled around in a little jig. "He is home, he is home," he yelled flailing his arms into the air and tilting his head back toward the ceiling. He sucked in a large breath of air through his nostrils and let out an equally sized gasp back out through his grinning teeth. The air hissed upon release.

Clapping his hands together one last time, he turned toward one of his work tables and leaned upon it. A tear ran down from his right eye as he slowly looked at his surroundings.

This room was where it all started. It was a new place, a new beginning to put together all of his years of experience to the test. It took him a while to find it; but indeed, was the best location for it. No one would ever want to wander in here nor want to brave the attempt.   It had built a reputation over the years as a death trap, an area to avoid.

It was all because of him.

The first part of his experiments in this new world was the hard part because he did not have easy excess to his subjects like he did in the past. Here, he had to hunt for them. Here, he was not part of a faction or had to answer to anybody. Here he was in charge, here he was able to do anything he pleased, and here he was not held accountable. The only downside of it was that here, he was alone.

Being alone, though, he wasn't held back. He could go at his own speed and do whatever he pleased. He would pay for help; find locals who were either too stupid to understand or just plain didn't care. He had found loyal ones; beings that came back again and again to help and they became resourceful.

The news about Heptor bothered him; he had been there for years and he was one of the most productive people he had hired. His feeble mind never questioned his job; he did what he was told to do, and completed the assignments on time. Heptor reminded Medico a lot about the old country. Men who worked for him there were productive as well, but had to follow the wishes of their superiors. He had to answer to them as well and also, produce results.

But his wishes were limited then and he was not allowed to expand beyond the perimeters of the complex. He wanted to try other ideas but his superiors feared he was out of control. They tried to set him up for failure, to frame him for all the tests, but he escaped and broke free of their grasp. His work and equipment were all saved and made the trip to this place.

He glanced around the room once again. He smiled knowing that this place let him break out of his chains beyond the locked doors and beyond the iron hand. Through technology that was offered him and the skills to work it, he was delivered here.

This was his domain and his kingdom.

Large steps echoing closer to the entrance made him slowly break his dream and concentrate on the approaching sound. He turned around and leaned his back onto the table and watched the shadow on the floor get larger and larger as the creature emerged.

The Klebit walked into the room and then stopped just inside the door. It saw Medico and smiled at him.

"Ahhh, 210!" Medico said as he lightly put his hands together, "How are we feeling my friend? Do you feel better after your rest?"

The large Klebit nodded its head and returned the smile.

"I'm so glad to hear that," Medico stated as he made his way toward a table on the other side of the room. The table had two chairs and upon it were two glasses with a bottle of liquid next to them. "Come, my friend, sit down."

The Klebit slowly walked over and turned its large body and sized up the chair. It turned its head left and then right showing a confused look. It let out a little whine.

"You'll be fine," Medico said as he sat down in the other chair, "Don't worry, 210, you vill fit."

The Klebit sat down and the chair creaked due to the weight. The Klebit first looked concerned, but once it was adjusted, the Klebit looked up and smiled at Medico. It was pleased with its accomplishment.

Medico reached for the bottle and started to pour its contents into the two glasses. "Vould you like some drink? I make this myself." He finished filling the glasses and sat the bottle back down. He then picked up one of the glasses and handed it to the Klebit. The Klebit gently took it from his hand as Medico picked up the remaining one and lifted it into the air.

"A toast," he said with a proud look upon his face, "to you, my friend."

As Medico took a drink of his, he looked sideways at the Klebit to watch his response. The Klebit copied him and drank as well. Half of the liquid poured down its cheek but most of it made its way into the mouth. After the drink was finished, the Klebit turned his head and smiled. It held out the empty glass toward Medico.

"More?" The Klebit slowly grunted out the question in hopes to get a refill.

Medico's inner ego ignited hearing the Klebit's voice. This was another success toward his ultimate goal and there was only one piece missing. That piece was 217.

"Yes, my friend," Medico answered while lifting up the bottle again, "you may have more."

The Klebit held on the glass with both hands as Medico filled it to the top.

****

Steve took another gulp of his glass of water. He could feel that the tingling in his skin had dissipated and he wasn't shaking as much. His hair, although, would have to grow back. In all the time that he was sitting in the chair, Remy was sitting next to him holding onto his arm. The concern on her face was heavy and she wasn't going to leave his side, that's why Aiden was running all the errands. She was the one that got the water; put the cold wet cloth on his forehead, and the one who called Jason. She was standing next to Steve's other side, waiting for her next task.

At first, they didn't know how to call Jason because Steve passed out after he stepped into the building. It was 20 taps later when he finally woke up. His words were groggy at first, but he quickly started to come around and recognize his surroundings.

The surroundings were a complete turnaround from the last time he was in here.

'Little Chicago' looked almost as good as new. The tables were all back in order and clean, the bar was repaired and even the lights were all functioning. It was surprising what these two ladies did overnight. At first, he didn't think he would see the ole girl open up again, but through their perseverance, it looked like a whole new life was polished into her. He did notice that the ceiling was going to have to be replaced.

When he was able to get his mind together, he told Aiden the Vid number to call and get ahold of Jason. And once again, was surprised to see that they had fixed it as well. He was really looking forward in working full throttle with the two ladies. All three of their talents together could really make this place hop.

But a speed bump was thrown into the road, in fact, several speed bumps. The situation with Hawk put everything on hold, and everyone on high alert. He didn't tell the girls what had happened; Remy wouldn't let him speak until he regained his strength. She said that it could wait until the others arrived. Waiting was not an option, and Steve knew that time was against them.

The front door creaked open and Jason walked in with Katrina; who wasn't looking well at all. Remy stood up from Steve's side and nodded her head toward them.

"It's about time, what took you so long?"

"Sorry to slow things down," Katrina said as she sat into another chair at the table, "I'm not feeling well today." She looked exhausted.

Aiden ran toward her side, "My word you look awful. Is there anything I can get you?"

Katrina only answered with a shaking her head no.

Jason grabbed the chair next to her and pulled it out to sit down. "So, what the hell happened?" He looked between Remy, Aiden and Steve for an answer.

"We don't know," Aiden replied. "Steve wanted to wait until you arrived to tell us."

"Not true," Remy added. "I wanted him to...."

"Hawk's in trouble!" Steve blurted out. "He's gone, taken from us. We have to get him back!"

Jason slowly sat down. "Taken how?"

Steve let out a long sigh and finished what was left in the glass. Aiden started to grab it to go refill it and Steve wave his hand over the glass, signifying that he didn't want any more. "No more. You need to sit and listen." She slowly pulled out another chair and sat down, the concern in her eyes, growing.

"Hawk and I was working on a few things around Sheila when an electrical current shocked the whole hanger and knocked me out." Steve's voice was raspy and sore as he continued, "I was in Sheila's bridge and he was just outside in front of her."

"Electrical charge?" Jason questioned. "What in the world could...."

Steve cut off Jason's next question, "Not my concern. But when I awoke, Hawk was gone. I tell you; he has been taken."

"What makes you think he's been taken?" Remy asked the question on everyone's mind.

Steve struggled to get something out of his right pants pocket and the painful movement alerted Remy to walk toward him. Steve raised his other hand to wave her off, that he was ok. Pulling his hand back from his pocket, he tossed on the table what he was reaching for; the small screen device that was on Sheila's bridge. The screen still had a blinking red dot.

"We don't have much time," Steve said pointing at the device. "That is your transmitter in his pocket," he said pointing toward Jason. "And soon it's going to be out of range. We have got to leave now if we're ever going to keep up with it."

Everyone at the table looked at the screen. The dot was blinking far off planet and almost to the end of the screen.

"Jason," Steve's voice sounded demanding and urgent, "we have to leave…. NOW!"

"Oh no," Remy protested, "Not in your condition. You need to rest and…."

"Fuck rest," Steve blurted out. He turned his head toward Jason and spoke sternly. "You know I'm right."

Jason stood up quick from his chair and went into action. "Aiden, make us a travel kit, simple necessities. Remy, get us a rental vessel. We can't chance hoping that a transport is going to follow him." He turned toward Katrina and the concern filled his face. "Honey, you need to stay with the ladies until you feel better. We will contact you." He turned toward Steve, "Can you stand?"

Steve grabbed both arms on the chair and pushed himself up to a standing position. He stomped his feet twice and flayed his hands out in front of him like he was shaking water off of his hands. "Let's rock," he said, nodding at Jason.

****

The more and more he looked around, the more his memory pierced his brain. Hawk tried so hard to forget this place, but the painful reality started to return and his mind was in turmoil. Life became so precious to him that the past became a distant nightmare and through his friends, he was able to put it completely out of his mind.

Now, he was back into the nightmare, only this time, he was trapped. Several courses ago, his restraints were released and he was able to walk around his enclosure. Medico took every precaution to keep him at bay for the restraints released on their own, electronically. The maniac wasn't even going to take the chance of walking in and manually unstrapping them.

After he was released from the holding board, he discovered a full room behind him containing a bed, a bathroom, and a small table with one chair. A small jail cell, you might say, but built like a holding tank. He had researched the entire containment room looking for a weakness, but there were none to be found. In each corner was an electrical current box, all connected by wires framing the ceiling and draped down to the floor. The floor held about two inches of water, wall to wall. The walls were a thick glass, in which he tried several times to punch, but found that they too, were electrically charged. Water slowly trickled down them making what should be non-conductive, very conductive.

The knowledge of the electrical weakness that he had ate at him for a solution. Thinking back to all the times that he had encountered electrical current, he never remembered getting electrocuted. He always took every precaution to make sure that it was safe to proceed. Odd, that something this small would be his downfall.

Medico was a butcher. Not only did Hawk remember all the tests that he was put through, but he had seen so many other creatures put through even worst conditions. Their screams echoed off the walls and sent shivers down one's spine. There were so many experiments and operations done that the creatures were not of their own anatomy anymore. They evolved into something different, something horrifying, and even appalling. Medico claimed that he was creating the ultimate race.

Medico, himself, was a freak. He had not only performed these experiments on them, but himself as well. Through his research and results, he had found a way to adjust his own physical properties. He was able to reverse his aging process, strengthen his bones and body, and keep himself free from any type of bacterial infection. His body was the ultimate god.

His mind, although, suffered the procedure. Over the time, Hawk observed Medico's mind deteriorating. He didn't remember much about time, or where he originally came from, but Hawk did remember Medico's change. The earliest he could remember, Medico was calm, even-tempered, and tranquil. As time went by, he started to notice a jittery uneasiness about the man. He would develop an on again, off again, twitch in his left cheek. His hands would at times start shaking uncontrollably, making his work harder to finish. Then there were the sudden outbursts that accompanied his inability to perform his tests. He'd throw things, break things and scream at the top of his lungs. Seeing this change in his behavior told Hawk that it was time to escape.

Sitting at the table, with his elbows propped up upon it, Hawk kept running through his mind several options on what to do. He was stumped about any possibility to escape, to even get by the electrical field. He saw that the control switch for the tank was outside of the front wall, and figured that the main feed to it was the large conduit cord connected to it. That cord ran across the room and out the far entrance hall, possibly toward the power room.

The layout plans for the area were slowly recovering in his mind as he pieced together an answer. If he remembered correctly, this room used to be a supply room which was at the end of the complex. Heading out the hall, if you turned to the right, it leads to the power room, and to the left was the main test room, or better yet, the torture chamber. After that room, further down the hall were the cells where all the test subjects were kept, where all the screams came from. After that, it was too vague to remember, but there were so many tunnels, one could get lost if you weren't careful.

Hawk leaned back into the chair and slapped his hands down onto his lap; and felt something hard in his pocket.

It was the transmitter.

If it was working, surely Jason and Steve knew where he was at, but by all means, he didn't want them here. If Medico got his hands on them the thought was too great to imagine.

Someone tapped on the front glass and Hawk looked up preparing to see Medico, but it was something entirely different.

It was a tall figure in a blue armored suit waving its hand to get Hawk to approach the glass.

"Go away," Hawk yelled, "leave me alone."

The figure reached up with its right hand and grabbed the power switch on the outside of the tank. The other hand waved Hawk forward again.

Hawk, protesting in his mind, stood up and approached the figure. He got up to the glass as close as he could without touching it, and sneered at the person.

"What?" Hawk asked.

The figure just stared and tilted its head to the right.

"What's wrong, can't you talk?"

The figure shook its head no.

"Great," Hawk sighed hoping to raise some information out of it. "I suppose you are one of the hired idiots that Medico has working for him."

The figure shook its head no, again.

"Really," Hawk continued. "You mean that you just float around here dressed up in combat armor for your own amusement?"

The figure didn't answer.

Hawk shook his head in disgust while the figure just stood there. Getting a deeper look into the armor, Hawk leaned forward and almost touched the glass with his nose. In the glass eyes of the helmet, he could see the reflection of the lights behind him and he could also see his own reflection, but he couldn't see into the helmet for it was too dark.

Hawk said slowly as if talking to a child, "Are you a human or you a test animal?"

The being tilted its head to the side again, a distinctive sign of not comprehending.

"One thing is for sure," Hawk said leaning back from the wall, "I'll bet you are true Dooferdoo."

The response that he got was unexpected as the being quickly reached up and slapped the switch.

The last thing Hawk remembered were lights flickering.

****

You really can't imagine the pain that someone else is experiencing until you yourself have the same common reference. You may have had the same symptoms, the same aches and the same ailments, but the difference between the individual's strength explains the intensity of the outcome. One person could break a toe and experience minor pain, but a weaker individual would scream for days. Determination and perseverance of any circumstance depends on the person's ability to deal with said problem. Injury is as common as illness, but both have different results.

Men are weenies when it comes to sickness. They completely fall apart and cannot function without help from someone else. You have seen it several times before; they become Wimps, wusses, sissies, and feeble-minded namby-pamby crybabies. They become as helpless as a sulking child and just as bad as a whiney assed bitch in heat. Their bullheaded attitude makes recovery longer and puts everyone else's schedule on hold. Of course, everyone will know of their symptoms because they continuously complain about them. 'My nose is so stuffed up....my throat is so sore.... I'm so hot I'm burning up....' are just a few of their lines. It just goes to prove that when men are sick, they are a bunch of candy asses.

But pain is a different story. Men can shake off bumps, bruises and even broken bones to continue on. They could be bleeding and not notice it until someone points it out or they see the drops hitting the floor. The, 'Shake it off' or 'Walk it off' mentality has always been the normal response to any pain situation, and most likely, the end of the discussion. Men don't talk about pain. Men, at times, welcome pain. It strengthens the soul, solidifies the drive, reinforces the muscles, and hardens the nerves. The more a man can take, the stronger he becomes. The bigger the pain the more gain. He becomes a beast, a savage brute and even an indestructible brick shithouse.

But when illness and pain are mixed together, it becomes an excruciating nightmare comparable to the fires of hell. Throwing everything at the body all at once makes a thundering roar of insensitive, never-ending turmoil which makes you wish that someone would shoot you and put you out of misery. Between the throwing up, the body aches and the fever your head performs a symphony of pain that plays all sorts of music, all at the same time. That pounding, piercing, burning pain in the ass condition brings on an entirely different problem. That problem can act on its own, or accompany any other malady that the body presents. That unwanted guest is called the headache.

Headaches could be explained in many forms from mild to extreme spontaneous combustion.

The first one, the Cluster, is a small spot behind one eye; a direct pinpoint of pressure that burns and makes. Any type of light is too bright and it makes you squint at everything. Being a true pain in the ass, this headache will make your eyes become puffy. The best thing to do for this remedy is to sit in a dark room and wait it out. Sleeping it off is another way around it.

Next up, is the tension headache. This sucker is brought on by many things and doesn't generally have a specific spot; it likes to move around. This annoying little shit messes with your neck, muscles and face as it swims behind your eyes and works its way down to your shoulders. Its dull, constant pain feels like someone has wrapped a tourniquet around your head and keeps twisting the stick. Although this is the most common one, it is nothing compared to the monster that you now carry within you.

The dreaded, first class, ultimate ballbuster called the migraine.

This headache effects everything you do; seeing, hearing, moving, drinking, breathing and walking. Both your temples throb to the beat of your heart and they feel like they could explode at any time. Your skin feels like pins and needles are being shoved into every pore and grinded deeper into you. The excruciating pain up the back of the neck is so tight that moving your head just the slightest sends jolts of pain to the eyes. This master of disaster is so unforgiving; it will not let you walk calmly to the bathroom, because with each step, the pressure pounds up through the balls of your feet and resounds to the top of your head. You get dizzy and the stomach churns wanting to spew out anything that it holds. Even though you have already thrown up everything you ate, just the thought of doing it again scares you. You have already reached the point where the only thing that comes out is the stomach acid, but the overwhelming pressure to the forehead while you heave intensifies the fever and the pain.

You are now to the point to where the only thing you wish to do is to crawl up into a booth in the dark part of the room and wait for death to take you.

"Do you think she will be ok?" Remy questioned Aiden as they looked at Katrina lying down in the far booth at the back of the bar.

"We need to keep pushing fluids in her and try to get that temperature down." Aiden replied as she started to soak a towel in a bath of cold ice water. "She hasn't broken that fever since she has arrived and that's the first thing, we need to get control of." She started to wring the water out of the towel and then folded it length wise. "Go get her another glass of water and I'll lay this on her forehead. Whatever bug she caught; I sure hope that we don't get it."

"That's for sure," Remy said as she walked behind the bar, "I hate being sick."

"That's stupid to say. Let me know if you know anyone who likes being sick!"

Remy gave her a disgruntled look and filled up a glass with ice and topped it off with water. "Should we get some food in her as well? She does look a little pale and has pretty much thrown up everything she's eaten."

"Soup would be the only thing I'd recommend," Aiden answered as she started walking toward Katrina. "She needs to regain her strength and that's one way to do it."

Remy walked out from behind the bar with the full glass and followed her. "Then I'll run down to the corner and get some dinner. It might be a good idea to just keep her here for the night until she gains some strength."

"Good idea," Aiden answered as she reached the booth.

Remy set the glass upon the table and then walked away. "I'll be right back, then," she said as she headed toward the front door. Aiden answered with a slight nod of the head.

Looking down at the pale face in front of her, Aiden flinched. Katrina looked so drained and weak. She had curled herself up into a little ball and was breathing very shallowly.

"Here, honey," Aiden said as she put the towel up toward her forehead, "lay this on so we can bring that fever down."

Katrina moaned as she stretched out across the booth and tilted her head up. "You two need to...."

"Shhhh," Aiden said quietly, "You need to rest and not exert yourself." She laid the towel across Katrina's forehead and the relief was instantly heard, for Katrina's sigh seamed relaxing. "This should help," Aiden continued. "And you need to just stay right here and rest. That means no walking, no talking and no dancing."

Katrina started to laugh but the pain was too intense for even a slight smile. She cringed and then put her arm across her eyes. The pressure upon them was intense and covering what light was hitting them helped.

"Remy went to pick us up some food and will be back soon."

Katrina started to shake her head no, but Aiden wouldn't hear anything of it. "You will eat if I have to shove it down your throat. I know your stomach is doing circles, but you have to get something in you to fight this. Soup will help you, even if it's just simple broth."

Katrina let out a slow breath and then nodded in agreement. She started to try to sit up and reach for the glass on the table, but Aiden stopped her. "I've got it," she said retrieving the glass.

"I'm not totally helpless," Katrina added, "at least, not yet."

Aiden smiled. "Let's hope it doesn't get to that, ok?"

CHAPTER 11

The red dot was getting closer, but still was a distance away. It had made its way past the orbit of Tego and picked up speed as it went deeper into the system. The course it was taking set it in line to cross through an asteroid field and then into deep space. Beyond that was nothing, at least nothing was on the charts. But just before the asteroids were reached, the dot did a quick jump to the left and set a new destination. It regained speed and then finally came to a stop.

It blinked unmoving on the planet Zeta. It had been there for some time.

Jason was sitting in one of the bridge seats of a rented transport jumper that they had picked up at Serin airport. Steve didn't want to spend much on it; for they really didn't need to splurge, but the condition it was in made both of them nervous. At first, it took three tries to get it started but when they finally lifted it off the ground, the vessel groaned as if the engine core was about to buckle. Steve regretted taking the pilot's seat when he found out how hard it was to control the directional shift. He literally had to use both hands to get it to move and the muscles in his wrist were aching from the strain. Even after they achieved space flight, the old bucket still popped and banged with each turn. The only thing probably holding the ship together was the rust that it was incased in.

"Zeta," Jason sighed, "it figures. I did tell you what happened the last time I was there, didn't I?"

Steve started laughing at the thought. "Yeah, an old man, a Klebit, winged creatures, and whatever that thing in the wall was." Steve smiled toward Jason, "you told me all about it. At first, I thought you were telling me about an old video game you used to play."

"I wish it would have been, then I would have surely used an extra power bar or weapons upgrade token." Jason sighed. "I'm really surprised that I didn't piss my pants."

An alarm that sounded like a baying dog startled both of them. A light above Jason's head flickered and sparked. Jason reached up and flipped off the switch next to it. "Shit, that was the directional alarm. I guess it's trying to tell us that we are about to approach Zeta."

"That or it's screaming for us to put it out of its misery," Steve added.

Another light flashed on the panel, but no sound accompanied it. Steve looked over and saw it was the sub light engines kicking on to slow them down, and then he noticed the planet closely approaching in front of them.

"I take it that's Zeta," Steve pointed toward the greenish blue orb.

"Yep," Jason answered. "She looks calm and serene from here, but the visit is sure no vacation."

Steve picked up the pad that was still tracing Hawk, "once we get parked, this should lead us straight to him, that is if it's still on him."

"Hopefully he didn't drop it or we have been chasing someone who had stolen it from him. "

The planet quickly filled their view and soon they found themselves landing in a clearing in the woods. The spot was only several thousand feet from Hawk's location.

Both men packed themselves with anything they would think could be useful. Food packs, liquid pouches, rags, and even a first aid kit. And of course, weapons, plenty of weapons. Steve had his AK-47 that he kept behind the bar, an old relic from times gone, and several knifes. He was very deadly with a knife. All his training that he had had throughout the years put him at the level of an elite combat soldier. Steve, when in action, was a lit stick of dynamite. He had everything tightly fitted into a backpack which he wore over his shoulders. The AK-47 was nuzzled into a rifle pouch on the right side of the bag.

Jason had his pistol and a pair of brass knuckles that he had never used. Also, strapped to his leg was a bowie knife. He had to be ready for anything.

When they opened the ship's gangway, it creaked and screeched loudly making Steve grimace. "Could never get over that feeling you get from nails on a chalkboard."

"Never bothered me," Jason added as they both walked out onto the ground. "It's the wooden stick across the tooth that gets me."

Steve stopped and looked at the pad and turned toward his left. "It's that way," he pointed as he held the device like a compass and followed its direction.

They had walked only a hundred feet when Steve noticed a large smoldering hole up ahead of them. Its circumference was at least 15 feet wide and white smoke was lightly billowing out of it. They both approached the edge of it and looked down into the Abyss.

"Shit," Jason "one of those damn entrance holes."

Steve noticed the dot blinking on the pad and looked toward Jason. "He's down there," he said as he shoved the pad into his back pocket.

"Of course, he is," Jason said sarcastically.

"I wonder if there is any rope onboard that rust can," Steve said pointing a thumb back toward the transport, "and possibly anything else we could use."

"Let's go see," Jason resounded.

****

Katrina didn't know what magic the ladies did, but it truly took care of the sickness that she was in. Her headache was gone, her temperature was back to normal and she felt refreshed. In fact, for the last couple of courses she was helping around the bar with the cleaning and maintenance. It was a lot later in the evening and the soup that Remy had brought to her for lunch cleared up the stomach pains as well. She was in a totally different frame of mind than she was when she first got up in the morning.

At first, Remy and Aiden wouldn't let her get up; they eventually gave in for her to do a little bit at a time, but they soon accepted that she was in a full recovery and eased up on her.

The bar was looking better and better with each passing moment. All the electrical equipment was in full repair and the drink station was functional. The front area still smelled like paint; for Remy had touched up all the smoke damaged spots and redid the trim. The bar was completely done and all the tables looked brand new. The only thing they had to do was stock the kitchen and drinks.

But their mind couldn't concentrate as much as they wanted to due to the fact of what had happened to Hawk. Speculation was in the air, but no real proof could support it. Where, what, who and why all haunted their minds. They could only hope that Steve and Jason would find him and bring him home.

All three of the ladies were sitting at one of the larger booths looking over their notes that they had created when they were at Steve's place. Most of the items on the list were crossed off, and the goal of reopening was closer than they thought. 'Little Chicago' was close to be reborn.

A low growl made everyone look up at each other.

"Was that your stomach?" Remy asked Aiden.

She smiled back and nodded at the same time. "I'm famished. Who wants to go get something to eat?"

"If the kitchen is in full operation," Katrina added, "I'd love to cook dinner for you two, my way of saying thanks for getting me out of that rut."

"Hell yea," Remy burst out. "It's been a long time since I've had a home cooked meal."

"Me too," Aiden added. "I've eaten out so many times that I forgot what a real kitchen is used for."

Katrina stood up from the booth and started walking toward the front door. "Fine, I still have a little time before 'The Harvester' closes up for the day. I'll run there and get us some stuff." She opened the front door and turned back toward them, "I'll be right back." And she shut the door behind her.

Aiden looked at Remy with a smile in her eyes. "She's really special. I'm glad Jason found her."

"Me too, and have you noticed the change in him since they have gotten together? It is if he had matured overnight."

"Yes, I have noticed it. He's not as childish anymore." Aiden thought about when she first met him, "He's come a long way."

Remy nodded in agreement.

Katrina's step was bouncy as ever as she made herself from 'Little Chicago' toward 'The Harvester.' She was happy about the direction her life was going, the friends she had and, of course, Jason. She was worried about Hawk, couldn't understand the depth of it, but knew that Steve and Jason would solve it.

But for the moment, her real concentration was on what to cook for dinner. She could get some fresh Mechay salad and add some spiced Guna steak, or make a large pot of stew. Or maybe she could make baked Rulante casserole. She had not made that for a long time and she could get all the ingredients she needed at 'The Harvester'.

The thoughts of the taste and aroma of Rulante solved her dilemma and she made her decision. She changed her mindset toward what ingredients she needed to pick up. Corsca beans, Louve sauce, Melon Terdonna, Kranslon leaves and Anglieon cheese were just a few of the items dancing throughout her head. Of course, fresh Rulante was also needed.

It then dawned on her that there might not be a sufficient cooking pan back at the bar for her to cook it in. She knew that she had one back at the cabin, but that was too far to go. Perhaps, Emmatt would have one for her to borrow.

When she turned the corner next to her destination, a cold chill ran up her back from the scene that now folded out in front of her.

Standing in front of 'The Harvester' was a large crowd and several base security police officers. Her once happy step turned into a cautious slow walk toward the front entrance. That's when she noticed the police tape across the front door.

"Excuse me," she said getting one of the officer's attention, "what happened here?"

"Can't really say anything, Ma'am," he answered. "We can't release any information until we notify the next of kin."

Katrina swallowed hard, "next of kin?"

"Yes, we are looking for a Katrina Williams. If you know of her, we need to talk to her."

Katrina's life took another wrong turn. "I'm Katrina Williams," she managed to say.

****

"I don't hear you laughing now!" Jason yelled toward Steve as he desperately held tight to his rope.

"No, but I did manage to piss my pants!"

The large roar from the wall creature in front of them startled both men and saliva spewed all over them. The stench of the air that accompanied it didn't smell good either.

They had found two ropes onboard the transport and now each of them was at the same level of the creature's mouth, dangling for dear life. Tentacles were wiggling all around them and they had to keep kicking at them, hoping to not get into their grasp. This creature was three times larger than the one Jason first encountered, as he had pointed out, and last time he was on a ladder.

Its greenish color was barely visible in the light even though the large opening above could still be seen. The creature was about fifty feet from the top, just enough to be hidden from view. They didn't notice it a first because it was receded into its hole in the wall, waiting for some poor unexpecting shmuck to cross in front of it.

They were the shmucks.

"Tell me again how you got out of this?" Steve questioned.

"I shot it in the eye with my pistol."

"Which one," Steve questioned again.

Good point. This thing had six eyes and all of them were bright yellow with a splash of orange as the pupil. It roared again, spitting more saliva and extending its open mouth closer toward them. The spot that it nested in on the wall had lots of fungus and algae growing around it, adding to the air a rotten smell of death. Each tentacle was about six feet in length and there were lots of them.

"Well, now would be a good time to try it," Steve pushed. "I can't reach the AK; it's strapped to my back and I'll lose my grip if I try!"

"That why I always carried a smaller gun, easier to handle." Jason tried to reach down and grab his pistol from its holder on the right while trying to hold onto the rope. "I don't think I can reach it."

"Well, how in the hell did you do it last time?"

"I WAS ON A FRIGGEN LADDER!" Jason yelled.

The loud sound made the creature stop moving, as if startled. Jason and Steve exchanged glances and looked back toward it. That's when Jason sucked in a big gulp of air and then yelled as loud as he could toward it.

"AHHHHHHHH!" Jason yelled toward the creature.

It answered back with a louder roar and almost knocked Steve from his rope. The drooling was more intense as before, and smelled even worse.

"You idiot, what the shit," Steve yelled back. "Are you trying to kill us both?"

Jason gave him a sideways smirk and wrapped the rope around his left arm twice. "Twice is a charm, right?" Steve's reaction was only a sneer. Jason took a deep breath and tightened his grip.

"Here goes nothing," he said as he quickly tried to get the gun without falling off of the rope.

In his first attempt, he missed and grabbed back onto the rope with both hands. His weight distribution gave more work to his arm than he expected, but on his next try, he would be ready for it. The creature roared as Jason tried again, this time succeeding in grasping it and pulling it out of its holster.

Jason's cocky smile toward Steve looked vainglorious. He turned his attention back toward the creature but it only took one swift hit from a tentacle to knock it out of his hands and he dropped it to the darkness below.

"SHIT!" Jason yelled as he could hear the gun clank twice during its fall, then nothing.

"Is the bottom that close?" Steve questioned as he looked down.

"It could be, but...." Jason paused because he had heard a familiar sound. "Do you hear that?"

The creature roared again as tentacles started to wildly flay around them again.

"I can't hear anything but this damn thing." Steve pointed out. "How the hell are we going to get past it?"

And in that next moment, one of the tentacles grabbed a hold of Steve's left leg and pulled.

"Shit, it's got me!" He started to frantically kick at it with his other foot but it wouldn't let go.

Jason started swinging on his rope in an attempt to kick at it as well but to no prevail. He swung back harder and harder as Steve was pulled closer and closer to its gaping mouth. Steve could hear the clacking of its teeth as he was drawn closer. Its chomping sounded like a large dog chewing on a meat bone, and this thing had the razor-sharp teeth to do it.

Jason, on the other hand, could hear the other sound he heard getting closer and closer as well. He tried to recollect what it was, but by the time he remembered, it was too late.

A large swarm of Hellgars came flying up from below, no doubt disturbed by his pistol falling. The high pitch screeching was piercing their ears and the swarm started circling both men so thickly that they almost lost their grip. The wall creature did lose its grip, though. It let Steve's leg go due to all the confusion that the Hellgars were causing and it frantically tried to catch some. The darkness started to close in on them because there was such a large swarm that they started to block out the light from above.

The creature roared again and the speed of the Hellgars frenzy doubled.

Steve looked up at the top and then back to Jason. "I'm taking advantage of this." And in one sift move, Steve slid down the rope burning his hands in the process.

Jason followed behind.

****

The sensation of crying never ceases to amaze me. At the first experience, I thought it to be all summed up perfectly, but there are different conditions. Before, the feeling of embarrassment, insecurity, and helplessness was overwhelming, but this time it is totally uncontrollable.

First, when the news hit you, the lungs run out of air. You can't catch a breath and the rest of the body doesn't realize what has happened. You need to take in a breath, but your full attention is trying to comprehend the situation. It is truly amazing how long one can hold their breath.

Second, your whole skin becomes clammy and cold. A blank look develops across your face and your expression has no meaning. You look chalky, colorless, bloodless, pasty –faced and pale as a ghost. You are white as a sheet. Your mind is shocked and startled beyond belief and will not accept the facts given to it.

Third, your body completely shuts down. It becomes aghast, bewildered, awestricken, and dazed. This part could best be explained as stupefied, dumbfounded, and floored. The news is that powerful. Your mind will not accept it, and tries to shrug it off, but it can't.
Then, that one teardrop runs down the cheek and the ball game is over.

The crying hits hard, harder than you have ever done in a lifetime. You scream so loud that it rips the lining in your throat. The sounds emitting from you is a combination of squalls, howls, squeals, and an agonizing wail of pain. Your knees start to buckle and you start to fall down to the floor but someone nearby quickly catches you and sets you down.

You cry endlessly, hoping that this is just a nightmare that you will soon wake up from. You quickly find yourself out of tears; your face muscles sore from the strain, and your eyes circled in red dry lines. Your nose is running down to your upper lip, but you have no wish to wipe it. In fact, all your usual clean cut, nice and tidy appearance doesn't matter to you at all. You could piss your pants right now, and it wouldn't phase you.

Your outburst starts losing its momentum and it turns into whimper, because that was the only energy left that your body could provide. You feel drained, exhausted and so overwhelmed that you might pass out. Your body trembles all over and it starts to shake, quiver, shudder, and twitch. You just want to crawl up into a corner once again and cut yourself off from the world. You didn't even feel the blanket that someone had draped across your shoulders. Your body and mind wish to hide, but your eyes will not cooperate. They still hold the gaze that they made when you first walked into the room.

That gaze was the sight of the body lying upon the bed.

Emmatt had died peacefully in her sleep. Her hands were still folded over her breasts and she looked like she could wake up at any moment. There were no signs of struggle in her face nor were there any signs of possible pain. She still had a smile on her face.

The port police were notified when the shop hadn't opened for business and the locals were worried that something was wrong. The police forced an entry through the front doors and worked their way back to the aft living spaces. They found her in the back bedroom about two courses ago. The coroner was called, and it was ruled as death by natural causes. She was 73.

Through a legal document order that was filed at the station, Katrina was listed as the beneficiary; an order that was placed by Emmatt over two cycles ago. Once the order was open, a call was placed to her residency and they found out that she no longer lived there. No forward address was submitted so they were about to contact local stations to broadcast a search but then Katrina appeared before they started the process.

The crowd outside the shop slowly dissipated as the coroner's transport pulled up to the front entrance to pick up the body. It didn't take long for them to bring in the gurney and lift it to the level of the bed frame. It only took two of them to lift the frail body and slide it into place.

Katrina was still in a dazed stare at the situation unfolding in front of her. The cozy little room around her had developed a gloomy, cold atmosphere that created the feeling of misery. She felt like her life was invaded; her one pleasant place of comfort now felt violated. The place that she had known for many cycles has now developed an eeriness that tainted the very foundation within. She felt cold, shaky and useless. It was too crowded and she felt like she was being suffocated. Even the thickness of the air was heavy; not like its usual, cozy, fresh, and relaxed state.

When the two men started to wheel Emmatt past her, Katrina jumped up from the chair. The blanket covering her shoulders fell to the floor, and she threw herself onto the covered body. The tears and the wailing started again. Her grasp onto the lifeless body was so tight that if alive, Emmatt would probably not be able to get a breath of air. Katrina's head was planted upon Emmatt's chest and her tears were starting to soak into the nightgown she wore.

Two pairs of hands lightly touched Katrina's shoulders and slowly started to pull her back. Katrina's grasp would not let go as it started to lift Emmatt's body partially off of the gurney. She did not want to let go, ever.

"Come on sweetie," Remy said as she lightly helped Katrina's grasp off of Emmatt, "Let's get you out of the way so that they can take care of her."

Katrina let her grip go and turned to see both Remy and Aiden standing behind her. She sniffled twice and then wrapped herself around Remy and started to bawl again. Aiden rubbed

Katrina's back as she watched them wheel the body past her and out to the waiting transport.

****

It was dark, really dark. The illumination stick that Steve had activated only gave off enough light to brighten a ten-foot radius around them. What appeared before them was pretty much what they had been experiencing the last two hours; condensation filled the walls and dampness was in the air, accompanied by the smell of dying flesh. A muggy mist covered their skin and the air itself made the mouth dry and bland. The maze that they had found themselves in was endless and they felt lost. The only reassurance that they had was the blinking light on the tracker. It was getting stronger and brighter.

The task first started when they had reached the bottom of the entrance hole, which was about twenty feet down from the creature they had left, and they both had rope burns in the palms of the hands. After Steve lit the stick, Jason was able to find his pistol and re-holster it. Another dent was added to its barrel due to the fall but the dent didn't bother him, the smell that surrounded them did. The cave that they were now in brought up bad memories and that smell only intensified the feelings. Jason remembered the mold, the endless tunnels, the moisture, and the Klebits. He didn't want to experience it all again but Hawk was down here, somewhere.

The tracker had led them to dead ends, twice, and once it even blinked out, only to return a minute later. The tracker's display listed Hawk as close as one hundred feet as they came up to another turn in the tunnel.

That turn led into another dead end.

"Son of a bitch," Steve yelled. "If we had some explosives, we could blow into this wall and he should be about seventy feet further."

Jason walked up to the dead end and looked at the gate that was imbedded into it. It was rusty and so old that the moss had grown around its outer rim and you could not see a handle or a keyhole to pick. The rock itself had managed to bury itself deeper around the iron bars making it nearly impossible to break through. He brought his face up within inches of the bars so that he could see beyond them and saw that a trickle of water was running on the other side. Its sound was echoing off the walls as it ran downward into the darkness. The wind beyond it brought up a smell that was worse than anything they had yet to encounter.

"Even if we did get through," Jason said, "that's a long way down. And that smell sure isn't inviting. There's got to be another way."

The illuminating stick in Steve's hand fizzled and sparked, indicating that it was at the end of its use. Before it completely went out, he pulled another full stick out of his back pocket and lit it with the dying one. The new one flashed to life and he threw the old one on the cave's floor. That made the third stick that he had to light, only four left in his pocket.

"We better find something," Steve added, "or we are going to be stuck in this darkness forever."

Jason grabbed the tracker out of Steve's hand and looked at its screen. "He's close; we just have to find the right path."

Steve turned and pointed the stick back down the direction that they came. "Well, we didn't go left at that last turn. That should be our next move."

Jason shook his head in agreement, "I'm right beyond you."

Steve started in the direction that he pointed at and a smile crossed his face. "Hey, remember that movie about that group of kids that got lost in that cave where the creatures of spawn lived?"

Jason stopped in his tracks. "Nice time to bring a reference like that up."

"No really," he said continuing. "Horror movies were always fun to watch. My wife would scream so loud she could wake the whole neighborhood." Steve continued down the hall and waved the stick around the room. "This area reminds me of that movie, in fact, that gate back there looked like the part where that girl wiggled her way out."

"If I remember it right," Jason grimaced, "everyone else didn't make it."

"Yeah, it was a nail biter. The musical score was just as intense." Steve's words went silent but he started humming a song that got louder and louder.

"I was more of a science fiction fan," Jason added. "The more aliens, spaceships and electronic gizmos the better." Steve's humming continued as Jason's words accompanied it. "There was this movie about an attack on earth from aliens,"

"Which one," Steve blurted out at the end of his tune, "thousands of movies had that plot."

"I know, I know, but this one had fighter jets against space ships, huge alien crafts blowing up major cities,"

"Is that the one where the White House gets blown up?" Steve interrupted.

"Yeah, that's the one. That was a fun movie."

They both continued walking in silence, and then Steve stopped short. Turning toward Jason he said, "I never would have thought that all that shit could be real."

Jason nodded his head, "tell me about it. I still wonder what's next."

Steve nodded his head and followed the curve to the left which started a downhill angle. It was about two feet full of water.

"Well," Steve said with a sigh, "there's what's next."

Jason's face expressed frustration. "Swell, and me without my trunks."

"Next time," Steve said as he held up the tracker, "I'm going to make him put a directional program in this thing. And a distance meter."

"Next time," Jason repeated. His mind started to think again about Hawk and what could be happening to him right now. Hawk didn't talk much about his past, but what he did mention seemed incomprehensible.

Jason looked toward the darkened end of the tunnel and gestured toward Steve. "You're the one with the light, after you."

174

"This reminds me of another movie," Steve said as he started sloshing his way forward.

"Several, actually," Jason said. "Just to let you know, if darts start to shoot out from the walls, or things start making waves in the water, you'll be the first to know."

"That's reassuring."

They started the forward pace again, the light from the stick dancing off the waves, and the water level never rose. It didn't really fall, either. The entire walk through the water was about eighty feet and when the stepped up to a higher level, the tunnel made a quick turn to the right.

Steve stopped and sat down on a large rock just before the next tunnel. He let out a long gasping sigh and looked up at Jason as he arrived next to him.

"Now comes the annoying part," Steve said.

"What could be more annoying than everything we've been through?"

Steve turned his head up toward Jason, "walking in wet socks."

CHAPTER 12

Hawk's eyes opened up and, in his vision, he saw sparkles. Zingers, as he recalled, is what Jason called them. Many tiny dancing light squiggles that flash throughout your eyes when you stand up too fast. Only this time, it wasn't from standing up, it was from that damn switch.

As his eyes started to clear, he saw that he was staring at the ceiling of his cage and that he was lying on the floor on his back. His entire back side was soaked due to the water inside, and he could hear the water dripping off as he slowly sat up. The pounding pain in his temples became worse as he tried to stand but lost his balance and fell back down onto the floor. Water splashed around him. He heard a laugh. Looking up toward the glass, he saw Medico standing there with a look on his face of enjoyment and amusement.

"Good," Medico said from the other side, "I see that you're avake. You vere out for a very long time, this time," he said as he shook his head. "You should learn your manners."

"You should go fuck yourself," Hawk said still sitting on the wet floor.

"Tsk, tsk, tsk," Medico said as he grabbed a chair from behind him and brought it up close to the glass. "Manners are not your strong point," he said as he walked to the front of the chair and sat down. "So," he stated loudly as he slapped his hands upon his knees, "ve need to talk."

"I have nothing to say to you," Hawk responded.

"You have plenty to say to me!" Medico yelled at the top of his lungs as he slapped his knees once again, only harder. "I brought life to your lungs! I gave you purpose!" His face started to redden with his anger and his fists gripped so tight that his knuckles were turning white. "I vorked for years to develop you, and to fail was not an option!"

His outburst continued as Hawk painfully stood himself off of the floor and sat down into his prison chair.

"I vorked till my fingers bled and my energy was pushed to its extreme," he yelled as his tantrum continued, and he repeatedly pounded his fists onto his knees. "I have achieved such greatness that is beyond men's comprehension." His words were getting louder and louder as spit was now spraying from his mouth with the rage that continued to engulf him. "I have created life, improved life and strengthened the inner vorkings of the mind! YOU OWE ME!"

Hawk's eyes widened with a sensation that he had never experienced: the feeling of fear and comprehension on how truly mad this man was.

"YOU OWE ME! YOU OWE ME! YOU OWE ME!"

His words barely made it out of his mouth because it was using the last breath of his lungs to produce it. When his words finished, he gulped in a large breath of air and then clenched his fists.

Silence took over the room. The only sound that could be heard was Medico's heavy breathing trying to recompose himself. The last 'Me' hung in the air like an echo from a deep cave and left a slight ring in Hawk's ears.

The two stared at each other for a long time. Not a word was spoken but several were said in the eye contact they had. Hawk's eyes were lightly red; not entirely burning with hate, but just enough to put him on edge. His breaths were long and deep, but in control.

Medico was right, after all. Hawk existed because of him. He didn't know how he started or where he came from, only that his beginnings were here, in this place. All the tests and procedures made it a torturous dungeon of experiments with no end in sight. With the taste of freedom, he had experienced out of this hellhole and the life he had developed with Jason and Steve, gave him a different purpose. But in true reality, this was where it all started. This was home.

Medico stared at his creation. He was angry that the entire situation got out of control but at the same time excited that it became so independent. 217 was his best developed specimen and his answer to his mortality. With the secrets that 217 carried in his veins, Medico could add that to his own solution and become even more resilient. The strength and power that 217 held could be his. He could control it and regulate it to others. He could increase or decrease its use and be the alpha. He would be the beginning of a new race, a new breed, and new being.

He could be God.

The silence continued on. They never broke connection between their eyes which reminded Hawk about another time with Jason. He had a weird game he called, 'A staring contest.' Whoever broke their concentration had to buy the next round of drinks. A small smile came across Hawk's face when he realized that Jason never won one.

"Vhat is so amusing," Medico questioned in a light voice.

Hawk wasn't going to give him the pleasure, "I'm hungry. Can I get something to eat?"

Medico nodded his head, "yes, you can get something, but I vant something in return. I need a sample of your blood."

Hawk smiled even wider, "Come and get it."

"Oh," Medico said as he stood up from the chair, "I vill have no problem getting it from you. I have several vays of getting it from you."

Loud footsteps started to resound from the back hallways as Medico continued.

"I could alvays pull the svitch," he said as he speedily rushed his hand to the lever and he saw Hawk jump in a startle. "But that vouldn't be good for the blood. I need it pure, unfazed."

The footsteps became louder.

"I need you clean, vithout any, shall ve say, tampering."

A Klebit walked in and Medico turned his head toward it.

"Yes, vat is it?"

The Klebit walked up to medico and whispered in his ear. Medico's eyes widened with a slight surprise but then regained their regular appearance. He nodded his head to the creature and then pointed toward the hall. The Klebit walked back out.

"It Vould seam that ve have some visitors." Medico picked up a rag off the back of the chair and diligently wiped his hands with it. "Ve shall velcome them." He threw the rag down and walked out of the room.

Hawk quickly stood up out of the chair and pulled the transmitter out of his pocket. The unit was glowing bright green. Someone with the tracker was in the area. It was either Jason, Steve or both.

His eyes started to burn red.

****

You are so overwhelmed that you can't think straight right now. The emotions that are jumping around can't solidify their presence within you making it impossible to concentrate. You can't even function correctly. You had a problem untying your shoes, brushing your teeth and even going to the bathroom. You lack the concentration on anything and it is making you one horrendous mess.

The tales of events that led up to your condition gives good cause for all the feelings you have.   At this moment, you can't even understand what is going on. Your mind knows the facts, but will not accept them. Combined with the body, all sort of emotions is coming into play with no real coherent separation of each. You feel spooked, uptight, uneasy, restless, and all shook up, but at the same time you wish to be in social isolation. You wish to sleep but insomnia won't let you. You're anxious, discontented, and discombobulated. You don't know if you hunger or have no appetite. You become tormented, hopeless, and so mixed up that even trying to understand it all has made you a nervous wreck.

You have become a bundle of nerves, shot to pieces, a couple of cans short of a six pack, an elevator that doesn't go all the way up, and not the sharpest knife in the drawer. You are a complete basket case. Your lights are on but no one is home.

But this condition has really brought some light to the subject. Most people in this condition who has had a lot of hardships, usually follows with a meltdown or total breakdown of emotion. Anxiety, guilt, depression, and stress all become an uncontrollable world of chaos that can build up and not only destroy you but the people around you.

It's hard to comprehend. Other people truly can't understand what you are going through. How could they? The pain and suffering that you have endured has created a mix of uncertainty that no one could be at the same level with it. Your body starts to sink lower, down a darkened hole with no return, and wonders if it will ever know happiness again. The moment has you in despair.

This situation has been known to become a disorder that few people recover from. It is viewed as a horrible disease that can destroy everything. It becomes a malady so extreme that when no help is there, it can send a being drifting down into an unconscious state of dread with no end in sight. That's when things become scary. Suicide, mental illness and even total memory blockage can occur making that one fine, beautiful human being into a complete an utter vegetable.

Depression is an ugly word. It's also hateful, unstable, dangerous, and deadly. Someone lost deep in depression feels that death would be better than life. They have no concern for themselves anymore and can become very lost.

But you are still strong inside and even with everything that has presented itself to you in the last several rotations, you are together. Your inner strength is being supported by the love that has been shown to you and the love that you express to others. Your excessive crying still continues, but it has slowed down quite a bit. Your body is still giving off shudders and shakes making it unclear that you are either too cold or just too scared to continue. These emotional feelings when mixed together make it very hard to think, to move, to concentrate and at times to even breathe.

You will be fine. The people around you will help you, guide you, and hold you up. The best recovery from anything is the support and love from others, particularly family. And you are most certainly surrounded by family.

Katrina sat unresponsive in a recliner in Aiden's apartment. It had been two courses since they left "The Harvester", and she still was in a state of shock. Aiden and Remy had tried everything they could to get her comfortable; they took off her coat and shoes, wrapped her up in a blanket, made some Kedy brew and lightly massaged her shoulders. They couldn't get her to talk nor could they get her to eat anything, but they did notice that she was becoming more attentive to the surroundings. Her breathing had also returned to normal.

Aiden and Remy were sitting at the kitchen table, across the room from Katrina, where they watched her guardedly. The lady had been through a lot and they were both afraid that they would end up taking her to the emergency station. A Port officer took all their information before they left the shop and gave them vid numbers to contact in case they needed help. The numbers for Port police station, the Med Emergency Evac, a hot line for victims, and for the officer in charge was listed on the sheet. The morgue was also included.

Remy finished the brew in her cup and stood up to refill it. She pointed to Aiden's empty cup in which she replied with a nod and handed the cup to her. Remy was only two steps into the kitchen when the silence was broken.

"It's amazing how people can find beauty in so many different things," Katrina softly said.

Both the girls looked at her and noticed that her head was turned toward Aiden's collection of glass animals. They were on display in a curio cabinet that hung on the wall and was illuminated from within. The light sparkled off the many colors in the cabinet; the greens, the blues, the reds, the oranges, and the pinks and made them dance together into a rainbow of effects. The mixture of birds, land and water animals indeed was a collection, one that Aiden started when she was very young, and she tried to add to it whenever she could. It was her get away spot, a place that she could stare at for courses and relieve the stresses of the day.

"Would you like a closer look?" Aiden said cautiously as she got out of her chair and walked toward her. Katrina nodded her head and slowly stood up. She still held onto the blanket that was upon her shoulders and even wrapped it tighter around herself as she moved.

Aiden met her at the chair, wrapped her arm around Katrina's shoulders, and they walked up to the display. "I've been collecting ever since I was five," she said while smiling, "and always had it in my head that someday it would be worth something."

The lights glistened in Katrina's eyes as she took in each piece, scanning them from the top shelf on through to the bottom. "How many do you have?"

"Last time I counted," she replied as she let go of Katrina, "it was at about two hundred. I first started to get a piece from each new place I visited, then it became harder and harder to find something that I didn't have."

"Not to mention on how hard it was to get her a present," Remy added as she joined them alongside. "At first it was easy to get her a gift, but then after so many, 'Oh I already have that', I gave up."

"So that's why you stopped," Aiden said.

Remy smiled at her then turned her attention toward Katrina. Her face looked better, it wasn't as pale as it was, and it also looked like energy was returning. Katrina's face looked like a child who had discovered a large candy shop. Her eyes sparkled, her cheeks glowed, and she was smiling. She was smiling.

"Of course, when you do research," Aiden continued, "you find out that there are so many of these that they will probably never have value."

Katrina turned and looked at Aiden's face. "You're wrong." Her face became determined and serious. "The value of an object is not measured in rolets, but what is in here." Katrina pointed at Aiden's heart. "Your experiences and everyday actions can be tied to an object. Your emotions can be triggered by the slightest gesture or smallest item. Take this for instance," Katrina said as she reached up and picked up a small four-legged animal. It was blue and had a head that looked like a bird, but a body like a land mammal. The tail was long and looked like a fishtail.

"It's a Berdish," Aiden said. "They look mean, but are so gentle." She started to smile as the memory flooded her mind. "I was fishing off an island on Tego, a small resort area, and this thing came swimming upstream. At first, I thought it was a huge fish and was ready to cast toward it, but then it stood up and completely caught me off guard." She smiled at the experience. "It cautiously wandered up toward me and begged for food. By the time I left, I was able to pet it, and in the process lost all my catch to it. It was hungry." She looked down at the item in Katrina's hand, "I bought that at the resort's shop."

Katrina returned the animal back to the shelf and let out a sigh. "You see, value is not measured on how much you own, but what you experience with the time and family that you have. Look at the memory that holds you just to that piece," she expressed while she pointed at it, "a memory that will always be with you. I'm not much of a material person; I value my life with the people, the places, and the family I grow with."

Remy reached up and put her hand on Katrina's shoulder, "Are you ok?"

Katrina sighed again, "no, but in time I'll be fine. I'm not alone. You two are part of the values of my life and no amount of rolets could ever buy that."

All three girls embraced in a hug and this time, the other two started to cry. Katrina's smile was so intense that it started to hurt her cheek muscles. As the hug continued, Katrina spotted something in the cabinet. It was a small red Trill.

"I hope the boys come home soon," she said. "But in the meantime, I'm hungry."

The other two let go of their grip and wiped the tears from their eyes. "It's a bout damn time," Remy added, "we've been waiting for you to say that."

They all three turned and went to the kitchen.

****

"I wonder how old I am," Steve said in the darkness.

"Old?" Jason's curiosity took his concentration from the tunnel ahead to Steve's face. "What did you mean old? Don't you know?"

"Well, think about it for a moment," Steve said still guiding the light stick in front of them. "We judge our age by Earth's yearly rotation around the sun and since we have been away for so long, and of course it doesn't exist anymore, how do you really know? We can't judge it by Largo's years..."

"Cycles," Jason corrected, "they call the planet's year rotation a cycle. The day is a rotation."

"Pfh," Steve spats back. "Don't get me twisted in that shit again. I mean really, doesn't it make you wonder? I was forty-seven when we met. We stopped trying to use Earth's calculations a couple of years after that, so it's hard telling how old we are."

Jason stopped in his tracks and turned toward Steve. "I've got an idea. Let's cut you in half and count the rings."

Steve let out a laugh without opening his mouth and it came out as a loud snort. "I don't think we'll have enough light for you to thoroughly cut through. This is our last stick."

Jason let out a sigh and then back down at the tracker. They were very close to Hawk and should be there soon. He glanced back up and something caught his attention.

"Look," he said as he put his hand over the glow stick to block out its light, "there's a light up ahead."

Steve's eyes widened with excitement and he started walking forward at a quicker pace. "It's about damn time." He proceeded to approach the end of the tunnel where it started to get wider, brighter, and warmer. That's when Jason grabbed him by the back of his shirt and horse collared him to a halt.

"Stop," Jason said at a whisper, "do you smell that?"

Steve's startled reaction to the quick grab changed to an expression of disgust. "Yeah, smells like, like rotting flesh. Once you first experience that smell, you never forget it."

Both men casually walked up toward the opening; the light from within casting a glowing orange upon their faces. Jason had his pistol drawn as he stepped into the opening. Steve followed closely behind.

They walked into the opening and found themselves standing in a room of bones and rotting flesh. The smell was overwhelming. Bugs were crawling all over the half-eaten carcasses, and blood glittered in the light; a light that was emanating from the next room. The bodies were unidentifiable, nothing looked human, but nothing looked intact either. Just massive clumps of meat, skin, hair and bones were scattered about. The temperature in the room was hotter and the air current was coming from the other entrance across the room.

Jason pointed toward that opening and they headed toward it. The floor squished and snapped with each of their steps up to the opening. The heat emitting from it was overwhelming.

Jason stepped in first and then stopped in his tracks. He put his hand back and laid it on Steve's chest to stop him.

"Will you stop doing that?" Steve said.

"I've been here before, just not on this side," Jason said astonished. His glance toward the bridge that extended over the lava creek flashed in his mind. Even though it was only last month when he was here, it felt like only yesterday. The lava was a little lower since the last time, but it still lit up the room like a flaming barn at night. It was here when all the trouble started.

Jason started walking out onto the bridge, waving Steve to follow him. As Steve stepped into the opening, he felt the heat and the thickness of the air. His scorched skin from the electrocution started to tingle and rise to a stinging burn.

"Well, welcome to hell's kitchen," Steve said.

Jason quickly turned and covered Steve's mouth with his left hand. Steve' reaction, once again, was annoyance.

185

"Shhhh," Jason said as he let go of Steve's mouth and then pointed up. Steve's gaze followed the direction. The tan walls lead up toward the darkened ceiling above, a ceiling that was slightly moving. Something was up there and disturbing it would be a bad idea according to Jason's reaction.

They started to cross again, as quietly as possible, and even though the heat rising from the river was starting to cook them, they made it to the other side.

That's when Klebits came out of nowhere.

Jason was hit hard from the left side and was knocked down onto a landing next to the river. The Klebit was on top of him slashing toward him with its clawed hands as Jason struggled to get his pistol, but the weight was too great. Both of his legs were folded up against him and the only thing that was keeping his face from being slashed was the distance of his knees. Then swiftly, with one great push, Jason kicked the Klebit off of him and its projection sent it into the lava river below. The scream was ear piercing.

Steve was hit so hard that he spun backwards and the next swinging claw ripped his backpack in half. All of its contents flew wildly about the room as Steve fell toward the ground. He didn't see his AK-47 anywhere, but he did manage to find his hunting knife. His first swing put a slash across one of the attacker's throats and it grabbed its open wound with both of its hands and fell to the ground. Blood sprayed everywhere. The next Klebit jumped from his right and ended up with a large slash across its arm and by the time the third one was upon him; Steve found the AK-47.

The sounds of rapid fire silenced the roars around them and echoed throughout the area. Klebits fell down dead or badly wounded as Steve continued his attack. The gun was doing its job but it also woke up the sleeping blackness from above.

Hellgars flew down from everywhere. They swarmed the area so thick that you couldn't see across to the other side but it didn't slow down the Klebits' attack. They continued coming even though Steve was rapid firing at everything that moved. He was knocking down not only Klebits, but several of the Hellgars out of the air. It was a free for all shooting gallery.

Jason started climbing up the side wall from the ledge that he had fallen to, and wasn't really pursued. He was low enough from the flying Hellgars and the Klebits didn't know that he had fallen. It seemed like all their attention was on Steve. Just as he pulled out his pistol, a large rock hit Steve in the arm and knocked the AK-47 out of his hands.

Several Klebits wrapped themselves around Steve and carried him out of the room.

Yelling would be a bad idea and taking a bunch of shots at them could possibly hit Steve, so Jason pulled himself up from the ledge and cautiously made his way through what was left of the Hellgar swam. He started to follow in the direction that Steve was taken.

****

What possibly could be the hardest emotion or understanding that anyone could possess? When experiencing the different directions that one's emotions can take you, it becomes mindboggling. The humanity mix is beyond understanding

At first, when someone gets mad, you become enraged, angry, irritated, sullen, fierce, fuming, hateful, riled and ill tempered. You get pushed too far and explode. To others you become a hot headed, unkind, high strung, grumpy, crabby, bad-mannered asshole. Nobody wants to be with you, near you or even in the same hemisphere as you. Your manner just brings others down to the miserable shit that you are. You are seriously mentally disturbed.

In a complete turnaround, you can be the sweetest thing on the planet. You are compassionate, kind, friendly, appreciative, sympathetic, all listening, affectionate, and caring individual. Happiness follows you wherever you go and you become a complete joy to be around. Everyone wants to be with you, or become a part of your life. You end up being an inspiration to many and always full of enthusiasm.

Other experiences can make you give up on everything, including yourself. Your life becomes such a complication because of the pressure that is put upon you makes you lose hope. Every time you try to move ahead, you get knocked back down. You get to the point that you are so used to failing, that your self-esteem becomes low, even nonexistent. Your health declines, as does your mind. You find that the little things that used to make you happy have now become another burden you must bear. You become depressed, pitiful, miserable, soulless, unhappy, dejected, and grief-stricken. Your life has become crippled, overpowered and destroyed to the point where you don't want to try anymore. You get bummed-out, dragged through the mud, ripped to shreds, down in the dumps, at the end of your rope and heavy because the weight of the world is on your shoulders.

All these different extremes all mash together into one being that tries every morning to wake up and start all over. Only you know what you have been through, how you experience it, how you deal with it, and how you try to move forward. The ups, the downs and all the moments in between can't possibly run smoothly together, but you try. Some things that should make you laugh makes you cry instead. Objects and ideas that bring happy thoughts to others, brings painful thoughts to you. Nobody will ever understand what you feel or what you are going through.

What possibly could be the hardest emotion or understanding that anyone could possess?

Empathy.

I'm here for you no matter what. I don't feel your fear, your anger, your sadness, your joy, your disgust, your surprise, or you trust, but I can understand you have them. I can comfort you and be there when you need an ear to chew on, or a place to let off some steam. I will not criticize you because of them and I will not hold it against you for having them. I will not freak out on you, or shut you off from my world because I need you in mine.
Please believe me that I understand and its ok.

Katrina sat on the ground in front of the new grave not wanting to ever get up. The air around her still contained the smell of dirt; that wormy, crisp, fresh sent that tickled the nose enough to make it sneeze. The wind was almost to a standstill but every once in a while, a light gust would rustle the leaves in the tree above. The birds were singing and the sun was dancing its light across the lake as it was slowly setting into it. The sky was a mixture of blues, grays, and silver as the clouds mingled together to create a light storm around the cabin. Small drops of rain started to fall; not enough to drench, but light enough to glisten the area around her.

She kept her promise and buried Emmatt next to Harland. The burial crew didn't take too long to complete the job, but the engraver was finished before they left. The name "Emmatt" was centered below "Harland" and in the same word style. The vegetable design around it balanced the two together well.

The flowers that Katrina had picked were a mix of varieties that was always available at the Harvester and were standing up in a vase in front of the tombstone. Laying in front of the vase were two cups; the two tea cups that Katrina and Emmatt always drank out of when they got together.

Light rain started to cover her face but she didn't take a notice to it. She turned her head toward the left and saw Veronica's grave and for the first time noticed the engraving upon it. Hawk must have had it done before he went missing.

It had a very simple carving of heart with a pair of wings at the top center of the stone. Below it was written; "My Forever Love". Many flowers adorned the ground below it.

Katrina looked back at Emmatt's grave and started to cry again as the light sprinkles turned into a steady rain.

"Look, Mom," she said with a smile, "the planet's crying for you as well." She reached out with her right palm and placed it on the pile of dirt in front of her. "I'm going to truly miss you."

Aiden and Remy were standing on the porch of the cabin watching Katrina by the tree. Aiden looked up toward the sky at the darkening clouds above and ran her left hand through her wet hair. "Looks like it's going to really cut loose here in a couple of taps, should we go get her?"

"Let her sit a while longer," Remy answered. "When it really comes down, we'll get her. We don't need her sick again."

Just as she said that, the steady rain turned into a solid downpour and they both ran out to get Katrina inside.

CHAPTER 13

Steve woke up dazed. The last thing that he remembered is being grabbed by several Klebits and dragged off down a hall. How he became unconscious, he didn't know, but he felt no head injury was present. As his clouded mind started to clear, he started experiencing other forms of feelings. Both of his wrists felt tight, as did his waist and legs as well.

He tried to sit up, but couldn't. With his head now fully clear, that's when he realized that he was strapped down on a table. He was able to turn his head around to look at the soundings in the room; chairs, tables overfilling with piles of junk, and a large spot lamp on a stand. Next to the spot light was another table where someone was standing with their back toward him.

"Hey," Steve shouted, "who the hell are you?"

Medico turned from the table and clapped his hands together. "I am me, and you are you," he stated as his wicked smile added to the crazy comment. "So, you think that you vere being sneaky by coming in here to get 217?"

Steve's ruffled brow displayed his confusion. "What the fuck's a 217?"

Medico smiled again and walked toward the table. "That doesn't matter now. What matters is that I can do things for you, you know, better things."

"No thanks," Steve said as he turned his attention away, "I've heard of your methods, shithead."

"Oh, I'm sure you have, I'm a monster," he said as he waved his hands in the air. "I'm a terror that preys on poor defenseless creatures and does unspeakable things to them." Medico sighed out loud. "But these people who say this don't realize the greatness I've done for them. Like 217," Medico smiled big and tilted his head back, "HE'S VONDERFULL!"

"And you're a fucking nutcase," Steve added. "That I do know."

"217 is the answer to everything, the beginning of everything, and the secret to everything!" Medico's attention wasn't even directed at Steve anymore. It was if he was speaking to someone above him, at the ceiling, or at his own inflated ego.

"Once again, your ability to be a blooming Ass hat has me in confusion."

"Yes, yes, in due time you vill know." Medico walked closer up to the table, "In the meantime, it's been a long time since I've had a subject of color."

"Color," Steve questioned. "Do you mean my skin or my glowing vocabulary, fucktard?"

Medico smiled and walked back to the table. "Why you vere unconscious, I took the liberty of taking some blood from you."

Steve's reaction made him jerk and test the strength of his restraints, but to no prevail.

Medico turned his head toward him, "You von't get loose," he said coyly, "you vill only succeed in hurting yourself more." Steve stopped his struggle.

Medico bent over to look into a lit instrument on his work table. "I vas just getting ready to look at your blood under the scanner and......." His demeanor froze and stiffened. "VHAT'S THIS?" He quickly spun around and his face lit up as if the greatest achievement had bestowed him.

"YOU ARE EARTHLING?"

"Yeah, so," Steve said shrugging it off. "What's it to you, Dickhead?"

Medico slowly walked toward him rubbing his hands together. If it was even possible, his grin enlarged with each step. "I am Earthling too."

"Bullshit."

"No, no bullshit. Everything I learned vas from experimenting, testing, probing, mixing, and vorking with all medical aspects of the human body. And it all started on Earth. I vas greatness!" He stood firm and pounded his right fist into his chest. "I vas the best that they had during the var!"

Steve's eyes lit up. "You Davi piece of shit," he said struggling at his straps again, "when I get out of this, I'll break your fucking neck!"

"Davi? Vhat is this Davi?" Medico looked puzzled.

"The war with the Davi, and don't act like you're ignorant of it."

"In fact," he said as he started walking closer to Steve, "I am ignorant to this Davi you speak of, I vas talking about Vorld Var two."

Steve's eyes expanded twice their size. "Can't be, that was years ago."

"Oh yes, many, many years ago," Medico added as he stopped next to the table and put his hands upon it. "Through my experiments, should I say, I became immortal."

"I don't believe you," Steve shook his head, "you would be...."

"Very, very old," Medico finished as he nodded his head. "Yes, very old. People here in this planet system call me 'Medico', but let me tell you vhat my real name is."

Medico bent down toward Steve's ear and whispered the name. He obviously didn't want anyone else to know or was that proud to hide it.

Upon hearing it, Steve's face went pale.

****

Jason was pacing himself at a high speed. He was torn between the thoughts of Hawk and Steve and who to go after first, but since the Transmitter was lost in the struggle, the only thing he had to follow was the tracks left in the dirt from the Klebit's exit.

Steve was the only lead he had. It was also getting harder and harder to track because more prints were interfering with the original set. He had followed them as far as he could and then found himself at an impasse.

There were just too many tracks to follow.

The most apparent thing to him was to follow the heaviest set, which would lead him to the most used rooms, or into a trap. He continued for what seemed hours until he encountered a really bright lite in one of the corridors. He decided to head toward it.

When he stepped into the room, it was empty. He saw a couple of chairs, and a table with a few items on it and to his right was a glass wall.

"JASON!" Hawk yelled running up to the glass, "I'm mad that you're here but also damn glad to see you."

Jason ran up to the glass. "Are you ok? Have you seen Steve?"

"Steve's here as well?" Hawk's expression changed. "What happened?"

"We were attacked by Klebits, and he was dragged off. I haven't the slightest Idea where to go."

"I do," he answered while in deep concentration, "If it's like all the others……" His thoughts drifted to scenes of terror. Shaking his head he looked back at Jason, "First, I need to get out of here."

Jason looked around at the glass wall and took note of the electrical box in the corner. "Can't you punch through?"

Hawk shook his head no. "There is a tiny trickle of water lining the inside walls, if I touch it, I get zapped. Not like a regular current, though, but a high dangerous voltage."

Jason stood back and pulled out his pistol, "Well let's blow a hole in this thing and…."

"WAIT," Hawk yelled putting his hands up. "The power signature from your laser would set of the electrical current."

Jason sighed. "Well, so much for that," he said as he reached behind his back. "They probably were not expecting this." He pulled out the AK-47. He had found it on the ground near Steve's capture point. "Stand back."

Hawk stepped to the side of the cell as Jason let loose with the trigger. Glass shattered everywhere as he did a complete circle design around the wall. When he finished, Hawk easily stepped through the opening.

"Ok," Jason said as he still felt the reverberation throughout his hands from the gun, "you said that you knew where to go?"

Hawk lifted up his right arm and pointed down the tunnel on the left. "Go down that hall and on the third opening on the left, follow that toward the second one on the right. He's probably there."

"How are you so sure?" Jason asked quizzically.

"That's the operating room," Hawk said in a hateful tone. "He's probably in there, hurry."

Jason started moving toward the tunnel but then turned back toward Hawk. "Aren't you coming?"

"I'll catch up," Hawk said as his eyes started to turn red, "I'm waiting for someone. With the sound you just made with that thing, I'm sure he'll be along soon."

Jason sighed. "Don't be long," Jason said as he headed toward the direction Hawk pointed out. "I'll be there waiting, hopefully with Steve."

****

Medico was bending over to get ready to inject a red liquid into Steve's veins when he heard the sounds of gunfire. His head jerked up and he dropped the needle on the floor, shattering the container.

"217!" He yelled. "NO! YOU VILL NOT GET HIM!" He quickly ran out of the room leaving Steve all alone.

****

Hawk stood just outside of the wall taking in slow calming breaths. His eyes were burning red but he was in full control. Every time he encountered this anger, he grew more and more in control of it. At first, he was a violent rage that he could not manage nor understand, but as he progressed, he became more aware of himself and his abilities. He was calm, serene and capable.

Medico raced into the room and stopped in his tracks when he saw Hawk. "217," he said as he held out his palms, "you're still here! I thought I lost you!"

"No, I wanted to say goodbye," Hawk said as he lowered his voice, "One, last, time."

Medico slowly walked toward him. Tears were swelling up in his eyes and one ran down his left cheek. "217, I need you." His hands started to tremble and his voice started to stutter. "I n-n-need you. The world n-n-needs you. We could do so many greatness."

Medico stopped within inches of Hawk's face and smiled. "I love you, 217. You are family, you are us."

"Not anymore," Hawk calmly replied. Then in once swift move, Hawk grabbed Medico by the collar and flung him into the glass cell through the open hole. Medico fell down face first onto the floor and water splattered everywhere. He grunted and flipped himself over to a sitting position on the floor and glanced back at Hawk. A line of blood was running from his broken nose as he held up his hands in a plea.

"217," he said while he cried, "I need you."

Hawk repeated his last comment, only this time at a whisper. "Not anymore." He walked over and flipped the switch.

Medico's body bounced all over the floor as the electrical charges danced all over the room. He kept smiling during the entire process. He groaned several times and bit his tongue but not once screamed. It almost looked like he was enjoying it.

Hawk stood there and watched. He had no feelings of pity, remorse or regret. He only felt satisfaction; satisfaction for all the pain he had put him through, satisfaction for all the pain he had put others through, and a complete satisfaction of getting rid of a menace to life itself.

He could see that the hair on top of Medico's head started to smoke, and his skin tone was slowly darkening. The scent of burning flesh started to hit the air even though Hawk's mind felt clean and fresh. Medico's body didn't bounce around as much anymore but slowed down to an occasional twitch.

All during the time, Medico never took his eye sight off of Hawk. He still held the stare of someone who was proud at what he saw.

Hawk walked away leaving the switch on and started walking in the direction he sent Jason.

****

Jason was almost to the end of the tunnel when he had to duck into an opening in the wall when Medico ran by, hiding from his view. Once the area was clear, he continued on down the hall. He was still holding out the AK-47 just in case he would run into any more surprises; but there were none the rest of the way. When he reached the room at the end, he peered around the corner and saw Steve strapped on a table in the center of the room.

"Steve," Jason yelled running in, "are you ok?"

"Yeah," he blurted, "get me the hell out of here before that maniac comes back."

Jason ran up and started fumbling at the straps holding Steve's arms down. "I found Hawk and got him out of his holding cell, but he's waiting for that freak doctor, or whatever it was that Hawk called him." Jason's concentration turned toward the straps because he couldn't figure out how the release clamps worked.

"Forget that name, you won't believe who he really is," Steve added. "He's...."

"...not coming back," interrupted Hawk as he stepped into the room.

Steve got a large grin on his face and his energy started to return. "Good to see you, young man. I'd give you a big hug, but I'm a little tied down." Steve lifted up his arms as far as he could to express his condition.

"Hold still will ya, I can't get this undone with you flapping around like that." Jason said as he tried to regain his grasp on the clamps.

Steve looked up at Hawk, "Can you get me off of this meat plate?"

Hawk stepped up and easily snapped the restraints with his hands and the broken straps fell to the floor. Steve sat up on the table and a quick dizziness hit him. As he blinked his eyes several times and tried to steady himself, and the other two took note of it.

"Can you walk?" Jason asked while grabbing Steve's shoulder.

"Yes," Steve answered shaking his head, "but don't ask me to dance."

Hawk leaned forward with concern in his eyes, "He didn't stick you with anything, did he?"

Steve shook his head, "He never got the chance, at least while I was awake. I don't know if he did anything to me while I was unconscious."

"You would know," Hawk added, "you would know for sure if he did."

"If you mean I'd feel really weird and shit, no. I don't." Steve looked around his arms for anything that would resemble a needle entry. "I don't feel any sore spots either," he concluded as he hopped of the table. The other two steadied him around his waist in case he couldn't stand. Steve held out his arms straight forward, "I'm fine, I've got it."

"Good, then let's get the hell out of here," Jason added.

"I know where the main entrance is at," Hawk added. "Let's go."

CHAPTER 14

Small electric light strings stopped dancing when the power switch was clicked off. The room was infused with the smell of burnt meat as the water in the cell slowed its wave to a ripple. Half the water had evaporated and it left a musty smell in the air creating a mist that engulfed the entire room. Several drips pitter-pattered down onto the floor from the furniture, wires, and the ceiling creating the environment of a light misty rain. Moisture was everywhere and every object was covered in condensation.

A low groan came from the floor.

Something large started to walk toward it; stomping its way through the water and cutting its way through the mist. Each step splattered the remaining water into the air and as it got closer, the location of the groan became clearer. The sound was emanating from a body on the floor.

The body was so black that at first it didn't look human. The arms were curled up against the torso and the fingers had been crimpled into small stumps. What clothes that covered the body had burned into a substance that melted to the flesh behind it. The legs were pulled up under the body and also unrecognizable.

The face still held a familiar look but it too was so distorted that it was hard to see it. All the hair was gone and the skin had peeled in several places around the skull. The blood that spotted it was black and hardened. The nose had very little skin left hanging on it and the nostril holes were fully exposed. The lips had melted away exposing a set of blackened teeth with no gums surrounding them.

A groan escaped the mouth again.

210 knelt down toward Medico; several teardrops were falling from his eyes, and he tried to lift the damaged body up but the crackling of bones frightened the Klebit and he quickly released his grasp. In his sorrow, the creature sat down into the water next to the body and looked deep into what was left of his maker's eyes.

They were both pure white and so glazed that there was no color left in them.

"Father," 210 gurgled out from his mouth. His chest was heavy with pain and he started to sniffle. He wanted to pick him up and carry him into the repair room so that everything could be made better, but the body was just too fragile to lift.

Light crackling noises occurred as he saw Medico's mouth start open. The muscles snapped and popped around the jaw and 210 could clearly see that the tongue was completely gone. The inside was just as black as the skin that surrounded it. Even though the lips were gone, it looked like Medico was trying to smile.

A loud gust of air released from the chest as Medico's head tipped to the right. The hiss of breath slowly came to a stop.

210 started shaking his head and waving his arms in the air. "No, No, No," he repeated over and over again. Then in one swift move, he grabbed the body and pulled it toward him for a last loving embrace.

The body cracked, snapped and shattered under the pressure.

****

The way out was fast, efficient and trouble free; no lava, no Klebits, and no creatures trying to eat them. It didn't take long for Hawk to remember his escape the last time and he knew where the main entrance to the underground was. When they began, it was hard at first. Steve was trying to regain his strength, but after several feet, it was a task for him and Jason just to keep up with Hawk. Hawk wanted to get out of there as fast as he could and didn't want to look back. The two men just followed Hawk's direction and soon found themselves exiting out between two large boulders in a cliff side. The opening was tight but Steve, the heaviest of the three, managed to squeeze through.

It was night and they could barely see ten feet in front of them. The trees surrounding the area cut out what glow that could come from the stars above and the night creatures were all making noise. There was a cool breeze that blew fresh air into their faces and it was refreshing, but the smell of the underground still hung around them like bad body odor. The wind whistling through the trees gave a calming effect to the chaos that they had just left.

Hawk stopped and turned toward the other two. "Are you guys ok," he asked. "Do you need to rest a bit?"

Steve was bending over with his hands on his knees taking deep breaths. "Just a couple of minutes," he sighed. "I haven't run like that since...."

"That time you streaked through the girl's dormitory," Jason added with a laugh.

Steve started laughing and then noticed that Hawk was quizzically looking at them.

Steve waved his hands in the air, "I'll explain that one later," he said to Hawk.

"Oh, I'm sure you will," Hawk replied. He started looking around the area; to the left, to the right and above. "So, where to next," he questioned.

Jason pulled a tracking unit out of his front pocket that gave the location of the rented transport and turned it on. The green glow lit up the area around Jason's face as he read the display. "Well, this is a sign of good luck; the vessel is a few hundred yards that way," Jason said as he pointed toward their right. "It shouldn't take us that long to get there."

Steve started laughing, "Hey Hawk, wait to you see this piece of shit we rented. Looks like someone's Grandmother knitted it together."

"It's held together by chewing gum and duct tape," Jason added. Steve and Jason started laughing and again, Hawk was confused.

"I'm sure you'll explain that one as well," Hawk said with a smile.

Steve stood back up straight and rubbed his hands together and looked back toward the opening they just came out of. "I really think we ought to set the place on fire. Burn it all out and put them out of their misery."

Hawk started to shake his head no. "This may sound weird, but Medico was right."

Jason and Steve got perplexed looks on their faces.

"They are family to me," Hawk said as he tilted his head down. "They suffered the same treatments, agony, and experiences that I went through. I know that I was human when I started out; how old or who I was I do not know, but they could be just as innocent as I was in the beginning. I owe them that."

Jason and Steve nodded in agreement. "But that wacko of a brain fart," Steve said, "are you sure he's dead?"

Hawk slowly nodded his head, "oh, yeah, I'm sure of it. I watched him burn in front of me."

"Medico was his name, right?" Jason asked.

"Yes, it was," Hawk said in a low tone.

"Oh shit," Steve exclaimed suddenly realizing what he was told, "That reminds me. Guess who he really is?"

All three of the men were interrupted by a loud roar from the trees and 210 came running at them in full speed. He ran between Jason and Steve; swatting each of them out of the way like they were annoying insects, and then fully lunged at Hawk. Jason was thrown ten feet to the left, and Steve was thrown to the right, but Hawk was caught completely off guard.

210 struck the side of Hawk's head once; causing his right ear to ring and bleed. When the Klebit tried to swing again, Hawk caught the claw and twisted it back, breaking it at the joint. 210 yelled in agony and punched Hawk into the chest. Bones cracked. 210 swung again and connected to Hawk's left shoulder ripping a large gash in it. Blood started to soak through his jacket as they continued to struggle on the ground. More and more blows were delivered by both and more wounds appeared. Hawk had cracked several ribs in 210's chest and more gashes appeared on Hawk.

In the struggle, Hawk ended up pinned on his back as 210 pushed all his weight upon him. The spit from the mouth of the Klebit dripped down into Hawk's face below, stinging his eyes in the process. Hawk pushed as hard as he could against the massive body, but 210 proved to be just as strong as he was. The Klebit slowly overpowered Hawk and started to lean forward to bite Hawk in the neck. Its jagged teeth inched closer and closer bringing the foul stench of breath with it. Hawk struggled to break the attack and then managed to get his hands around 210's throat. He put all the strength he had into squeezing as hard as he could.

210 couldn't breathe. The grip that was upon him was so strong that he had to let go of Hawk and try to pry off the choke hold. He was only able to use his left claw because the right claw had been broken so severely that the bone was protruding out and he could not move his fingers. He tried to pull up and away, but once again, Hawk's grip was so tight that he couldn't gain the momentum and was starting to lose consciousness. His eyes started to get blurry and his breathing became more non-existent. In one last attempt he tried to push again but it was useless. Hawk's grip started to crunch 210's windpipe and blood accompanied the saliva dripping out of the mouth.

In one last gasp for air, 210 died on top of Hawk pinning all his weight down upon him. He had barely enough energy to roll him off and once he did, Hawk laid on his back trying to catch his breath. This was the first time he had ever been this worn out, this defeated, this stunned.

Hawk slowly rolled over to his right side and the pain that emanated everywhere was excruciating. The Klebit had managed to slash him five times; two in the shoulders, once on the head and two in the torso. Blood was everywhere. As he was trying to regain his strength, he saw Jason trying to sit up over by a group of trees. With no strength in his legs, Hawk started to pull himself toward Jason.

"Jason," he yelled, "Jason. Are you alright?" With each pull a stabbing pain hit his right ribs.

Jason turned toward him while holding his waist. "Ouch," he yelled. "I think that fucker broke my ribs."

"Where's Steve?" Hawk Asked.

Jason started to look around. "Steve," he yelled as good as he could through the pain, "Where are you?"

There was no answer.

Both men managed to stand but had to depend on each other for support. Once they were on their feet, they held onto each other as they limped around searching the area. They finally spotted Steve by a group of rocks on the far right.   He was lying face down.

Jason let go of Hawk and fell hard on his knees next to Steve. He leaned over him and grabbed his right shoulder. "Steve," he said as he rolled him over. "STEVE!" Jason yelled.

Steve's face had blood all over it and by the look of it; he had hit the rock that was next to him. It too was covered in blood.

"Shit," Steve sputtered as blood sprayed out of his mouth, "is this a bitch or what?"

"Take it easy, old man," Jason said, "we all had the shit kicked out of us, so don't try to make sound like your wounds are the worst."

Steve smiled through the blood in his teeth, "hell, this is just nearly a flesh wound, boy. You too pansies will be crying for a week. Besides, I think he knocked out at least two of my teeth." Steve closed his eyes tightly and then swallowed hard. "My head feels like...."

"A busted watermelon," Jason added.
Steve smiled and more blood came from his lips. "Probably looks like one too."

"Ahhh," Jason said, "it's an improvement."

Hawk now joined them on the ground and took note of Steve's condition. "Damn, dude. You look like how I feel."

Steve noticed all the blood and cuts all over Hawk and took attention to it, "if you could only see it through my eyes." He started coughing and more blood came up. He glanced back toward Jason and continued. "And if I could have that last bottle of Whiskey."

Jason put his hand on Steve shoulder, "We'll drink it when we get home."

Steve smiled again.

****

The emotions that combine together to build the human experience is the most complex system ever created. Take the emotions and combine them with the ever-changing life around you and it becomes a game. Each individual reacts differently because of how they were raised. The teachings and the life style of a child's first years will set the stage for which direction they will go.

Take for example a person who has a loving family, friends and support. They are taught patience, sensibility, understanding, caution, judgement, practicality and kindness. Skills are developed by those and become the backbone of their existence. It builds wisdom, maturity, familiarity, manners, proficiency, good taste, nobility, and politeness. Everything becomes a blessing for them and life is an enjoyment. They become someone you can count on, a tower of strength, a crutch, a person of their word, a mainstay, a lifeline, a straight arrow, and someone who would lend you the shirt off their back.

But if a child were to be brought up into a world of chaos it would become an entirely different situation. If they were surrounded by a world of hate, greed, corruption, obscenity, offensiveness, unpleasantness, and cruelty, they would have different results. Once again, their skills are developed by those and become the backbone of their existence. It would make them bitter, angry, resentful, belligerent, bad-tempered, vicious, and wicked. They become a person that is untrustworthy, treacherous, disloyal, self-centered, unreliable, arrogant, conceited, and vainglorious.

Each upbringing can change as they grow older depending on what reality slaps them with. It's a struggle no matter what life throws at you and your foundation is how you are going to perceive the direction of your outcome.   Personalities are built by the combination of their upbringing, training, skills, and what life throws at them.

Life is made by how an individual wants it.

Throughout their lives they become known by other descriptions according to their personalities.

One set is known to brighten up the room when they walk in and can make you feel better just by interacting with them. They are pleasant to be around, social, happy go lucky, fancy free, light hearted, cheerful, and bright-eyed and bushy-tailed. Not many words are available to call a person like this; only Angel and sweetie come to mind.

The other set can bring down morale and turn a pleasant room into a darkened disaster. The mere appearance of this individual can make people want to leave the building and build up the feelings of distrust, annoyance, and hatred. They are uncomfortable to be around, antisocial, miserable, cranky, mean, downhearted, and despicable. Many words are available to describe this type of person. This being is known as a jerk, bugger, douche, a real SOB, a dick, a pain in the ass, an asshat, an asshole, a shit head, and fucking prick.

The only true safe haven from all of this is pure ignorance. You can't be held accountable if you are ignorant to the subject. You could be uneducated, oblivious, innocent, inexperienced, uninformed, naïve, witless, unaware, foolish, and untaught. This also brings on another slew of name calling. You are called stupid, a dolt, a Dooferdoo, a simpleton, a blithering idiot, an imbecile, a bonehead, dummy, dork, nincompoop, blockhead, and a complete dipshit.

In all of this, it's strange to find that there are more descriptions for bad people and ignorance than there is for people who really brighten the lives of others. People are too quick to judge with hate or inappropriate behavior toward things that they don't understand. Once again, all things have a different upbringing, and according to what they encounter, it brings in different responses.

There is one common thing that they all share. Even after all the pain, the sacrifices, the emotional scars, the everyday conflicts, and the unknown future ahead, all of them carry this within them. Hope.

They hope for the better, they hope for an end, they hope for a new beginning, they hope for a cure, they hope for reason, they hope for an understanding, and they hope for a brighter day. All creatures, no matter what or who they are have hope. Hope gives them something to look forward to. Hope gives them confidence in themselves and makes them stronger to carry on. The spirit in one's soul brings life to the body, and an energy that sets forth a power from within to enlighten that person to achieve anything. It builds character, it builds faith, and it builds confidence.

If empathy is the most powerful emotion to possess, then Hope is the machine that drives it.

Katrina sat in the rocking chair on the porch of her cabin drinking a large glass of speckle tea. The last four rotations had been very rough, and if it wasn't for Remy and Aiden by her side, she didn't know what she would have done. The girls stayed at the cabin the entire time, taking care of her like she was invalid. They cooked for her, did her laundry, cleaned the house and even took her to Serin base to see a doctor for her illness that came and went frequently. The results were surprising and pleasing at the same time.

She took another sip and the warm liquid soothed her sore throat as it went down. The warmth continued to her chest as it went deeper into her body and it made her fell calm and serine. The thoughts of what had taken place over the last term were now becoming a distant memory, but for a while she thought she would never recover from them. The love and support from friends gave her the strength to continue on and she felt cleansed and renewed.

She had hope.

Her faith was strong knowing that the men would all return safely and they would start a life together. A new beginning was on the rise and her anticipation was digging at her like a knife. They had heard nothing from them and each of them were growing more impatient. It already had been eleven rotations since they left, and trying to keep busy wasn't burning the time any faster. For the other two ladies, it might have, but for Katrina, time was moving backwards.

The door squeaked behind her and the other two women walked out onto the porch. Aiden spoke first.

"Jason just called and said that they were landing at Serin base within the next two taps."

Katrina's inside didn't need the tea anymore to warm her up. A fire lit in her heart and started to inflame her entire body. The reaction made her voice chipper. "Are they all three arriving?"

Aiden glanced at Remy with a concerned look in her eyes, prompting a response.

"Yes," Remy said. "All three of them will be there."

Katrina stood up and sat her empty cup on the table next to the chair.

"Great," she said with a smile. "Then let's not waste any time."

CHAPTER 15

The tree by the lake started to get crowded. Where there was once only one grave, now stood four. The smell of fresh dug dirt hit the air once again and the rain was lightly falling. Everything was very quiet with the exception of the wind blowing through the leaves. No insects or animals were making any sound. But occasionally, a rumble of thunder occurred, but it was off in the distance and getting farther away.

The rain was colder than normal because the sun was setting fast and the wind was blowing inland from the lake. The casual sound of the waves hit the bank and splashed water into the air adding a fine mist to the rain droplets coming down. Everything was wet, including the five people standing by the graves. Some of them were wearing sweaters and some of them were wearing bandages, but all of them were as silent as the area around them.

They stood there for a long time, so long that the sun had set and the only light provided to them was the occasional flicker of lightning. With the darkening of the day, the night creatures started their mating calls. Clacks, chirps, clicks, and buzzing was filling the air around them and every once in a while, a Fana bird would echo from across the lake.

Remy and Aiden were hugging each other, still stunned from the news that they received that morning. They had both cried so hard that their sides were sore, and they were so exhausted from the emotional stress that they could hardly move, nor get any sleep. Their throats were tight and dry; their eyes couldn't produce any more tears and were stinging from the pain. Their noses were clogged and it was hard to breathe. Everything came to a standstill.

But there was still hope.

Katrina held her ground. Through everything that she had experienced, she had become stronger. She couldn't believe that it happened again, and she tried to make sense of it. A death always changes the perspective on how a person looks at their own life. It makes them ask the questions, 'Is this all that I can be or is there more?' 'Do I feel complete?' 'Do I still have time to do the things I want to do?' Death has always been a wakeup call to the living.

But there will be hope.

Jason had a hard time accepting this outcome. His concentration was fuzzy, his eyes to dry to cry, and his ribs were still sore from the attack. He too had several bandages; most of them around his chest, but he had to take short breaths due to the pain. It was hard to do when you were crying. Katrina was wrapped around him lightly; she didn't want to cause more pain to the wounds, and his love for her continued to grow. He wished that he could have been here to support her in her time of need, but the two ladies proved to be a blessing in disguise. Katrina seemed different, though, but in a good way. Even after everything that they all had been through, tomorrow was another day.

But there is hope.

Hawk was in total control. His emotions that plagued him still were burning inside, but he had better control of them. His eyes had been blazing red ever since they had left Zeta, and they still continued to burn. He was wrapped up in several bandages; one around his head, one covering his right shoulder, and several around his waist. He was wearing the jacket he wore during 210's attack, and even though it was ripped and torn, it still felt comfortable. The wings on the back gave off a light sparkle from the rain that covered them and it symbolized his flight through life. Its condition showed the glamor and the pain. His life had been one of extreme and up until he met everyone here, it felt reckless and lost. He learned to trust, to laugh, to enjoy, to dream, and to love. The death of Veronica hit him hard, but not as hard as this death. He lost a mentor, a father, and a friend.

But……….

They all continued to look at the new stone in front of them which had several carvings upon it. Located on the bottom were several glasses; each of them filled with different colors. Lining up both sides were ropes twisted together to symbolize unity, and at the top were Captain's bars under a carving of an OAJ fighter jet. Under it and in the middle was;

Steve Morris
Husband, Father, Boss, Friend

Jason wrapped his arm tightly around Katrina and sighed. His eyes started to tear up again because the thought of not having Steve around anymore made him feel lost, and oddly alone. He swallowed hard, "I guess this makes me the last Earthling," he said to Katrina.

Katrina smiled and turned her head toward him. She took a deep breath to compose herself, and spoke at a whisper. "That's not entirely true," she said.

A quizzical look engulfed Jason's expression and he turned toward her, "What do you mean, not entirely true?"

She smiled again and looked deep into his eyes. "I'm pregnant."

EPILOGUE

"Ahhh!" Jason screamed, "this pain is killing me!" His expression across his face said it all as Katrina was crushing his hand. "Hurry up before you break every bone in my hand!"

"Killing you?" Katrina yelled back, "How would you like to have my pain? I feel like...." Another contraction hit her and she lost all of her air as her face turned bright red.

Jason's concern deepened. "I'm just trying to make you laugh, Honey."

Her death stare toward him told him to stop trying and she squeezed harder. He could see that his fingertips were turning white and the feelings in them were getting numb. He might need the Doctor as well when this is all over.

She had been sitting in the birthing chair for almost nine courses, and he had been by her side the whole time. Even with the proper breathing techniques, if there is such a thing, she ran out of energy fast. The baby was being difficult and was taking its time to arrive into the world. As far as Katrina was concerned, it was time to get a pressure vice and pop that child out. She wanted to just lay back and sleep.

"Push again," stated the Doctor down by her knees. "The head is just about to come out and when that happens it will be over quickly."

"Quickly," Katrina echoed. She turned to Jason and sneered at him. "You did this to me. When this is over, I'm going to hit you in the head with a bar mug."

"With the circulation cut off in my hand, I probably won't feel it." Jason stated. "Besides, breaking a perfectly good glass will piss off the ladies. You know how much of a tightwad they are."

That line made her laugh, and then another wave hit her. Her breath cut short again and the Doctor stood up and leaned his hand onto her belly.

"Ok, one last time. Now push!"

She leaned forward and pushed at the same time as the Doctor. She gave everything that she could. Just when she thought she didn't succeed, she felt like she had relieved herself on the toilet and the sound of gushing liquid splattered all over the room. It sounded like someone had busted a large water balloon. She felt embarrassed, exhausted, and happy all at the same time. Now, completely out of energy, she plopped her head back onto the support pillow and released her grip on Jason.

They both sighed.

The crew in the delivery room quickly cleaned up the area and the child. Their efficient speed demonstrated that this wasn't the first time, or the last. Within taps, they had left the room and the only one remaining was the Doctor walking up with the baby wrapped in his arms.

"Congratulations, it's a girl." He said as he lightly laid the baby into the mother's arms. "I'll leave you three alone for a while. The nurse will be in to get the child later while you get some rest."

"Thanks Doctor," Jason said as the man left the room.

The small face that starred up at them was clean and full of color. Her eyes darted back and forth between Jason and Katrina as if she was taking everything in. She slowly poked her tongue in and out of her mouth, like she was testing its movement.

Mother and Father were glowing inside at the new life they had brought into the world. It was a fresh new beginning for them all, for they all get to experience life again together. They would experience it from the first cry, the first tooth, the first walk, the first bruise, and the first word.

The baby crunched up its face in confusion like it was trying to understand something and her lips started to jitter. She started to suck in air and open her mouth wide.

"Get ready," Jason said, "here comes her first cry."

The new parents leaned closer to the child when the sound came out.

Hum* "Hello Father, hello Mother," she said.

The following is a sample chapter from **"TAINTED"**, by Richard Crane. It is now available on all e-reader formats and in print through Amazon.

THURSDAY

Day 23, Thursday May 4th, 2000, 4:15 a.m.

Damn, am I ever tired, seriously tired. This is Dean and I never knew that this project could drain so much energy. Last night, as I reported in my last entry, Brad brought over the EC-380. It took us forever to drag the sucker downstairs and into the basement, but it's finally resting in the pool room. How Brad took it from Mckinley Hall without anyone helping him, I'll never know, but he did. With all that extra weight, I bet his SUV bottomed out a few times on the way over here.

Oh, by the way, I've got another word to add to Brad's verbal dictionary. This one is a gut buster. We had the unit half way down the steps when he mentioned that he has never snaffled anyone before. Snaffled; what a word. It caught an odd look from me, but I still don't know what it means. I'll have to look it up later. Since he was born at least forty years before me, I should expect a generation in there.

Well, anyway, the unit wasn't as complicated as I thought it would be, in fact, to set it up was nothing. It's as easy as plugging in a toaster. The power drained down most of the lights in the house so everything that wasn't needed was turned off. God, I could just imagine the power bill for this month. Brad said he could get the University to pay for it since it is a project for them.

I'm so glad that he got me involved in this project. When he showed me the matrix on the robot, at first, I was skeptical but after all the progress we have made over the last three weeks, I'm as excited as he is. After we got the 380 into place and grounded, we hooked up DD. When we were certain that everything was on backup, I wired myself into the transfer line.

Oh, yeah, I forgot to explain how the 380 works. It consists of a brain wave transfer unit and a thought pattern analyzer. I'm plugged up with six recorder suction tubes, and then the 380 transfers the pattern into DD's memory board. This unit is normally used to transfer computer readouts and programs to a main collector, but we integrated a brain scan machine into the buffer. I was first really scared about doing this but with all the safety precautions Brad took, he said that failure was impossible. It still gave me the heebie-jeebies, (a Brad word). So, in conclusion, all that the 380 does is take my brain wave patterns and my personality and transfers it into DD. Hell, he already has my great looks, might as well give him my great personality as well, if you know what I mean.

When Brad turned it on, everything I saw was doubled. I told Brad about it, and he said it was natural because it's working with the robot's imagery. He also mentioned that I would pass out, and I did.

When I woke up seven hours later, Brad wasn't in the room. My head was fuzzy and my mouth was really dry. I saw Brad's glass of milk on the work table and took a swig of it. That's how I found out it had been seven hours. Needless to say, I'm going to have to clean the area after I'm done with this entry because I spit it out all over the desk.

After that, I pulled off the suction cups from my forehead, and that's when I noticed the great smell of bacon drifting from upstairs. I groggily walked up the steps to find Brad in the kitchen fixing breakfast for me. The clock on the wall said it was half past ten, and Brad informed me that Curt had called wondering why I wasn't in the lab. Brad covered for me and told him that we were working on his SUV.

Speaking of Curt, I wonder if it's time to tell him about what we have been doing. It's been seriously hard to keep him out of the project for he is my best friend, and I'm running out of excuses. Brad and I didn't want him to know because we are going to test our invention on him and Lynette, in fact, Lynette is my first target. If we could fool her, we could fool him. But if we were to run into any problem with completing DD, Curt could help us. In fact, we probably would have finished a lot faster. He didn't receive a full grant from the college for his dashing good looks and the way he is with the women, he happens to be the highest ranked IQ in college history. Of course, his mouth and his attitude don't reflect the IQ. He'll say out loud what others only think because it drives him nuts to be around people who don't use their common sense and he's very arrogant because he knows that people will always need his intelligence. In fact, he's created such a stir with campus police and the board of trustees that I'm surprised that he hasn't been expelled yet. He's crude obnoxious, gross, vulgar and a pervert but I wouldn't trade his friendship for anything. He's always been there for me.

Anyway, back to our progress. I'm sitting in my recliner upstairs writing this and enjoying a cold glass of orange juice. Brad told me he had fallen asleep in the chair next to the 380 downstairs and woke up about thirty minutes before I did. He said that his stomach was growling and came upstairs to fix something to eat. When he heard me rustling downstairs, he cooked more bacon and eggs.

Man, I'm tired. My body feels like it has no energy, but my mind is wide awake. I hate that. While I'm writing this (and eating), I've been watching an old black and white movie on TV. So far three people and one horse has been shot. I'm giving this entry an end.

close: 4:56am

Day 23, Thursday May 4th, 2000, 5:57 a.m.

Brad here with a few words. Dean didn't make the rest of the movie; he fell asleep on the couch. The transfer really wiped him out and hopefully he'll regain his strength before he goes back on it again. I'm calculating that he should only have to be on it two more times for it to complete all transfers. By then we should be able to do a dry run and have DD walk around the house by himself. He should be able to speak as well and voice Dean's vocal patterns. I don't know if Dean had already said this in the Diary or not, but the hardest part is over. Making the body skin and the animatronics was the hardest part. Programming the robot will be easy. Once the patterns are transferred, we should see major results. This whole project is getting really nifty and fun. I can't wait to present it at the Seattle conference next Saturday. Hopefully the project will go well this week, and my report will have significant data to impress them all. Well, now would be a good time for me to get forty winks while Dean is doing the same. I'll retire to his guest room and later we can start round two.

close: 6:11 a.m.

Day 23, Thursday May 4th, 2000, 8:37 a.m.

Oooo, is my head pounding. I woke up to find the TV off and Brad gone. My mouth was so dry I went to the kitchen to get a drink of water. It was a task to even walk. You know those headaches that pound every time you take a step? Exactly, that's what I have. Going to the bathroom was even a bigger pain. I was going to go upstairs to my comfy waterbed, but no energy to do so. After I put this pen down, I'm going to pass out once again in this recliner.

close: 8:52 a.m.

Day 23, Thursday May 4th, 2000, 12:42 p.m.

I'm alive and ready to go! Boy, do I feel great. The headache is gone; Brad and I just filled our stomachs with pasta and I had a long visit with the bathroom. We are getting ready to go back downstairs to do round two. I hope I don't have another one of those headaches again, you know what I mean?

close: 12:59 p.m.

217

Day 23, Thursday May 4th, 2000, 1: 32 p.m.

Brad here with a few lines. It didn't take long to plug up Dean into the chair; he was very excited to continue. The way we made the 380 resulted in a real handy dandy hook up. The robot sits in one chair while Dean sits in the other one. The 380 is between them, and the hook up is just a few electron suction cups that I fasten to Dean's forehead. DD just plugs into his servo, which by the way, connects between his butt cheeks. We had to find an area where nobody would notice it and could get easy access. Of course, pulling his pants down is odd but it would only happen here. Besides, he doesn't have a tally Wacker, so it's not like we are being weird.

While Dean is out, I think it would be best to detail everything about him I can. After all, if this report is going to be the ground foundation of this project, it has to have all the information in it to compare how the robot operates and what it actually receives in the transfer.

Dean Mitchell is an honor student at Tandam institute of Technology. He is in his sixth year and studying mechanical electronics. He is six feet tall, with dark brown hair, hazel eyes, and medium build. He rarely curses, and he always is the nice guy to be around. He always loves to give to others and never asks for things for himself. In fact, he would rather put himself on the spot rather than point out that someone else has a problem. He loves a good movie and enjoys eating out a lot. In fact, he is a hot sauce junkie and loves to take challenges when it comes to hot food. I couldn't last a second on some of the stuff I have seen him eat. I would end up with a wiz bang of stomach problem even if I smelled some of those concoctions. Just the other day at the Pizza Pub, he must have put on at least 20 jalapenos on his pizza. An old geezer like me would have had a cardiac arrest, not to mention the pain that would come from my derriere the next day.

Dean was very well set when his parents died in a car fire about ten years ago during a really nasty snow storm on I-72 heading toward Decatur. It was blizzard conditions, and they just finished a seminar in Decatur when the storm hit. A six-car pileup resulted in two cars burning and the loss of four lives. Due to the white out conditions, rescue teams couldn't see and by the time they were reached, it was too late. I didn't know Dean then, but I do remember reading about it in the paper. They were very wealthy because Dean's father owned a pump company and designed all the pumps himself. His mother handled the office operations, and they had several clients including the United States Navy. Dean wasn't interested in the pump aspect of the business but spent his time understanding the equipment and the technical aspects of the machinery. His cravings for information lead him into mechanical engineering and beyond that. When his parents died, he inherited everything they owned which included the house, cars and the business. He sold the business to his father's silent partner and he immediately went into schooling. This year will be his sixth and final year at Tandem.

He has a lovely relationship with a lady named Lynette Ashbury, and they have been engaged for over six months now. No date is set yet: they are waiting for Dean's graduation, but yours truly gets to give away the bride. Her father died several years ago, and she has no other male figures in her family. Since I have no ankle-biters of my own, it would be an honor to play the part. She is a manager at the Book Nook, and I can tell you she can cast an eyeball. Not only is she very attractive, but she walks very daintily and presents herself as a classy gal. She loves dresses, and I rarely have seen her in jeans. When she walks, her posture is very upright, as if she was taught to walk with books on her head. Even when she sits down, she doesn't slouch. Her speech is very articulate and precise which is refreshing to hear in this world we now live in. One thing is for sure, Dean and she are both hooked on each other pretty good. She is our main target with DD. If we can go the whole week fooling her, then it's made in the shade.

The other target is Dean's best friend Curt Johnson. This dude is a person for the history books. He has the highest IQ that Tandam has ever encountered and is very aware of his surroundings. Getting past him is going to be a real pickle, but if we could pull it off, it would be the bee's knees. The main problem with Curt is that he is very outspoken. He's very arrogant, and he knows it. He has been in a lot of trouble with the university and I personally had to pull some strings to keep him from getting kicked out. One of the saves he had was to design a security system for the entire university. It ended up being so good the government looked into hiring him but found out his character was too much of a problem. The university paid him a lot of bread for it, and eventually he designed several more systems for local businesses. He's got a great cash flow which gives him a lot of free time. I wanted to have him help us with this project, but Dean insisted on using Curt as one of the test subjects. I hope he doesn't blow a gasket when he finds out.

One thing is for sure, not only is he unpredictable but he has the good looks to go with it. He can pick up women faster than a bent eight on a quarter mile strip. His favorite hangout is a strip club called Marvin's, and he probably has nailed every dancer in the club; twice. Being cocky, intelligent and, overbearing can make a person into one loaded cocktail. He has been in trouble with the authorities because he doesn't back down from a fight. He has been trained in Taekwondo, by a private instructor, and is always a comfort when trouble surfaces. He has been running his own school for about five years now. One time I had two boys cut me off on the campus one night, to try to rob me. Curt, just so happened, to be sitting on a bench a few leaps away from us. By the time campus security arrived, one boy was unconscious and the other one was in real bad shape. I'll never forget that night.

Anyway, I thought it might be a good idea to get some information in this dairy about the parties involved so if certain instances occur, we can cross reference the spots. I haven't really read most of Dean's entries and hopefully we are not repeating each other, but soon we are going to have to get another book for this one is filling up. It is now later in the afternoon and I need to run to my office to get something, but I hate leaving Dean plugged into that thing with no observer. Sitting in this recliner across from him is starting to stiffen up my back and I may have to get up and walk around at least.

Well, I'm going to stretch my legs by going to the kitchen and get something to drink. I'll probably not go to the office. I just don't feel comfortable leaving.

close: 4:42 p.m.

Day 23, Thursday May 4th, 2000, 5:21 p.m.

A loud shout from downstairs had me taking two steps at a time, and I almost broke my foot at the bottom. When I got to Dean, it seems that he was having a nightmare. I checked all the stats on the 380, and the brain activity as well, and everything checked out. The transfer is still working. I'm going back upstairs to get my stew before it burns and change my pants.

close: 5:37 p.m.

Day 23, Thursday May 4th, 2000, 8: 11 p.m.

My God! What seemed like only 20 minutes was a little over 8 hours! Fascinating! I have no headache, and Brad even said that I had more color in my face. The odd thing was how I woke up. It was quick and sudden like someone just slapped me in the face. I shook my head a couple of times to clear things and that's when I noticed DD and called Brad downstairs.

Surprisingly, DD had stood up and walked a couple of feet away from his chair. It was just enough to break the connection from the 380 and wake me up. COOL! I must have been dreaming in my sleep about walking in order for him to do that. Brad might be right after all. We might only need one more down load and he will be finished. After working on this project for almost a month now, my confidence has doubled. Doubled, funny joke, huh? I finish the download then all we would have to do is work the voice stabilizer and test him around the house. I don't want to take him out too early and have him break down on us at school or even worse around Lynette. She'd freak out.

By the way, that reminds me that we have a date Saturday night to go to a late dinner and a movie. She said that she would be over about 7:30 after she gets off of work. She really needs a break from that place. One thing about being salaried, a company will work you to death. I can't wait to see her though; I haven't spent much time with her recently. Outside of her working full time at the bookstore and me doing this, we've only had phone conversations. Not to mention that her x-boyfriend is back in town, and she has been on edge ever since. That guy has to be one of the biggest jerks I know. He had a very beautiful, sophisticated lady and treated her like crap. Some guys just don't get it. At times I'd love to punch him in the face, but unfortunately my strongest muscles are in my brains, so I normally wimp out and walk away when I have to deal with the bully. Man, it's been almost three years since she dumped him, you'd think by now he'd move on with his life. I still remember all the things she had to do to make her life more comfortable. She had to move, make her address and phone number unlisted, and even move her lazy butt sister in for security reasons. Don't even start me up about her sister, Kimberly.

Anyway, back to the project at hand. Brad was sitting in the recliner reading a book when this all happened with DD, so he didn't witness it. Brad had twisted his ankle earlier and had it propped up with an ice bag on it. One thing about Brad, he always has his nose in a book. Once he got all the suction cups off my forehead, we backed DD up into his chair. He moved a lot easier and didn't feel as stiff anymore. It still freaks me out how real his skin feels. Not only does the feel freak me out, but if you get up close to his face, it really creeps me out. I seriously think I'm looking at a mirror. I can still remember all that wet plaster Brad put all over my head to make the mold for his face. Boy did that stuff stink. Well, after we secured DD, we ran a test pattern on the

380 and found out that almost 75% of my brain patterns have been transferred into him. Ha, look at me; it's so close that I'm actually calling DD "Him". So, according to Brad one more download ought to finish it, but we have to be careful. There is no telling what DD will do once fully loaded, so for safety reasons, we placed him inside one of my empty metal lockers and padlocked the door. He shouldn't overheat in it and I feel more relaxed knowing that he is secure. Ha, "He". So, to top off this evening with a short celebration, Brad and I are going out to the Pizza Pub, have some pie and a couple of beers.

close: 8:57 p.m.

Day 23, Thursday May 4th, 2000, 11: 41 p.m.

Brad here with a couple of lines. After watching Dean have four beers and almost a whole Buffalo chicken pizza by himself, I thought it might be a good idea that we rest tonight and do the final download tomorrow. I'll sleep here again tonight, but tomorrow I have to get to the office and start getting things together for next weekend. I'm about to bust a gut on this, and it's beginning to become a total blast!

close: 11:57 p.m.

AUTHOR PAGE

Richard Crane Is the author of three books. He is a veteran of the United States Navy and spends most of his time watching movies, drawing, or supporting his favorite sports team. He's a diehard Science-fiction fan and also enjoys a good horror movie. He's a collector of many movie items and enjoys long walks with his dog. He currently lives with his family in Central Illinois.

Other books by Richard Crane;

"The Sacrifice"

"Tainted"

"The Angel"

www.ingramcontent.com/pod-product-compliance
Lightning Source LLC
Chambersburg PA
CBHW032212190626
46810CB00019B/2751